9. 23. 13

Dear Rae,

What can I say to express my abundant gratitude for all your help over the years and all your support. You are such an amazing woman and such an inspiration!

love you,

Riki

The Messiah Chronicles
Book 1

Have You Seen the Signs?

The Messiah Chronicles Book 1

Have You Seen the Signs?

Rivka Sarah Horowitz

Library of Congress Control Number:		2013908600
ISBN:	Hardcover	978-1-4836-3995-6
	Softcover	978-1-4836-3994-9
	Ebook	978-1-4836-3996-3

Rev. date: 08/19/2013

To order additional copies of this book, contact:
Xlibris LLC
1-888-795-4274
www.Xlibris.com
Orders@Xlibris.com
120893

Dedication

Thanks and blessings to my father and mother for their continued love, support, and faith in me, and to my son, Raphael, for keeping me grounded in this world and for coaxing me out to play. I love you!

Acknowledgments

I thank all those who helped me in my research and gave generously of their time, knowledge, and opinions. Any misrepresentations or inaccuracies are solely mine.

I wish to thank all those who helped me in the writing of the book: to Linda Lee and all the members of her writing groups, particularly Ed Harris (of blessed memory), Ken Oguss, Mac, Phyllis, Ed Morris, Margaret Kolman, Ahmet and Esther, Susan Lawson, Ed and Susan Alley. It's been an honor and a privilege to write with all of you. To Shoshana Hurwitz, for your assistance, editing, and advice on the first draft of this project.

I wish to also thank all those who've listened to me go on about the book or acted as readers for the various versions of the manuscript: first and foremost, my mother, Temi Horowitz; my father, Al Horowitz; my uncle, Dr. Abraham Speiser; Davida Nugiel; Paula Saffire; Katherine Soskin; Sarah Goldstein; Eliyahu Lotzar; Yakov Nagar; Judith Friedman; Rev. Ed Harris (obm); Linda Lee, Dorethea Goold; Ken Oguss; and Margaret Kolman.

To Chaitanya Dave, for your spiritual and intuitive guidance, friendship and support, and to Rehka and all those who join together at the table; to Rae Kridel; special thanks to Rabbi and Fraidel Schusterman and all the Schusterman family; to Rachel Rose; Joyce Rose Weissberger; Shirah Eliyashiv; Harriet Ross; and Cassia Margolis, for your support. I thank you all for your friendship and your honesty in this process. I couldn't have done it without you.

Additional thanks go to Janette Cothrel; John F; and Janet Speck, Lorie Brown; Michele Chabin; Tracey Shipley; D'vorah Goodman; Laya Saul; Cay El Nemr; Rahima Jill Moore; Munir Peter Reynolds; Debbie Sayre and Rahmana Elizabeth Sayre; Eliana Gilad, and the readers of my blog.

The list of teachers who have influenced me and to whom I owe a a depth of gratitude is too long to include them all here. Please forgive me for any people I have omitted. I have appreciated all your teachings. Some of them include Rebbetzin Faiga Ashlag, Rabbi Shalom and Judy Brodt, Rabbi Shlomo Carlebach, Rabbi Shai Cherry, Rabbi David A. Cooper, Rabbi Arthur Green, Emmunah Witt Halevy, Rabbi Ruth and Dr. Michael Kagan, Melinda Ribner, Sarah Yehudit Schneider, and Rabbi Dovid Zeller (of blessed memory).

MOSHIACH BAH

On Sunday, the 17th of Sivan, 5747 (June 14, 1987), the Messiah will come to our city.

With the rising of the sun, he will pass over the Mount of Olives and raise the sleeping.

He will rise and come to the Mercy Gate to the Temple Mount.

He will rise over Mount Zion and arrive at Zion Square at noon.

There we will join him and go together to the Knesset.

The redeemer will come to Jerusalem and the children will return to their borders.

Foreword

They say the best fiction is based on fact. In spring of 1987, I saw a sign at the exact corner of King George and Hillel streets as described in these pages. The wording of the sign, which I have included is an exact translation of what was written. Some of Arielle's experiences are based on my own life as a master's student majoring in communications at Hebrew University on Mount Scopus. Like Arielle, one of the main characters of the story, I took courses in journalism and screenwriting and wrote a documentary screenplay and an article based on this experience. It was, in fact, one of my first times interviewing people. I've featured most of the interviews, that were part of the original documentary script, which also included people's comments about the poster, and their beliefs about the Messiah in general and the possibility that the Messiah was coming.

We weren't required to film the script, and I didn't have a video camera and have often thought, both at that time and over the years to follow, that it's a shame that I hadn't captured those interviews on tape or film.

Twenty-three years later, in the middle of a long night spent meditating and praying for guidance, a voice came to me that said it was time to write the story of that process and what would happen if the Messiah were here trying to make his presence known to the world. The story was to include that event and other times in our history that a potential Messiah had tried to reveal himself and what might have happened. In addition, I was told to write a story about what might happen the next time around, in our current generation, should a new potential Messiah attempt to make his presence known to the world. The ideas and scenarios started to flow, and I wrote them down. This book is based on what I was shown and asked to write that night.

The ideas are also based on additional interviews I've conducted over the past few years formally and informally with people across the religious and political spectrum, along with research about the Messiah, messianism, and the end-of-times prophecies of many, if not all, faiths, especially in the Jewish tradition. Names have been changed: characters fictionalized or consolidated, lots of stories expounded upon, and whole fabrics woven from my imagination.

It was at about that time that the Lubavitcher Rebbe (*zt"l*) started his focused campaign to do all we can to bring the Messiah through our deeds and fervent prayers and increasing our *kavanah, devotion,* and desire for the Messiah and all that his coming will mean for the Jewish people and for the world.

Some of the stories I've attributed to Rabbi Yehuda are Chassidic tales that I heard or learned over the years from many rabbis and teachers. I have done my best to remain true to their character, spirit, and teachings; but the exact words and the circumstances are fictionalized. May what is written herein show my deep love, appreciation, and gratitude to them and their teachings. It is not my intent to disparage any sect or denomination; therefore, I have not specified what sects the fictitious David and Aryeh might have been born to.

I am not a great scholar. I have done a lot of research on the subject; but even more so, this has been an act of great faith, love, and some might call *chutzpah,* I hope *holy chutzpah,* to bring forth. Any inaccuracies are mine alone.

The signs are all around us, but it's not enough just to see them. We must recognize them and go out of our way to do all we can to promote his success. We must not only believe that he'll come. We must do all we can to hasten the coming, not put obstacles and stumbling blocks before the blind. All those who don't see the signs are like the blind referred to in the biblical passage. All those who don't believe are like a *tinok shenishba,* a child who is taken captive before he has a chance to learn the ways of Torah.

May this endeavor bring a *tikun* to all those who read it. May it fill us with the knowledge of G'd and bring us closer to the time of Moshiach, enabling us all to live lives filled with holiness and divine inspiration, in a world filled with peace, free from suffering.

I never did find out who put the sign up or why, but it started a journey that continues to transform my life, and I would like to say thank you. I really did go to Zion Square that day and waited from noon to about 1:00 p.m. I found only a smattering of people there, no more than usual at noon on a Sunday, no one discernibly there to greet the Messiah or join a rally. I don't know if there was a gathering at the Knesset. I didn't get that far. I headed back to campus when no one showed up at Zion Square. My mind filled with speculation, and I continued to wonder what would it take for people to believe? What must we do to be worthy for the Messiah to come? These questions have been with me most of my life, even before this event, and other questions like, Will people really believe and accept him or her when the Messiah comes? What will people be willing to do to change their lives in keeping with what we've been taught will happen at the time of the Messiah?

*   *   *

Chapter 1

The redeemer will come to Jerusalem and the children will return to their borders.

—Jeremiah 31:16

Arielle
Jerusalem, May 1987

What first caught my eye about the sign hanging on a lamppost on the corner of King George and Hillel streets was the white writing on a blue background, the exact shade of blue we call *techelet* in Hebrew. The sky was that color today, a deep, rich azure blue. The words were in an ornate, old-fashioned font generally reserved for prayer books and Bibles, not often seen hanging from lampposts. They were what held my attention. They read:

MOSHIACH BAH

On Sunday, the 17th of Sivan, 5747 (June 14, 1987), the Messiah will come to our city.

With the rising of the sun, he will pass over the Mount of Olives and raise the sleeping.

He will rise and come to the Mercy Gate to the Temple Mount.

He will rise over Mount Zion and arrive at Zion Square at noon.

There we will join him and go together to the Knesset.

The redeemer will come to Jerusalem, and the children will return to their borders.

Moshiach Bah. This could mean that the Messiah is coming or that he has already come. The Hebrew is not clear. I say *he* because what is clear from the Hebrew is that it's masculine, not feminine, but I wouldn't be opposed to a woman redeemer. Does it mean that he's already here in Israel but hasn't yet been proclaimed or that he'll be arriving on June 14? Is he a regular person coming in a regular way, or is some miracle going to happen? It doesn't really matter how the Messiah comes, at least not to me, as long as he comes. Is there any chance that it's for real that the Messiah will actually be here in less than three weeks?

We pray every day for his coming. It's in so many of our prayers. I've often wondered, how we'll know when it happens. Will it be clear? Will the people accept him, or will there be dissension about it again, as in the past? I was so curious to know what people thought or might know about it that I started asking people for their opinions, which is really out of character for me. I don't usually talk to strangers, let alone walk up to them out of the blue and start asking questions, but I couldn't help myself.

I know it's good for me to do since I want to be a journalist, but up until I saw the sign, I was always too inhibited, too afraid. Today, for the first time, I walked up to complete strangers and started to interview them. It wasn't like I suddenly had courage. It was more of a compulsion. I couldn't stop myself, not that I wanted to. It was exciting and liberating. I had a purpose. I felt free and alive.

"Excuse me. Can I trouble you for a moment?" I cleared my throat, trying to gain the attention of a young Chassid passing by. He seemed startled, which was understandable. I'm sure it wasn't often that strangers, let alone young female strangers, called out to him in the middle of the street. "Did you see the sign?" I inquired, pointing to the poster he'd just walked by without so much as a glance. I could tell he was a Chassid by his *peyot,* which came down in dark, tight, symmetrical curls in front of his ears, and by his long black suit jacket and hat. He rushed by without answering.

"Uh, pardon me," I called with a bit more force, trying to get the attention of another young man wearing similar attire. "What do you think of this sign? Have you noticed it?"

Unlike the first young man, this one stopped to see what I was referring to and then responded, "I don't believe it. It's a fraud. We would know if he was coming. There would be signs." He stroked his scraggly beard as he answered.

"There are signs, look," I said, playing innocent, though I knew what he meant. "Here's a sign."

"Not that kind of sign, I'm talking about *simanim*—things happening in the world, clear indicators that it's time. The rabbis would know. They'd tell us."

"You're kidding me, right. You don't think there are indicators? What, things haven't gotten bad enough for you yet? They've been saying for years that we're in the birthpangs of the Messiah. If not now, when? When will he come?" I asked emphatically. I took a deep breath, regaining my calm. "So, will you come?" I asked.

He clicked his tongue in an Israeli slang gesture meaning *no*. "Sorry. I have class at that time. Besides, I already told you, it's not for real," he called out as he hurried on his way.

"How can you be sure? Isn't it more important to be there to support him in case it is real than to assume you know the truth? Don't you believe that anything is possible? Don't you believe the prayers you recite every day?" I yelled after him. Having been raised in a modern Orthodox family, I've often wondered what will happen when the Messiah comes. Will people believe? Will it happen immediately? Automatically? Or will we have to help him? Will there suddenly be peace on earth? Will people suddenly be healed from all illness? Will people really rise from the dead? If the holy temple doesn't just drop from the sky, will people help to rebuild it? What will people be willing to do to help him succeed? Will they be willing to change their lives? If they don't live in Israel already, will Jews be willing to leave everything behind and move here, as it says will happen when the Messiah comes? The questions came to me, one after another. I didn't have to plan it out. They just kept coming. And is there something we could or should already be doing on our own to bring about the kind of world we long for? When I asked myself this question in my teens, I had answered, *yes*. I vowed that I would make aliyah and be a part of the Zionist dream, building the Jewish homeland and readying it for the ingathering of diaspora Jewry.

I spent hours interviewing people as I stood near the sign. Very few, if any, believed there was even a remote possibility that it was true. Most just laughed or shook their heads, saying it must be a hoax or a marketing ploy. I approached religious and secular people alike, men and women across the religious spectrum. A group of young ultra-Orthodox men walked toward me, and I asked them too if they'd seen the sign. "It says the Messiah is coming," I pointed out.

"Don't pay any attention to those signs. It's nonsense," said another yeshiva student.

"But how can you be sure? Don't you think it's worth checking it out for yourself?" I questioned, repeating the arguments I'd made earlier with arrogant, know-it-all ultra-Orthodox men.

"It would be a waste of time. We have class." He used a phrase stressing the religious imperative to maximize one's time and that it was a transgression to misuse it on fruitless or unworthy endeavors.

The closest I got to a believer was a middle-aged American man with a felt black yarmulke who asked, "Is it the Lubavitcher Rebbe? A lot of people believe it's him. Did you see him? He even has a house at Kfar Chabad."

I shrugged. "I don't know. It could be."

"You believe this man could really be the Messiah?" challenged another young Orthodox student. "On what basis?"

"Why shouldn't we believe?" I challenged in response. He shrugged and clicked his tongue then headed on his way. That tongue click could mean many things, none of them positive. It's Israeli slang for *no, no way, you've got to be kidding, don't be ridiculous,* and other choice put-downs that might be used in English depending on the volume and duration of the click. Sometimes those put-downs are used in addition. I can't say that I've entirely mastered how to interpret it in every situation, suffice it to say, that it never means anything in the affirmative.

Next, I approached a couple who were clearly tourists who had stopped in front of the sign. Both were tall, elegant and strikingly attractive. He looked like Richard Gere, she like Geena Davis. I wondered what they were doing in Jerusalem. He wore dark jeans and a polo shirt: she wore a flowery pink sundress. Atop his head sat a small crocheted yarmulke; atop hers, a pink wide-brimmed floppy hat that matched her dress and sandals. They were looking down at a street map when I approached. "Hi, can I help you?" I inquired with a smile.

"We're looking for the Mashbir. We're supposed to meet our group there." From his raspy bass voice, it was clear that he wasn't the man who turned millions of women's legs to jelly, including my own.

"Oh, you're on a tour? Where are you from?" I inquired. I love to connect with tourists, love hearing their impressions of Israel.

"We're from Los Angeles," the woman said.

"Really, how interesting. Is this your first time here?"

"Yes, it's my first time, but my husband has been here many times. We're on our honeymoon," she answered with a smile.

"Congratulations! How wonderful—to spend your honeymoon in Israel," I exclaimed. "The Mashbir is just down the road. Cross this street, then the next, and it's the big department store right at that corner."

"Thank you so much." The husband smiled.

"Before you go, can I ask you a couple of questions?" Optimistic, I turned to a new page in my notepad.

"Sure."

Yes! I thought, psyched that they'd help. "That sign you're standing in front of. It says the Messiah is coming on June 14 at noon and asks people to come to Zion Square then to the Knesset." I translated the wording for them and asked, "What do you think?"

"We'll be gone by then. We're only here for another week." The husband frowned.

"But what do you think? Do you think it could be true?"

"I have no idea," the wife shrugged her tanned shoulders.

"Would you consider changing your plans and staying longer?"

They both laughed as if I'd told a fantastic joke. "We'd love to stay longer. Who wouldn't? But, no. We have to get back to work," the husband said once he'd caught his breath.

"Unfortunately, there's no way we can extend our honeymoon." The wife shook her head. "Our lives are there. We just put our things into our new apartment, and haven't even finished unpacking—there's just so much time we could take off from work."

"As it is I'll have a tremendous backload. It will probably take me weeks to catch up," he added.

"Well, if the Messiah were to come, would you come back? Would you be willing to move here? To make aliyah?" I asked.

Again they laughed. "I don't think so," the husband blurted. "Look, Israel is a great place. I really love it, but I'm a lawyer. How on Earth would I make a living here? I can read a *siddur* and pray, but I can't speak the language. I'd have to retrain completely. There's no way we could leave everything behind and come. Maybe when I retire, but not until then."

"Unless we win the lottery!"

"I barely spoke the language when I came. You could take an *ulpan* and learn Hebrew. Many people retrain. I have cousins who did it when they were older than you are. Now they're practicing law here and love it. I'm sure you could do it," I encouraged.

They looked at me as if I were from outer space. "Um, sure, we could, but I don't think so." The husband smirked. The wife shrugged her shoulders and tried to keep her lips from twitching.

"You mean to tell me that if the Messiah came and said that all the Jews should move to Israel, you wouldn't come?" I don't know why I was shocked. I should have expected it.

"You really think that's likely to happen?" he challenged, raising an eyebrow.

"I don't know, but if it did, or when it does, what will you be willing to do to change your lives? Will you answer the call?"

They looked at each other this time. "We've really got to run," she said. "We were supposed to meet up with our group five minutes ago. I hope they didn't leave without us. Well, it was nice meeting you."

"It was nice meeting you too. Good luck to you both. Thanks for your honesty. Think about it though, okay? Israel is your home, just as it's the home of every Jew," I said. "Living here is a choice you could make at any time . . ." I continued calling after them as they raced across the street to meet their group.

*   *   *

On my way back to campus, I thought about all the people I'd just spoken with and decided to use the interviews for my final journalism class project. Over the course of the next week, I first asked questions while standing at the corner next to the sign then progressed to interviewing people about it wherever I go, whether on the bus, in the dorms, or in my classes. I ask if they've seen the sign. If they've seen it, I ask what they think about it. If not, I tell them about it. Then I ask what they think about the possibility that the Messiah might really come in two weeks' time.

Here we are, in the heart of the holiest city on Earth and, according to the sign, the anointed one we've been waiting for, for millennia is about to come. Do they believe it? Do they think others will believe it? Will they come? What do they think will happen if the Messiah really comes? How will it change our lives? We've waited for so long. Are people ready? Do they think we're worthy? One thing is for sure, in my opinion, we really need him now!

The next time I took a taxi, I asked the driver if he'd seen the sign. When he said he hadn't noticed it, I told him what it said. "So?" I questioned. "Do you think it could really happen?"

"It would be entertaining. I don't think people are ready for it. At least I'm not." He laughed. He wasn't bothered by the idea of animal sacrifices being renewed but thought that the city was not equipped to handle all the traffic. "Getting to the Old City would be a madhouse. And what would happen to the Moslem Quarter? I can't see the Muslims allowing us back on the Temple Mount, let alone putting up a new temple."

"You have a point." I smiled.

"That alone would start a war," he said, suddenly serious.

"G'd forbid, *chas v'shalom*," I said.

"*Chas v'chalilah,* believe me," he said.

"You'd be called up for reserve duty?" I asked.

"Of course. It wreaks havoc with your life—work, finances, puts a lot of pressure on a marriage, and the kids don't understand why Daddy's away for so long. My mother still worries, even at my age."

"Sounds like you've been through it before."

"Many times, wars and *koninut*." He was silent for a minute. Then he lightened up. "G'd willing, it would bring peace. That's what the *meforshim* say, isn't it?" The rest of the cab ride passed with each of us making more speculations about the likelihood of the Messiah coming and what would happen if he/she did.

When I got to town, I stood by *my corner* and took out my notepad. It took me a minute to work up my courage and then choose someone to interview. I thought it would be good to get a different perspective, so I first chose to approach a couple of young women who were wearing pants and tank tops, who looked to be on their way to lunch or to go shopping.

"Excuse me," I said. "Can I ask you a couple of questions? Have you seen the sign up around town? What do you think of it?"

"*That* sign?" One pointed. "*Aizeh shtuyot.* How ridiculous!"

"I don't know. Wouldn't it be nice if it were true? The rabbis say he could come any day, at any time," said her friend.

"You've got to be kidding. You really believe that nonsense?" The first raised her voice.

Her friend seemed stunned by the angry response. "*Mah pitom?* What are you talking about? The Messiah coming is not ridiculous nonsense. I doubt it's the time, but I hope I'm wrong. I believe the Messiah will come someday," she said. "G'd willing, it will be soon. Why not now?"

"I can't imagine it," said the first with a click of her tongue.

"Why not? We've been waiting for him throughout history. He has to come sometime. They've been saying since the establishment of the state that we're experiencing the birth pangs of the Messiah. It's been a long labor. It's time that he comes," concluded the second.

"If he were to come," I asked, "what do you think would happen? Would the Holy Temple be rebuilt? Do you think there will be a renewal of animal sacrifices? Would you want there to be?"

"Animal sacrifices? You must be kidding. What do you think? That we're in the Middle Ages? It would set progress back hundreds of years," the second practically screamed. "We have prayer now. Prayer replaced sacrifices. There's no reason to go back to all that."

"It's out of the question. It's completely barbaric and gruesome." The first was adamant in her insistence.

"It seems barbaric to me too, but think about it," I replied in a calm, soft tone, doing my best to bring the conversation back down to a normal pitch and decibel level. "Why not? If people eat meat, isn't it better to sanctify and consecrate it to G'd instead of mindlessly eating it with no thought as to where it came from?"

"Maybe you're right. If we give a part to the priests or to the poor versus devouring it two or three times a day, wouldn't that be better? Look at the way meat is processed and eaten today. It's gone to the extreme. Why is it barbaric for us to burn some of that for G'd before we eat the rest? Most of the animal sacrifices were eaten. Is it that much different than a barbecue? And who doesn't love a barbecue?" agreed the second young woman.

The first shook her head vigorously. "It still sounds horrendous to me. I don't think it's necessary at all. If they're going to insist on having sacrifices, I don't want the temple to be rebuilt at all."

"Well, I would." said the second. "May it come speedily in our day! *Halevai*—it would be great, if only the signs are true."

"Thank you for your time," I said. "Will either of you come on the fourteenth?"

They both laughed. "I don't think so," said the first derisively.

The second raised her eyebrows and tilted her head to the side. "I'll think about it."

"Well, thank you for your time." I let them go, sensing that the first was getting antsy, and I didn't want to deal with more of her annoyance. I could hear them arguing about it as they crossed the street and continued on their way.

The next person I approached was a middle-aged man wearing a small colorful crocheted yarmulke, indicating that he was probably modern Orthodox and a Zionist. "I think it could be true." He nodded.

"Really, so you believe it?"

"We'll know soon enough, won't we?"

"Will you come?"

"No. I'm very busy. It's in the middle of the workday. I'll wait to see what the news says about it."

"Well, thank you for your time," I said. I smiled, despite my frustration. *Why won't anyone agree to come, even people who say they believe it could be true?*

He smiled a genuine smile that lit his green eyes. "My pleasure. Good luck."

I spoke with several more people that afternoon before heading off on errands to the bank and the central post office. While in town, I stopped in to visit my cousins who live in Nachlaot. Their home has become my home away from home since making aliyah. As usual, my cousin Shirah insisted that I stay for dinner, and as usual, I gladly accepted. She's a great cook, and I love spending time with her and her family. Shirah and her family are my closest relatives in Israel and my only relatives in Jerusalem. I also have some friends from college who now live here, and I just heard that my cousin Shaina and her husband Yossi will be arriving during the summer. Yossi is going to study at a yeshiva in Arzei HaBirah, a very religious Jerusalem neighborhood. I'm really looking forward to them coming, even though I heard they're only planning to stay for a year. Shirah is my father's first cousin. Shaina is my first cousin—our mothers are sisters—so Shaina is even closer to me than Shirah, and she's closer to my age.

Shirah grew up religious but left it all when she was in college in the sixties. In some ways, she and her husband Andy still have that radical sixties lifestyle. It's funny, Shirah and Shaina are on opposite sides of the religious spectrum. Shaina and her family are ultra-Orthodox, while Shirah and her family are totally secular. I am more of a moderate. Each probably thinks I'm more similar to them than I really am.

Over dinner we talked about family, and their daughters, Adina and Aliza, showed off some of their art projects. As always, the food was fantastic—wholesome and delicious. Before making aliyah, Shirah owned a restaurant in the Boston area. It's always great to spend time with them. I feel completely at home. Being in their little house is like being in a warm, loving embrace. I asked them if they'd seen any posters about the Messiah coming. Neither had noticed them.

"You must have seen it. It's right at the corner of King George and Hillel streets. You pass by there at least twice a day," I said.

Shirah shook her head. "Nope. Never noticed it. I'll be on the lookout now that you've told us about it, but I'm sure it's not for real. Sounds pretty bizarre."

Her attitude didn't surprise me since I doubt she believes in the Messiah, G'd yes, just not all the rules and regulations of the religion, which she considers to be based on a bunch of myths.

They wished me luck with the project, and, in response to my questions, Shirah said, "I'll be thrilled to find out I'm wrong. World peace and an end to suffering—what could be bad about that? I'm not thrilled with the whole third temple idea. I'd probably lead protests against animal sacrifices, and the traffic would be horrendous. Can you imagine?"

"That's what my cab driver said," I told her.

"And the parking?" Andy chimed in, and we all laughed. "Real estate prices would shoot through the roof, as if they're not high enough already!"

"Why did you want to live in Jerusalem, seeing that neither of you are religious at all? What was the attraction?" I asked, on a serious note.

"It was the weather, wouldn't you agree, honey?"

"Yes. The Jerusalem winters were the closest we could find to Boston," Andy joked.

"No, really. Why Jerusalem?"

"It's a beautiful place. When we came on our pilot trip, we fell in love with the architecture and the history of it, the old and new worlds, the Middle Eastern and the European cosmopolitan styles interwoven into a bizarre mesh that bustles and vibrates with life." Shirah feigned a sophisticated, upper-crust New England accent, the one she used in her Katherine Hepburn impersonation.

"Can I quote you on that?" I asked.

"But of course." She switched to a French accent, sounding like Bridget Bardot, which differed from her Italian femme fatale impression of Sophia Loren.

"Plus, it's where I got the best job offer," Andy piped in.

"That makes sense," I said.

"It's where we wanted to live," Shirah added quickly.

"It made the most sense to us. We love being in the heart of things, right downtown, with easy access to businesses and restaurants, shopping and culture," Andy explained.

"Yes, it's just *maahvalous, dahling*," Shirah chimed. "We can walk practically everywhere we want to go, so we don't need a car. That's been amazing. There's great bus service to anywhere in the city, and we almost never have to transfer. The perfect school we wanted for the girls is within a five-minute walk, and everyone comes to see us, which we adore."

"They just drop by, like you did today, and if we're here, great, if not, so be it, they'll try again in an hour or two if they still have time."

"If we're still not home, they'll try again the next time they're in town and feel like dropping by . . . it's perfect for us, actually."

"That *is* pretty cool," I said.

"We love it," Shirah enthused, cleaning as she spoke. I joined her, straightening things up alongside her.

"But I do wish we were a bit closer to the sea, especially on Shabbat, since there's no bus service. That's the only time I miss having a car," she said. "But we discovered that there are *moni'ot sherut*, special taxis, that go to Tel Aviv, and they leave from right here, downtown. We don't even have to get to the Central Bus Station."

"That's wonderful."

"Yes, it's brilliant," Shirah said, reverting to her mock British accent.

It was starting to get dark out, and I had lots of reading to do before classes tomorrow, so I took my leave.

"Stop by anytime," said Andy, as he did every time I visited. "You're always welcome."

"Thanks, I know. It means a lot to me." I thanked him with a hug and a kiss on each cheek.

"And to us too." Shirah's eyes started to mist. I hugged her too then picked up each of the girls and whirled them around as I gave them each a kiss good-bye. "I'll see you soon. I promise," I said, kissing the mezuzah as I walked through the blue metal gate, that color *techelet* that you find all over the Middle East that is believed to ward against the evil eye.

On my way back up Rechov Betzalel, I saw an elderly man in black Chassidic garb putting up more blue signs. He had a big pile of posters and was putting them up on Betzalel near the original corner I'd seen the sign. In my thick American-accented Hebrew, I asked if I could help him. He looked surprised but gave me a few posters to put up on campus and around town.

I felt self-conscious talking to the Chassid dressed as I was in a short-sleeved, scoop-necked top and jeans. I hoped he wasn't offended, but I wanted to help. I didn't know if he'd be offended to have a woman speaking to him and taking posters from him either. Having posters up around campus would also make my project easier, but I really did want to help. *I hope that the Messiah is coming. It's not just my project that's motivating me.* I was encouraged to see that it was a Chassid hanging up the posters. I doubted that he was promoting a play or some product, so he must be genuine.

"Are you him?" I questioned in Hebrew.

He laughed. *"Lo, ani ozer lo."* The wizened Chassid with white hair and a long white beard let me know, in his Yiddish accent, that he was not the Messiah, but his helper. "We can speak in English. My English is actually better than my Hebrew."

"Really. Why is that?"

"I've been living in America since the war," he said. "We're here now and, G'd willing, will remain here from now on."

"Oh. Is there a way I can reach you?"

"We're staying at the Ram Hotel on Rechov Yaffo, room 211."

"Is it okay to call? Is he there too?"

The old man smiled but remained silent for a moment. Then he responded, "If you put up the signs and come at the time and to the place indicated on the posters . . . that will be enough."

"But I'd like to do more. Is it possible to interview him? I'm a journalism student at Hebrew University. I'd like to write an article about him and possibly do a documentary on this . . ."

"Call the hotel. I'll see if he'll agree to it." He shrugged noncommittally.

"Can I ask you some questions at least?"

"Not right now. I have to put up more signs, and then I have a meeting. If you want, call. Oh, there is one more thing you can do," he said.

"What's that?"

"Tell people about it. Talk to as many people as you can and bring them."

"So it's okay if I write an article?"

"Of course, but I can't promise you an interview."

I looked at the phone number he'd given me and saw he'd also written his name on the little scrap of paper. It read, "Eliyahu." Tingles went up and down my spine. It was too strange a coincidence. Could he be *the* Eliyahu, coming in advance to tell that the Messiah is on his way?

As I told Eliyahu, I plan to make a documentary about the event, whatever might happen. For the final in my screenwriting class, we have to write the script for a ten-minute documentary. We're only required to write the script, but it would be amazing to film it too. Unfortunately, I know nothing about filming. I'm going to use the answers I've gotten over the past week and continue to get over the next two weeks for the script.

I wish I had a video camera. Even if I had one, I'd have to learn how to use it or bring a crew with me. It's more than the class calls for, but why not? It would be great to be there with a video camera and film it for posterity. I wonder if other journalists will be there or any television crews. It would be amazing to have it all on film.

*   *   *

Chapter 2

The details about how Moshiach will unfold cannot be definitely known until they occur for these matters are undefined in the prophets' words and even the wise men have no established tradition regarding this . . . and neither the order of these events or their details are fundamental to our faith.

—Maimonides, Mishne Torah, Malachim 12:2

David

Jerusalem, May 1987

"What else can we do? I feel like I haven't done enough," I asked Miri Roth, my fiancé, one Sunday night while eating dinner at her apartment. "I'm going to call my father again and my other uncles and their families. Do you think I should contact Uncle Yehoshua's children? More than anyone they should be here."

"But it's been years since you've been in touch with them, hasn't it? Do you even know where they live?"

"I don't, but my parents know."

"Haven't they been estranged from their father? Didn't you tell me that they also followed their rebbe's edict?"

"Yes. They stopped talking to him—disregarded the commandment to honor their father and mother. Tell me, which is more important, upholding the rebbe's *cherem*, or honoring their parents or in my father's case, his uncle?" I finished and picked up the phone.

"Is that your father you're calling?" Miri asked. "Are you sure you want to call him now? Why don't you wait until you calm down? That argument you had before Shabbat was a big one. Are you ready to accept it if he says no or gets upset with you again?"

"I've got to try. I know it's a long shot, but if I don't try I'll never forgive myself if Uncle Yehoshua doesn't succeed," I explained.

"Ah, now I understand. Do whatever you have to do. I'm here if you need me," Miri kissed my cheek, got up from her chair and started clearing the table.

I dialed the phone. It rang twice before my father picked up. "Hi, Papa. How are you doing? . . . . Great, great. Good to hear . . . . Yes, that's why I'm calling again so soon . . . ."

"There's no way I can come," my father replied in Yiddish, sounding even more annoyed than he had when I'd called last. "How many times do I have to repeat myself?"

"Listen, Papa. I'm sorry I hung up on you, but please, Papa," I begged. "I think you should come. Uncle Yehoshua needs you."

"*Dovidel*," he said, using the childhood nickname my family still called me, "how many times do we have to go through this? I know what Uncle Yehoshua says. I know what he thinks, but our rebbe doesn't agree. He doesn't believe it's him. My hands are tied."

"Papa, he's your uncle. You've known him all your life. He's been like a father to you all these years. How can you abandon him? Please, he needs you here, and not just you, as many people as possible. It's time."

"I'm not abandoning him. He's still my uncle. I cannot condone let alone promote this. It's not time, regardless of what he says. I can't come to Israel right now."

"But it could be time," I insisted. "If you and others believed, maybe he could succeed. Maybe he still will. Don't you want to be here for that? Haven't you waited your whole life for it?"

"Dovid, this is crazy. I don't know why he's insisting on going through with it, and that friend of his is no help. He just encourages this *narishkeit*. You know as well as I do that he's in *cheirem*. Excommunication is not something to be taken lightly, and there's a question in many people's minds as to whether he should be institutionalized. They say it's something called Jerusalem syndrome. You live there, you must have heard of it. I can't defy my rebbe. I can't sanction what Uncle Yehoshua is doing if I'm not one hundred percent sure it's true."

"Pop, it's not Jerusalem syndrome. The rebbe is wrong. Jerusalem syndrome happens to people when they come here, and it's out of the blue. Uncle Yehoshua already had visions and believed he was

Moshiach; not just believed, there were many indications that it was or is really the case. Look Pop, even if you're not one hundred percent sure, what if it is true? Think about it. How do you know that Uncle Yehoshua is not the Moshiach? We need this, the Jewish people and all the world. We need it to happen, and in order for it to happen, we must do everything it takes for him to succeed. What's the worst that could happen? In my mind, it's worse to stop him from trying than to let him see this through, even if he doesn't succeed. Can't you see? He'll never succeed without people's support. I know he gets confused sometimes, but he's not crazy."

"Really, Dovid. He's just a man. How could he be Moshiach? Do you see any indication whatsoever that Uncle Yehoshua is or could be Moshiach *tsidkainu*?"

"We have the lineage, Papa. You've always been so proud of it. Your whole family is proud of it. What are you so proud of if this is the way you treat someone who claims to have *ru'ach hakodesh*? What if it's true? How can you be so sure it's not him? Eliyahu says it's him. You've heard their stories. I grew up on those stories—the light around him in the camp, the miracle of how he came back from the brink of death, how he prayed for people and kept them alive, how their barracks had the fewest fatalities . . . you've heard them all, over and over again. I believe it's true, and I'll do everything in my power to help him succeed." If I hadn't already left the rebbe, I would have left him now. "I'm through with it," I told my father. "I have no regrets! If I had any before, they're completely gone now. I have no regrets at all that I left. He's not my rebbe. If I have a rebbe, it's Rabbi Yehuda, not that intransigent tyrant you hold by."

"G'd forbid, *tfoo, tfoo, tfoo*." I heard him spit at the other end of the line. "How can you say such a thing? How can you compare our rebbe with that heretic? Our rebbe is a righteous person, a *tzaddik*."

"Your rebbe might be very knowledgeable, a great scholar, but in my opinion, he is not a *tzaddik*."

"How could you say such a thing?"

"I say it because it's true. Whether you believe Uncle Yehoshua or not, he's family, the closest thing to a grandparent I have. You should be here at a time like this. He needs your support."

"There are a lot of people who need my support, people who are dependent on me. I have a lot of obligations. Your uncle's misguided notions are not for me to support. If I'm wrong, and he is the Moshiach, show me. Make it clear. I'll be thrilled to be proven wrong."

"Okay, Dad. I understand. *Zei gezunt*, be well. Send my love to Mama and to everyone else. I miss you."

"I miss you too. Should I get your mother?"

"Of course. Is she there?"

"Would I offer for you to speak with her if she weren't here?" he replied with a question of his own, with *talmudic* logic.

"Okay, Dad. Please put her on," I said, exasperated. I love my father, but he drives me crazy. I knew it was a long shot to get my father to come, but I had to try one more time. Of all the people in the world Hashem could have chosen, he'd chosen my great-uncle. My Great-Uncle, Yehoshua, a rabbi and scholar, teacher and *tzaddik*—in my opinion. Why do I think he's a *tzaddik?*

There are many reasons. I've never seen him angry or upset, even with all he's been through in his life. I never hear him say a mean or unkind word to or about anyone. I've never seen him do anything wrong, never seen him lose his temper, unlike my own father . . . unlike their rebbe.

I couldn't understand why they'd chosen him to be the rebbe. Just because he survived the war and made it to America, and none of his brothers had didn't seem like a good enough reason to appoint him to such a position, but they insisted on going by lineage and not merit. There was a time when the rebbes had chosen their successors by their worthiness, their knowledge and their *midot*—their attributes, but that had all but ended, and all the Chassidic sects seem to have developed into dynasties. The mantle of leadershp passes from father to son, or son-in-law, if there are no male heirs—like royalty.

"Are you okay?" Miri asked when I got off the phone.

"Great talk with my mother, not so great with my father."

"The usual." She frowned sympathetically.

"You could say that. I wish he'd come. His uncle is here—sick, in and out of the hospital, and planning to come out to the world at a rally in two weeks' time, and none of his own family, except me, will be there. It's insane. How can we hope to get anyone else to believe if his own family doesn't? And his own rebbe and the rebbe's Chassidim not only don't believe, but they've excommunicated him . . ." I repeated, despite knowing that she was quite familiar with the whole situation.

"Well, we'll be there, and we'll bring as many people with us as we can," Miri said in a soothing tone. It worked to bring my level of upset down. I don't know what I'd do without her. She has the ability to calm me down and get me to see the bright side of things in most situations.

"Thank you, honey. I love you so much. You're the greatest."

"I love you too. And I love your Uncle Yehoshua. He's such a sweet man. He has such a bright, radiant aura. His frequency is very high."

"If you say so. I don't see auras, but I'm sure you're right, and I agree, he's pretty terrific."

"He is. I really believe he is who he says he is. Won't it be incredible if he succeeds and this is it—that the *geulah* is finally here?"

"Yeah. It would be amazing. I pray every day that he'll succeed."

"So do I."

"I'm so glad you don't think he's crazy." I snuggled close to her, put my forehead against hers, and took a deep breath.

At first when I told Miri about my Uncle Yehoshua, she thought I was kidding. Then when she realized I wasn't joking, she thought he must be nuts. And when she realized that I believed him, she thought that I must be insane as well, but then she met him, and she was convinced.

An Orthodox Chassid who's been observant all his life, it's clear that he isn't lying. Whether or not he's correct, he truly believes that he's the Messiah and, in his mind, for good reason. Hashem told him so. Hashem told him that he's the Moshiach and told him that the time has come to let it be known that this is the time: the only chance he'll get in this lifetime to do whatever it is the Messiah will do. Now the issue is to get other people to give him the chance to prove it's true.

To meet him and speak with him, one would never think he's crazy, unless one got on this topic. When he starts to talk about it, most people think he's a little strange or all-out crazy; but still others, like his longtime friend, Eliyahu—yup, that's really his name—believe with all their hearts that it's true that my Uncle Yehoshua is really the Messiah—our generation's chance to bring redemption, to fulfill the ancient prophecies and bring peace on earth and an end to suffering.

Why is it so hard to get people to believe? To me he's always been the most wonderful uncle: soft-spoken, pious, G'd fearing, and loving G'd at the same time. He's taught me so much. From him I learned what a man should be. I model myself after him as much as I can, not the harsher, dogmatic, critical ways of my own father, but the sweet goodness of my Uncle Yehoshua. If I could only be more like him, life would be easy. I've always thought.

That's part of what makes Miri so perfect for me. She judges people favorably and reminds me to do the same, and along with finding the good in people and situations, she can find the humor in them as well. I'm so lucky to have found her, lucky she's agreed to be my wife, and lucky she introduced me to a whole new world filled with *chessed*, loving-kindness, and a community where everyone is welcome and cherished and a rebbe whose heart is overflowing with love.

*   *   *

When I got to the hospital, Eliyahu was sitting at Uncle Yehoshua's bedside reading *tehillim*. I didn't want to disturb him. He looked up at the monitors, saw me, and motioned for me to bring a chair over and sit, then went back to completing his recitations. Seeing my uncle hooked up to machines filled me with worry and concern for his survival. When I had dinner with him last week, he was happy, if a little disoriented. I thought he had just overdone it and needed to rest.

"*Shalom aleichem* Reb Eliyahu, good to see you again. Thank you for taking such good care of my uncle," I said.

"*Aleichem shalom* Reb Dovid, I'm so glad you came. He loves you so much. It's been wonderful to have you in his life again."

"I love him too. Thanks for calling to let me know. What happened this time?"

"He fainted. Luckily I was there. He didn't hurt himself, but he was disoriented, and his pulse felt weak, so I brought him in. They put him on oxygen and hooked him up to the IV and these other machines monitoring his heart rate, and I don't know what else. He's been sleeping most of the time. I don't know what's going to happen."

"Only G'd knows. We'll just take it one day at a time."

"Of course, but the event, there's so much depending on it," Eliyahu said. "I don't know if he'll be better in time. The posters are already up around the country. *Baruch Hashem* I've gotten help with that. We've waited so long, travelled so far, and now this. I pray that he'll recover," Eliyahu said.

"I know. G'd willing, he will."

"He's had heart trouble for years, as you know, but now this. The doctors explained that it's related. Now his respiratory system is contributing to the problem. With his breathing compromised, there's not enough oxygen getting into his bloodstream, so it's not getting to his organs properly, including his brain," Eliyahu explained.

"So that's what's been affecting his cognitive functioning. I've seen signs of it recently, moments of disorientation and forgetfulness," I said. "I've been worried about him."

"That's all it is. I'm sure of it. He isn't senile, he doesn't have Alzheimer's or another type of dementia, no matter what some people have been saying about him," Eliyahu defended.

"How long has this been going on?" I inquired.

"A few months."

"So it started before you came."

"Yes, but just a little. Very little. It was barely noticeable," Eliyahu insisted. "I don't know if he'll make it out of the hospital in time for the event. We have to have faith and continue to pray for his recovery. He has to be well enough to breathe on his own and make it on the walk. It will be taxing for him, I know, but we still have to try. Pray for a miracle that he'll be healed. If all people are to be healed, shouldn't it start now? With him?"

"B'ezrat Hashem," I said. "Eliyahu, thank you for all you've done. I know it's been hard for you with everyone turning on you both as they have."

"Yes. You know what happened when we tried to bring the message out before. It was in the 1970s."

"I remember. I was a young boy."

"I had a dream that it was time to make it known that Yehoshua was the Moshiach. The voice in my dream was very clear, and the images I saw were of wars that would plague us if we didn't succeed. War after war would continue with less than a decade between them, and conflict and turmoil among the Jewish people would escalate. There would be wars all around the world and big changes to come, some devastating, and not only for the Jewish people."

I got goose bumps listening to Eliyahu retell the story. I lived through it, but it was many years ago.

"Yehoshua had also gotten a message," he continued. "At first, he refused to do anything about it. He was still resisting his role. No matter how many times I'd told him of my visions—or seen first him and then others who were near him come back from death's door—he still didn't believe he could succeed, even if he was the one.

"I was twenty-two when we were taken to the camp. He had just turned thirty. Separated from the rest of our families, we came to depend on each other. He got very sick, and I did my best to take care of him, but I held little hope that he'd live through it. I'd seen too many people die by then who didn't seem nearly as sick as he was. Then, one night, I saw the light around him. It was a bright light that radiated through the bunk. He came back that night from the brink of death and was healed. I knew I'd witnessed a miracle, but that didn't mean he was to be Moshiach. But I heard a voice that night telling me that he was the one, the potential redeemer for our generation. I was told to protect him and to do all I could for him, to put my fate with him, like Ruth did with Naomi. True, Ruth was the one to follow Naomi, and Ruth was the one who is the progenitor of King David, thereby, the ancestor of the one who will be Moshiach, but nonetheless,

I was to stick by his side and to go wherever he went and to make sure he was always safe so that when the time came, he could fulfill his destiny.

"He was too humble. I reminded him that having too much humility is not always what's called for, like Moshe *rabeinu*. He was considered the most humble person of all time, but that didn't stop him from taking on the task of leading the Jewish people from slavery to freedom. True humility comes from knowing that everything comes from G'd and is not because of us. We can acknowledge what is true of our abilities and our position, but we must remain grateful to G'd for all of it. So finally, he accepted it and admitted that he'd had messages as well. He'd also been told that it was time, he just didn't know what to do about it. Neither did I, so we prayed for guidance, to be shown how to proceed.

"It was hard to keep it to myself all those years, but I did, until his children were old enough to understand. He refused to say a word, but finally, I told them and his wife and other relatives, the nieces and nephews who had survived and also come to America after the war. I told them all what had happened. None of his siblings had survived, nor his first wife and children. They were all gone. Actually, I did tell someone before then. I was luckier than Yehoshua had been. Masha, my wife, survived. We were reunited when the camp was liberated, thank G'd. She was gaunt, skeletally thin like we all were, barely recognizable, but I knew it was her from her eyes. We spent several years in the displaced persons camp and finally made it to America where we moved to the same neighborhood as Yehoshua. I told her that we needed to stay near him, and I told her why. She trusted me and agreed to do what I needed to do. When I told his family, Yehoshua said nothing. He didn't agree, but he also didn't disclaim it. I don't know what they thought at that point. Meanwhile, we lived our lives. Yehoshua remarried and had a new family, he got a job in a *cheider* teaching children, and I became a jeweler and found work in the diamond district. Eventually I got my own stall on Forty-seventh Street," Eliyahu recalled.

"I know. I bought Miri's engagement ring there, remember?"

"That's right, you did. Last Pesach. She's such a lovely girl. I'm so happy for you."

"Thank you. She likes you too," I said, patting his arm.

They were both Chassidim who followed a rebbe who died in the holocaust. All his descendants had perished in the war as well, and he had never named a successor, so we were Chassidim without a leader. They joined a shul with a different Chassidic rabbi as its head.

He had many followers. His great-grandfather had been our rebbe's grandfather, so we felt a connection. They had been sent to lead communities in different towns in Europe, back at the beginning of the twentieth century, so their ways were very similar, but their personalities were very different.

"Our rebbe had had an air of holiness about him. He was soft-spoken and thought things through before he spoke. He would go off into what seemed to be a trance before giving an answer to a question, whether of a personal nature, to help one of his Chassidim seeking direction, or on a theological topic, as if *ru'ach hakodesh*—the holy spirit—was coming to him right at that moment. It was a wonder to behold. If he didn't get an answer, he would admit it and say he'd look into it and get back to the person as soon as he had an answer. He was very approachable and very loving." Eliyahu smiled. "As a child and a teen, I was in awe of him. I prayed for that kind of guidance, to be worthy of it and privileged to receive it, and it finally came that night in the camps when I received my first personal experience of it. That was the message—to stay close to Yehoshua, to follow him and protect him. I've made it my life's mission to be there for him whatever the situation, no matter the sacrifice necessary. So we moved to the same neighborhood he did, though Masha had some distant relatives in another community. We got an apartment in the same building, we went to the same shul and saw each other at least once a day. Having lost so much family, we became each other's adopted family, celebrating holidays and *simchas*—happy occasions—together. His children were as close to me as my own. The difference was, mine didn't turn on me when our new rebbe tried to stop us.

"It was 1970 when we told him. I told him, actually, at Yehoshua's request. He wanted the rebbe's opinion before taking action on the visions or making it known, but once I did, the rebbe shouted at us to get out, that we'd obviously lost our minds. He wouldn't have a rational conversation with us that day or ever again. If only he'd kept it to himself, that would have been one thing, but he didn't. He called us a danger and a threat to the community and barred his followers from having any contact with us. It was terrible. After all we'd been through in our lives, we couldn't believe that a rabbi could do such a thing. I feel guilty that I involved Yehoshua at that point. If I had gone alone to the rebbe, maybe he would have only blamed me, not both of us. Maybe he would have only excommunicated me. Yehoshua lost his job, but my business was my own, so no one could fire me. It suffered, but other people came to me. I wasn't dependent on the community for my livelihood like he was."

"I remember," I said. "They were afraid to let him teach their children, so you gave him a job until he could find another position. They made it so uncomfortable for you that you moved to another community, found another shul, but the rumors followed you. I wish my family had been stronger, that they hadn't continued to follow the rebbe, hadn't capitulated to the *cheirem*."

"Thank you, Dovid. It means a lot to us that you've been back in touch as long as you have, since you went to college, isn't it?"

"Yes."

People ignored them. They crossed the street to avoid them. It had bothered me. I hadn't wanted to cross the street. I loved my Uncle Yehoshua, but my parents would pull me away, especially my father. On occasion, my mother let me say hello, even give him a hug or a kiss, but not if anyone was watching.

"I felt bad for my children and for Yehoshua." I heard the pain and sadness in Eliyahu's voice. "Perhaps that's why my sons moved out of town and my daughter moved to *Eretz Yisroel*. *Baruch Hashem*, it didn't turn them off to *yiddishkeit*, but it affected them all in their own ways.

"In the next town," Eliyahu continued. "Yehoshua was afraid to tell anyone. So we held off, and then the Yom Kippur War came. After all the victories of the Six Day War, the casualties in this war were unexpected. I was told to wait, the time could come again, with the help of G'd, if the circumstances were right. So we waited. And then, this year, around Chanukah time, I got another message. This one was to leave everything behind and go to *Eretz Yisroel* to announce that Moshiach is here and make it known that Yehoshua is Moshiach. He was already in his seventies. I was in my sixties, not quite ready to retire, but I did it. I handed over the business to two of my sons, liquidated what assets I could, and did what I needed to do to put the plan into action. The hardest part has been convincing Yehoshua that he could do it. In my opinion, he's too humble, too modest." He shook his head. "If he had been willing to promote himself, he could have been the rabbi of a big congregation, but he was content to teach in elementary school. Not that there's anything wrong with that, it's just that he had the potential for a much grander role. He loved working with children, and the children loved him. He had the brains, the knowledge, the scholarship, and the depth of understanding, he could have done so much more, made such an impact on our people, as I hope he will have now."

"So you packed up everything and came."

"I was told to keep going ahead with the plans; that this would be our last chance; that on the seventeenth of Sivan, we should go up to the Mount of Olives and come down, through the Old City, up to Zion Square to meet the people, and go together up to the Knesset, where we will formally announce his arrival. We got special insurance, and despite his doctor's warnings, we came. His children also thought it was a bad idea and asked him not to make a fool of himself. They blamed me, as you know."

"I'm sorry about that. I don't blame you. I think he needed you and still does,"

"Thank you, Dovid. That means a lot to me. As you know, our budget is small. We haven't had many contributors or many people to assist us. As a school teacher Yehoshua never made very much, so it was up to me to put up what money I could for us to fly to *Eretz Yisroel* and to pay for our headquarters. The posters were all we could afford in terms of advertising. I wish I could do more. I hope it will be enough."

"I hope so too," I said. *I wish I could do more to help them, but I'm just a student with a limited budget and lots of student loans, despite the scholarships I've received.*

"So how's Miriam?" he asked.

"She's doing well. She's working."

"Send her my regards. Such a nice girl. I'm so happy for you. May you be as happy together as I was with my Masha."

"Amen. Thank you."

Uncle Yehoshua didn't wake up during my visit that day or the next. It was yet to be seen if he'd be well enough to make his announcement on June 14 as planned. We'd just have to keep praying for his health to improve and take it one day at a time. In the meantime, Eliyahu was proceeding as scheduled.

*   *   *

Chapter 3

For He is our G'd and we can be the flock He pastures, and the sheep in His charge—even today if we but heed His call.

—Tehillim 95:7

Arielle
June 13, 1987

I called the hotel every day, but there was never an answer until yesterday, right before Shabbat. The man who answered the phone sounded like Eliyahu, with a thick Yiddish accent, though I wasn't one hundred percent sure. "There's no time to talk now," he said. "Come to the hotel on Sunday morning. We're meeting at 10:00 a.m."

"Thanks," I replied. "I'll be there. Shabbat shalom."

"A *gutten Shabbes*," he responded as he hung up the phone.

I'd already written the article and handed it in for my journalism class assignment. I got an A on it but couldn't get it published in any newspapers. I wish I'd succeeded in doing so prior to the event. That might attract more people. I plan to write another article. Depending on what happens, the *Jerusalem Post* editor agreed to consider publishing it.

My flatmate, Linda, and I had invited some friends for dinner Friday night in honor of having the apartment to ourselves. Our other two flatmates, both students on the one-year program, were away for the weekend. They'd be going back to the States within a few weeks, and though they're in the midst of finals, they decided to go away for the weekend.

Some of our guests for our big vegetarian Shabbat dinner, like Linda's boyfriend Elliot and my friend Jean Marc, met us at services at the Mount Scopus synagogue. Jean Marc had asked to bring his girlfriend, Leslie. I hadn't met his most recent conquest and was worried it could be awkward, considering my being one of his past flames that hasn't been completely extinguished. We'd dated when I was on the one-year program and decided not to continue the relationship long distance when I left. Neither of us wanted to be pining for someone so far away, and we figured we were still so young, it was unreasonable to expect each other to stay faithful and in love for two or more years before we'd see each other again. Besides, I'd been through it before, where I did try to have a long-distance relationship with someone I'd fallen in love with on kibbutz two years earlier, and I'd been heartbroken. Even if I hadn't felt that way, I couldn't imagine Jean Marc would have made it through two years alone. He's not the type, as far as I can tell, unless I've been completely mistaken about him.

I always feel blessed when I go to services at the Mount Scopus synagogue, especially on Friday evenings. *Kabbalat Shabbat* is my favorite service, and I have to pinch myself to believe I'm really here, in this beautiful synagogue with the most spectacular view imaginable. The front wall of the synagogue is all glass and overlooks Mount Moriah. As the sun set over the Old City, its light cast a rose pink and golden glow on the Jerusalem stone buildings with their rounded archways, and the silver and gold of the domes at this angle shine so brightly from the Temple Mount it's almost blinding, even at this late hour. All of the structures on the Temple Mount are clearly visible from this vantage point. Due to its location, northeast of where the holy temple once stood, we face southwest, instead of east, while praying.

The melodies transported me back to other times. Many were familiar to me from childhood, while others reminded me of my time on kibbutz, and still others of my year on the one-year program when I attended services here more regularly. Just that little extra distance from the Idelson dorms, as opposed to Resnick, makes it an easier trek to the Conservative synagogue on French Hill.

Walking back to the Idelson dorms on the other side of campus, we enjoyed the cool night air. We walked up the two flights to our apartment and waited for those of our guests who hadn't yet arrived. As soon as they did, Jean Marc made Kiddush for us all; then we washed our hands and said *hamotzi* together as we held the sweet challah I'd bought that afternoon at the Machane Yehuda open air market and tore off chunks then dipped them in salt before we ate them. No one spoke until they'd swallowed a bite of the special bread. Laughter and conversation flowed during dinner, along with the wine Elliot brought.

The late arrivals included Leslie, my friend Stacey and her longtime beau, Amram, a native Israeli pharmacy student she's been dating since her junior year at Hebrew University in 1982. Stacey, a native of Riverdale, New York, was getting her master's in psychology; Amram was finishing his last semester and would soon be looking for employment. Stacey and Amram had continued their relationship, staying in touch through letters, phone calls, and visits to see each other during the time we were back in the States finishing our undergraduate degrees in psychology; but Jean Marc, a Parisian of Moroccan descent, and I had barely been in contact then reconnected when I came back to Israel last fall, as if no time had passed, though our relationship had changed.

Over the course of the year, our friendship had grown stronger and though platonic, there was definitely sexual tension between us. Despite all the flirting and banter, I knew better than to go down that road with him again, at least not until he was finished breaking hearts and ready to settle down. Granted, the breakup had been mutual, but it had taken me a long time to get over him and move on. I often compared the men I met to him, and few were able to compete. They either weren't as handsome (okay, I could deal with that, it's just the external package,) or as intelligent (a few were) or as funny (that I'd really missed) or as romantic (how could any of those American boys compete with a Frenchman?). He'd been a regular student, with a double major in economics and international relations, in his first year after finishing the *mechina*, preparatory program, while I was on the one-year program.

I was surprised by Leslie's attire. She looked ready to go to a disco in her bright red miniskirt with a gold belt synched around her size-zero waist, matching red blouse with a low-cut bodice, and red stilettos. I don't know what I'd expected, if I'd expected anything, but she wasn't it. I'd been looking forward to meeting her and had hoped we'd become friends. It's easier to retain a friendship with an ex when you get along with his or her current partner, but something about her led me to think she wasn't the type of woman who has many female friends. I found her both intriguing and intimidating. Elliot and Amram did their best not to stare, but I'm sure it wasn't easy. Elliot, who'd been dating Linda since shortly after our arrival last summer was very attentive, asking Leslie all about herself, questions I wouldn't have thought to ask.

"How long have you been in Israel?" he inquired.

"For a little over a year. I've been teaching English at the Foreign Minsitry." So there was more to her than met the eye.

"That's impressive," Elliot commented.

"I guess," Leslie said. "It pays well."

"That's great. I'm sure it's very rewarding."

"It is, but I'm ready to go home. I have a job already lined up."

"Oh," Elliot said. "Where will you be working?"

"At a primary school in London."

"Really. What made you decide to leave?"

"I miss my family. We're very close. I never intended to make aliyah; it's just that once you're here it's hard to leave. There's a lot of pressure to stay and be part of all this. People act as if I'm deserting them, but in truth, I never planned to stay. Of course the thought crossed my mind, as a Jew, Israel is home, but England is also my home, and my family need me. My parents are getting on in years. They're survivors." She left it at that. There was a lull in the conversation leaving each of us with our thoughts. I could understand the pull of family and was relieved not to be in her position. I don't think I would have been selfless enough to leave and give up my dreams. But it hadn't been her dream to stay. It felt too personal, too invasive, to ask her more. I felt lucky that my parents were still young and in good health.

I wondered if Leslie and Jean Marc would continue their relationship when she left, and if he would wind up leaving too. I couldn't imagine him leaving. He's always been such a strong Zionist. I looked over at him and tried to read his expression, but couldn't. I felt for him. It was like déjà vu. How many times had he been through it? I know I hadn't been the first. Why did he keep dating women who didn't plan on staying? The thought crossed my mind that he'd be available in a few months, but I pushed it aside. When was she leaving? She hadn't said, but I wasn't about to ask. Who said it was easy keeping in touch with old boyfriends, especially a handsome *Casanova* like Jean Marc? To his credit, he has a lot more going for him than just his good looks and charm. He's extremely intelligent, a true Zionist, passionate about politics and philosophy, but at the same time lighthearted and funny, but even more important, he's caring and kind.

Over dessert, I broached the subject that was never far from my mind of late, and asked them all for their views on the prospect of the Messiah coming. "Have you seen the signs?" I asked.

Only Jean Marc and Amram have even noticed the posters.

"I thought it was an advertisement for Shalom Hanoch's new album," Jean Marc said.

"It said the Messiah is coming, not that he's *not* coming," I said, referring to the popular song by the Israeli rock singer that had been a huge hit.

"Yes, but still. It could be a ploy to sell more albums, or perhaps he's having a concert," Jean Marc said.

"No, there was nothing written about an album or concert on the posters. Besides, I saw a Chassid putting them up. I'll show you exactly what they said." I rushed to my room and came back with the text I'd copied from the poster for my interviews. "You should come. It could be the event of the millennium, and if not, it should be fun anyway. We can make an outing of it. I'll even let you bet on it and rib me if I'm wrong," I coaxed.

"You really believe this is true?" Leslie asked. She sounded shocked that anyone could believe it. In my mind, I heard her thinking *How gullible. It's preposterous* in that British accent. All right, I admit it. I was a bit jealous of her tall, willowy build and her long dirty-blonde hair and that figure that was to die for. And she was so much nicer than I'd thought at first impression.

"Well, I don't know, but I hope it's true. Wouldn't it be amazing? Haven't you ever thought about it? What will happen when the Messiah comes?" I asked.

"Not really," Leslie admitted.

Jean Marc, the most religious of us in some ways, despite his philandering ways with women, offered, "Of course I've thought about it, but to be honest, though I hate to admit it, I'm not ready for him to come tomorrow."

"Come with me, Jean Marc. Come on, it will be fun," I said.

Leslie gave me a look, which I did my best to ignore.

"Are you kidding? I have too many papers to write and finals to study for, plus my job. If it's true, we'll find out soon enough." Jean Marc laughed, clearly not believing that it's possibly the time.

"Do any of you, by any chance, have a video camera I could borrow?" I asked.

Our guests stayed until about midnight, except Elliot, who was still there when I excused myself to get ready for bed and the next morning.

*   *   *

When Shabbat ended, I attempted once again to procure a video camera. No one I knew had one, and the communications department refused to lend equipment out to students unless they were specifically in a class that involved television, video, or film production. I explained the situation to them, but of course, the bureaucrats stood by their positions, and due to privacy rules, they wouldn't give me the names of anyone with access to the cameras, so I didn't know if I even knew anyone in any of those classes whom I could have asked. So I took a bus downtown to see about buying one, even though I was sure I couldn't afford it, but I had to at least try.

I called Israel TV, and the editor I spoke with said no one had noticed the signs, and as far as she knew, they weren't planning to cover the story. The *Jerusalem Post* office said that they'd take the story if something actually happened, but they weren't going to send a reporter to cover it. "This is Jerusalem. We get reports about Messiah sightings by wackos all the time. Just because this one put up some posters doesn't make it true."

*　　*　　*

As I'd expected, video cameras were beyond my price range. Throughout Shabbat and when in town this evening I kept inviting people to join me, but everyone I asked had an excuse. Most, like Jean Marc, were studying for finals or working. I couldn't get anyone to come. Despite all the responses I'd gotten, I still believed the possibility existed that the Messiah was getting ready to reveal himself. None of the people I spoke with had seen Eliyahu. It felt surreal to think that the Messiah was on his way.

I feel grateful for the experience I've gained. Whether or not they succeed in ushering in a new era and ending the diaspora, I am certain Eliyahu and the one he claimed to be the Messiah sincerely believe they were following Hashem's will. I've found it very frustrating listening to all the naysayers and not being able to sway their opinions. Why can't they just be open to the possibility? I've felt even more disheartened to hear so many people say they don't want him to come, or that they don't even believe in the Messiah at all. Most people I've interviewed haven't even noticed the posters, and no one I've spoken with is planning to be there. Whenever I spoke to someone who didn't know about it, I took it as an opportunity to inform them, hoping that they'd be as excited as I was, but almost no one seems willing to even entertain the possibility that it might be true, let alone get excited about it. Even if they said they want the Messiah to come and that they pray for it every day, they still don't believe it could be true.

*　　*　　*

Sunday, June 14, 1987

Today's the day. I can't believe it's already here. I dressed with care making sure to wear something sufficiently modest by even the strictest standards. I chose a high-necked black cotton top and black skirt that reaches below my knees, with a long silk flowing black jacket with wide bands of periwinkle, violet, and turquoise over it. The jacket brightened the outfit, and its style was figure flattering, but not revealing. I didn't want to offend anyone at the gathering, and, though I never dress like Leslie, I regularly do wear short sleeves or sleeveless tops and dresses, as well as pants, of which the ultra-Orthodox don't approve, I don't generally worry about covering my collarbone, another of their specifications regarding acceptable, modest women's attire. I was both excited and nervous.

I reached the hotel by 10:00 a.m. When I arrived, several men were already present—all were dressed in ultra-Orthodox attire: black suits; white, button-down shirts; and black hats or large black yarmulkes. One of them answered the door and ushered me in. I looked around the cramped hotel room wondering if any of the people present were *him*. I searched for Eliyahu and just as I had that thought, he hurried in, a bright smile on his radiant face.

He greeted everyone enthusiastically. "Thank you all for coming. You've been such a help to us; we're grateful for your faith and trust in us and for all the prayers you have been saying for Rabbi Shapiro. I just wanted to let you know that he is out of the hospital and will be joining us later. We thought it best that he spend as much time as possible resting and preserving his strength, but thank G'd, we are going ahead with everything as planned." He spoke to several of the men individually then smiled when he saw me, "Ariella, you're here. I'm so glad you made it. Thank you for your help putting up the signs I gave you. I'm sorry I wasn't able to get that interview for you, and as you heard, he's not here yet. but G'd willing, all will go well today and you'll be able to talk to him later."

"Thank you. I'd appreciate that. I've tried to get people to come with me, but I'm sorry to say, no one I know said they could make it," I apologized.

He smiled and nodded slowly, as he looked deeply into my eyes, I felt as if he could truly see my soul, know my innermost thoughts and desires, hopes and fears. "That's alright. You did the best you could. That's all anyone can ask." He took out a handkerchief and as soon as he wiped away the beads of perspiration on his forehead more appeared. He swiped at the new ones, and some on either side of his nose. Self-conscious he smiled, "Please excuse me. I must sit down."

"Of course. Go right ahead." I moved aside so that he could take a seat near where I stood. I couldn't imagine wearing all the clothes they did.

From his seat he addressed the group, "As you all know, posters have been posted around the country in most cities. There's less than two hours to go. I want some of you to continue making banners and signs while the rest of you go out and talk to people. We need to bring as many people as we can, to let them know what's happening, or to remind them if they've already seen the signs."

It was hard to believe the Messiah was really here—that if all went according to plan, masses of people would ascend to the holy city from all over the country to hear him speak. But would anyone else really show up? Had the others been more successful at getting commitments from people to come? When he finished speaking, I asked Eliyahu for a moment of his time. I took out my notepad and gave him an open-ended question to provide him the opportunity to tell me, and G'd willing the public once my article is published, what he most wanted to convey. Unexpectedly, he explained the significance of why they'd chosen the exact shade of blue, *techelet*, for the signs.

While stroking his beard he said, "We wanted the signs to be eye-catching of course, and we wanted to evoke in people's minds a connection to all our hopes and dreams as a people. It's the color of the flag, and the color that symbolizes peace. To me, it's the color of the Jewish people. It's the color of the string on the *tzitzit* that can only be made by a special snail or by a mixture of herbs. It wasn't a coincidence. We chose *techelet* because of its historical significance, because of its use in holy temple, in both the *kohen gadol's* vestments and the color of the *parochet*, the curtains in the *beit hamikdash*. It's both a show of our patriotism; that we will not usurp the authority of the state, and our devotion to *HaKadosh Baruch Hu*. Yehoshua is not seeking power over anyone. He is here to bring peace. He would like to find the way to be included in matters of state, and to assist them in finding solutions to both the country's problems and problems all over the world. Honestly, I don't know how it will all be done."

"Is he expecting there to be miracles?" I asked.

"I don't know. We'll see. You know, there are different theories and beliefs as to what will happen. Isn't it exciting? He wants to work with all the religious factions and the secularists and bring peace, understanding, respect, acceptance and cooperation among them all.

Even though he's a Chassid, he is a Zionist. G'd wants the Jewish state to exist. He never wanted a king in the first place, so I don't believe that's what He'll ask for now. It's all about peace and cooperation in the world. No one needs to suffer. There's enough for everyone if we learn to dispense resources properly, and if we cooperate in growing and creating what's truly needed for everyone's benefit, not just those with power or those who seek it. Yehoshua will tell you more."

It was as if the holy spirit, *ru'ach hakodesh*, flowed through him as he spoke, and then it passed. I felt humbled. I knew I was standing in the presence of a true holy man. I felt I'd witnessed prophecy come through him. It was a completely new experience for me. I didn't want it to end. If Eliyahu had this ability, I couldn't imagine what it would be like to be in Rabbi Yehoshua's presence.

Did this happen all the time? Had others witnessed or experienced it? I looked around the room and outwardly nothing had changed. The small crew present was busy with what they were doing, buzzing with excitement, but no one seemed to have noticed. If Eliyahu had spoken to others as he'd just spoken to me, I'm sure they would all come. Optimism filled me, and I thanked him for his time.

"Is there anything else we can do?" a tall Chassid with a long black beard and *peyot* like bottle curls asked. "What do you need? Can I bring you a glass of water, sir?" He looked to be about twenty, thin and slight. He wore the traditional garb with a black hat firmly planted on his head.

"That would be nice. Thank you." Eliyahu turned back to me and said, "Maybe you should go out and talk to people." He turned to a tall dark-haired young man and said something that I never would have expected. "Aryeh Leib, why don't you go with her? Yes. That's a good idea," he continued. "Aryeh Leib, you and Ariella do that. Go out to the streets. That's where you're most needed. Meet us at Zion Square, like the poster lists. Put up more signs, hand out flyers, and talk to people. Get them to come, as many as you can. Do it however you think is best. I trust your judgment."

"If that's what you'd like, I'd be happy to," came the answer in a deep baritone that resonated like the voice of an FM disc jockey on late-night radio. I was taken aback to hear that voice coming out of the young Chassid, dressed like all the others. He sounded American, from New York, but not Brooklyn. I wasn't sure from where. He was taller than most, his beard a bit fuller, and he was perhaps a year or two older as well.

"May I ask you a few questions?" I asked as we walked up Ben Yehudah Street.

"Sure," Aryeh said. "Go right ahead."

"How did you get involved in this? How did you hear about it? Did you personally know Eliyahu or Rabbi Shapiro? What are your thoughts on the likelihood that we are really witnessing the coming of the Messiah?"

"Woa. That's a lot of questions all at once. I don't think I can keep track of all you asked." He smiled and his eyes sparkled. He had adorable dimples and I couldn't believe I was noticing such things about a Chassid. I brought my attention back to focus on what he was saying. "I saw the signs and was curious," he continued. "At first I thought it was strange that they would publicize the Messiah coming with signs on lampposts, but then, when I thought more about it, I figured it was as good a way as any to let people know about it and get them to come." He handed out flyers as he spoke. "I didn't see any of these until today. Did you? No? So anyway, I thought, *Why not put up signs?* People think that miracles are going to happen, and they'll know when the Messiah is here, but the Rambam says no, it will all happen in a natural way. So I figured it makes sense, putting up signs is a very natural way to make it known. I told everyone I know about it, but I didn't know what else I could do until one day, when I was shopping in Geulah, not far from my yeshiva, I saw Eliyahu posting a sign, so I quickly ran over to him and asked if I could help. I had never met either Eliyahu or Rabbi Shapiro before that."

"Something similar happened to me, but on Rechov Betzalel," I jumped in. "So you're studying in yeshiva?"

"Yes," he answered and continued. "Eliyahu gave me signs and asked me to post them around the city and to personally tell people what was happening. I gladly agreed. How could I say no? We've been waiting for this all our lives—at least I know I have. I asked how I could contact them to do more, and Eliyahu wrote down a phone number and said I could contact him at that number." I took notes as Aryeh talked, and he continued to hand out flyers as we walked up the street.

"By the way, my name is Arielle, not Ariella," I said. "It seemed too trivial to correct Eliyahu, but if we're going to spend the next couple of hours together, I thought you should know," I said.

"Nice to meet you, Arielle. You can call me Aryeh. I prefer it to Aryeh Leib, but I didn't want to make an issue of it with Eliyahu either." He laughed. "So tell me, how did *you* get involved?" he asked.

"In a similar way. I also saw a sign and was intrigued. I hoped that it was true, but honestly, I had no idea if it was really true or some ploy or scheme, which is what most people I speak with seem to think. I'm studying communications at Hebrew University, and I thought this would make an interesting project for my journalism class, so I started interviewing people about it, asking if they'd seen the signs, what they thought about it, that sort of thing. But after I finished the assignment, I still wanted to be involved. I wanted to help them succeed. With all the negative responses I received, I was afraid no one would come, and we'd miss the chance for the Messiah to be revealed. Like you did, I asked Eliyahu how I could help when I saw him putting up signs one day. He also gave me a pile of posters and his phone number, but when I called, there was never an answer, until this past Friday, I finally got through to someone, and he invited me to come this morning. I was planning to come at noon anyway and was excited to get the opportunity to come a few hours earlier and help out. I'm going to write another article about what happens today, G'd willing."

We continued up to King George and Hillel, where I'd first seen the poster. Notebook in hand, after I'd finished interviewing him, I questioned other people asking if they'd seen the signs and if they were planning to come at noon to Zion Square, simultaneously interviewing and encouraging them to come. "I know I'm not the most objective or unbiased reporter because I so want it to be true and for him to succeed, but some things are more important than objectivity, in my opinion," I said.

"Definitely."

After a few minutes interviewing and encouraging people, I took a break and watched Aryeh do what he could to catch people's attention. "Come join us, you won't be sorry. Moshiach is here. He's coming today. He's on his way now. Join us at Zion Square at noon. We'll all go up to the Knesset together. Don't miss it. He's here!"

Most people glanced at us, shook their heads, and kept walking. A few stopped to challenge us or to answer questions or ask their own.

"Huh," I sighed. "I wish I had been able to get a video camera! This would have made a great film, even all these nonbelievers. Some of their comments are so interesting, it's a shame I'm not getting all this on film. It would have been great to get my interview with Eliyahu on film this morning. I wish everyone could see it and experience what I did." Instead, I could only write it all in my notepad. "That would convince people. I'm sure of it."

"He is pretty believable," Aryeh agreed.

"More than that, he radiates holiness," I tried my best to express what I'd experienced while he spoke to me this morning. Aryeh smiled and nodded.

"Sounds like quite an experience." He went back to trying to catch the attention of people passing by us. "Excuse me, sir. Have you seen the posters?," he called out. "He's coming. Moshiach is coming;

actually, he's here. Today is the day," Aryeh called to another young Chassid passing by. "Come, see for yourself. All will be revealed. Join us at Zion Square at noon."

"Don't believe it. You're wasting your time. This is a fraud. We would have heard about it sooner if he was coming," the young man answered, readjusting his hat, and continuing on his way.

"He's not a fraud. Come see for yourself. What have you got to lose?" Aryeh asked.

"I have class," the young Chassid called as he hurried on his way.

"Ugh, this is so frustrating," Aryeh said clenching his fists at his sides. "If even most other Chassidim don't believe it, who will? I could only get a couple of my friends to help out putting up posters, and none of them would even come to the hotel with me this morning. They said they'd come to the rally but only if they can make it without missing class. I explained to them that this man claiming to be Moshiach, and Eliyahu, were very sincere. I urged them to come and see for themselves, but almost everyone I spoke with laughed at me. They don't believe it's really the time or that the right conditions have been met. They warned me of the dangers of falling prey to a false Messiah. I understand the risks, but I truly believe it *is* the time and that he *does* have the potential."

"It's been frustrating for me too," I said. "Very few people I've spoken with thought it could possibly be true. I don't understand it. Aren't we supposed to believe that it could happen at any time? Why not now?" I went back to my interviews, taking snapshots with my camera of whoever would agree to be photographed, but by this point, I was also encouraging people to come as persuasively as I could.

As I wrote down their answers, I was struck with a thought, *I should have seen if I could get a Dictaphone or a small tape recorder.* Why didn't I think of it earlier? That would have been better than all this writing. I must remember to get one as soon as possible. It will be important for me to have as a journalist—and to learn shorthand. The most positive response I heard all day was from a man in a business suit who looked to be in his thirties. He mused, "If he really is Moshiach, I think he's only here for preliminary meetings. Then he'll go to the States for a lecture tour and fly around lecturing in Jewish communities around the world for the next few years. There's a lot for him to do."

"So, will you come?" I asked.

"No. I have a meeting, but I wish him luck."

"He needs your support."

"Sorry. I wish I'd known sooner, but I can't change this meeting. It's very important."

"More important than Moshiach coming?" Aryeh joined the debate.

"I'll hear it on the news if it's truly the time. I'm sure my being there or not won't make a difference," the man insisted.

"But if everyone feels that way, there will be no one there, and if there's no one there, maybe Hashem will decide it's not the time," I said.

"So be it," the man said. Aryeh's mouth gaped and his eyebrows lifted. Mine probably did too.

"You're willing for that to happen?" Aryeh asked.

"What can I do? I already told you, I have a meeting," he shook his head at us and walked away. It took a minute for us to recover. I shrugged my shoulders and took a deep breath.

We heard many of the same responses I'd heard all along. Even after we told them about Eliyahu, they just clicked there tongues, grunted disbelievingly, shook their heads and went on their way.

"I think it could be true," said one middle-aged man with a crocheted yarmulke.

"Are you going to come?" Aryeh inquired.

"No, I'm working. I can't take the time off."

"Please come," Aryeh said. "We need your support. Aren't you curious? Don't you want to be there?"

We approached anyone who passed. Secular or religious, it didn't matter. We spoke to women in all modes of dress, something I'm sure Aryeh wouldn't normally have done, but this was too important to worry about propriety.

A group of young ultra-Orthodox men approached, and Aryeh asked, "Have you seen the signs? They say Moshiach is coming today."

"Don't pay any attention to those signs," said one.

"It's ridiculous," said another.

"If he's coming, he should have already been here last night. Tradition says he'll come on Saturday night after Shabbat ends, not on a Sunday afternoon," said a third.

"In Jerusalem, they say every day that he'll come. This happens all the time. I can't take time off from work every time someone claims the Messiah is coming. I'd never get any work done. So what? They put up some posters. Anyone can put up posters. You think that makes it real? Please! It's ridiculous. I want Moshiach to come of course, you understand, but I can't just leave the office and run whenever something like this happens," said a man in his late thirties with a crocheted yarmulke in a dark blue business suit.

Doing our best to keep getting the word out, we approached a nonreligious woman as she passed us. "Oh, it's the name of a play," she said. "Or maybe Candid Camera."

"No, it's not," I said. "Look. There's no name of a theatre listed. Nowhere to get tickets or get more details. How could it be a play?"

"You think they're serious? They've got to be kidding. Who did this? You believe this is real?" The woman laughed, shaking her head and proceeding on her way.

"It's *bupkes*, nonsense," said another yeshiva student.

"If Moshiach, the Messiah, was coming, Eliyahu Hanavi would already have been here. He's supposed to come to Jerusalem three days beforehand to announce the coming of Moshiach."

"Well, he has a helper named Eliyahu," I said. "Who knows?"

"That's just a coincidence," the man insisted. "I've never seen anything like it before, but I don't believe it." The man shook his head.

"If you really believe, the rabbis say, then when the Messiah comes, you won't have to ask what's going on, you'll know it's happening, and you'll run out to be there and greet him!" was one confident reply.

"That's why I'm going. How can you be sure it's not him? Don't you think it warrants checking it out for yourself?" Aryeh challenged. This young man like so many others said he couldn't miss class. "Tell your rebbe. Maybe he'll let you come. Maybe he'll come and bring the whole class," Aryeh suggested hopefully.

"Is it the Lubavitcher Rebbe? A lot of people believe it's him. Did you see him?" another asked.

"I saw him. It wasn't the rebbe," Aryeh informed them.

My eyes widened. "You saw him! Have you met and spoken with him? I've only met Eliyahu. You're sure it was him? What was he like?" I asked, incredulous.

"You believe this man could really be the Messiah? "On what basis?" challenged another of the young Orthodox students who'd gathered around us, ignoring my questions.

"He was with Eliyahu at one of the first meetings I attended. "He's a Chassid; he looks like a pious old man. His name is Yehoshua Shapiro. He's a rabbi and seemed completely sincere. He was very modest and humble. He didn't say much. Why are you so skeptical? Why shouldn't we believe?" Aryeh asked, answering the man's questions, doing his best not to get defensive.

"Well, did he do anything to prove it?" the youth asked.

"I didn't ask him to prove it." Aryeh let out a deep breath. "The Rambam says that he'll be a normal person, and we shouldn't expect him to perform miracles, so what is he supposed to do to prove it? I know many sources say that he will perform miracles, but some, like the Rambam, don't agree. Come with us. See for yourselves. What have you got to lose? Think of all you and *we all* have to gain." Aryeh posed the questions, "What if it's him and you're not there? What if people don't come and it could have been him?"

"What if the sky falls down," one of the students responded. His friends laughed.

"It says in the Gemara that if you're planting a tree and someone tells you that the Messiah has come, you should first finish planting the tree before you go to greet the Messiah," said another man with a black felt yarmulke.

"So what are you doing right now? Are you planting a tree? I don't see any tree." Aryeh chided him, then he blushed and he looked abashed for his sarcastic remarks.

"Literally no, but figurative. I have to get back to work. Work bears fruit. I'll see if I can come for a little bit on my lunch break. If I miss it, I'll listen to the news on the radio and watch it on television tonight. If Moshiach comes it will be a newsworthy story. I'm sure they'll at least mention it."

"But what if everyone has that attitude and no one comes? What if that's all it would take for the Messiah to reveal himself and bring salvation to the world?" I asked.

"What if?" he asked sarcastically.

"You're willing to take that risk?" Aryeh asked.

"What risk? If it's him, it's him. We'll know soon enough," the man reiterated.

"I hope you're right," I said, worried that Moshiach wouldn't succeed and wondering if we even deserve for him to come if this is the people's attitude even in the holiest of cities. It's clear to me why we're called "a stiff necked nation."

Finally, a young man listening to the conversation said, "I'll come, I'll talk to our rebbe. If he agrees, I'll come. I'll see if he'll come too and bring the whole class. Maybe the whole yeshiva!"

"Thank you! That's great! Hurry!" Aryeh prodded.

The group rushed off, back to their yeshiva. Aryeh looked at his watch and called to me that it was almost noon, time to head back to Zion Square. I would have loved to have seen it happen, to have watched the Messiah pass over the Mount of Olives and come to Mercy Gate, then to the Temple Mount, and descend with them to Zion Square instead of meeting the group there. We brought about a dozen people with us whom we'd managed to convince to come. Bursting with excitement, we arrived at Zion Square to find it looking no different than it usually does at noon on a Sunday, with some tourists, some students, and some businesspeople rushing up and down the busy intersection. Some seemed to be milling around, which was not out of the ordinary, but no one seemed to be congregating or waiting for a big event. Aryeh waved at someone around his age in similar attire, motioning for him to join us. "Hi, Shimmie, thanks for coming," he said.

"No problem. I tried to get some of the other guys to come with me, but as you can see . . ." He shrugged. He looked me up and down, then back at Aryeh when he spoke.

"I thought Mendy was going to come," Aryeh said.

"Yeah, he decided not to at the last minute."

"Well, I'm glad you came." Aryeh thanked him.

"Sure. It will be interesting to see what happens," Shimmie said.

"I can't believe there are so few people here," I said.

"Oh, Shimmie, this is Arielle. She's been helping publicize this with me. So what do you think? Are those people waiting for Moshiach?" Aryeh asked, motioning with his head to the people milling around the central square. "Where could they be?"

"They're not coming. I told you it's a fraud!" exclaimed an impatient dark-haired man in his late thirties who we had just spoken with and gotten to come. "Let's get out of here," he complained, trying to convince others to leave with him. It reminded me of how Datan and Aviram incited the people at the foot of Mt. Sinai when Moses was late coming down from the mountain.

"No, no, please don't leave yet. Give them time. I saw them this morning. I saw him. He's real. I promise you!" Aryeh raised his voice over the crowd that was growing impatient.

None of the yeshiva students came back with their classes as they'd said they would. The small group present grew more and more cantankerous. Neither Aryeh nor I could contain them. We couldn't convince them to have patience and wait. One by one, those assembled started to walk away. What was taking so long?

Aryeh, Shimmie, and I waited and waited. Finally, about an hour after we'd expected them to arrive, we glimpsed a small group of mostly men dressed in black with slumped shoulders coming down Rechov Yaffo from the direction of the Old City. If possible, they looked even more dejected as they saw so few of us waiting.

At the front of the group was an old man with Eliyahu. Eliyahu held one of his arms; a tall, broad-shouldered young Chassid, who looked to be in his late twenties, held his other. The old man seemed to be struggling just to stand after the trek from the Old City.

"Hello, sir," Aryeh said. "It's an honor to meet you." He bowed his head toward him in deference. The old man nodded, looking pale and tired. Aryeh turned to Eliyahu and asked, "What happened?"

"It took longer than expected. We walked, a few people joined us, but the dead didn't rise, it's hard to tell—maybe it will happen but didn't happen immediately. We thought it might, though as I'm sure you know, the Rambam said that the Messiah won't or doesn't have to perform miracles to be the redeemer, still—it's what people expect will happen. Maybe not enough people believed. I don't have any answers." Eliyahu shook his head.

"Should we go to the Knesset? There might be people waiting there?" someone asked excitedly.

"That's a good idea. Maybe there are people there. They didn't come to the Old City, or Zion Square, but they might be at the Knesset waiting," Eliyahu said, brightening visibly at this last possibility.

I'd thought that we'd walk, but they hailed a taxi, and the rest of us took a bus to the Knesset. It took a while to get there, and by the time we arrived, there were only a handful of people still present. Rabbi Shapiro made a speech to those assembled, his voice low and raspy and, I had to strain to hear him.

"Thank you all for coming. You are the chosen few, the faithful who chose to believe against the odds, against the advice and ridicule of others. Thank you for following your hearts and staying open to the possibility that I would succeed. For that you will be rewarded. We have waited for millennia for the redemption. Our people have lived through many hardships and struggles. We have dreamed throughout our history of the return to our homeland and for there to be true peace. We have suffered and been persecuted for our beliefs.

"Now, as a sovereign nation, we have the illusion of safety. With the state of Israel's successes has come a sense of security and pride among Jews throughout the world. Despite the wars that have been waged every decade since the establishment of the state, people have become complacent. It seems they are happy with their lives and have forgotten that there is more to life than the pursuit of our personal happiness and success. We have become like other countries, but that was never meant to be the case. We are meant to be a light unto the nations. We are meant to follow G'd's commandments, to stay true to the teachings of the Torah. Today, this generation has been tested. Once again we have failed. Once again we must repent or face the consequences. G'd was ready. G'd was willing to redeem his chosen people, to bring the masses still in exile home to our land, an act He's already begun, but the people have not come. Had they come today we would all be rejoicing. We might have even witnessed miracles," he finished, his voice even softer than it had been when he began. He seemed to have exhausted the last of his energy reserves. Two young men stepped toward him and held him up by his elbows. One whispered in his ear and he nodded. They walked him to the nearest bench and he eased himself down. We all followed.

"We just need more publicity. We'll try again," Aryeh offered.

"No. We'll have to wait another generation. I pray that people will accept it when the opportunity presents itself—that they will believe and they will come," he answered.

"We knew it was a risk, but we had to try. We were afraid if we didn't try now, we'd never get another chance. Thank you for all your help." Eliyahu sat down beside him. "Let's go back to the hotel, Yehoshua. You look tired."

"Keep doing good deeds." Rabbi Shapiro whispered as he got up from the bench with the mens' assistance. "I'm sorry." I thought I heard him say as he got into the waiting taxi. I'll never forget the look on his face, a mixture of sadness, disappointment, defeat, and dread for our future. It was clear to me that he was a hundred percent sincere. It wasn't a hoax. How was it that so few people were ready to believe?

Eliyahu asked if anyone else wanted a ride back to town. Several men got in with them and the rest of us waited for the bus. I was too upset to go straight back to campus; so I did a little window shopping, treated myself to a cappuccino, and headed over to Shirah and Andy's.

* * *

"Hello, anybody home?" I called entering the courtyard. Shirah opened the door and held her arms out to me. "So, *nu*? How did it go?" she asked after giving me a welcoming hug and kiss on each cheek. It was so good to see her and get that warm, caring hug.

"As you expected it would," I raised my arms in defeat.

"I'm sorry to hear that, honey. I know how much you were hoping it was the real deal." She opened the door wide and let me precede her back into the house.

"Thanks. That's just the thing, I think he was *the real deal*, but not enough people believed so he failed. That's it; it's over. Lucky for you, though, you won't have to worry about crazy traffic and the influx of millions of new immigrants and tourists on pilgrimage."

"*Halevai!* It would be amazing if the Moshiach would really come," Shirah said. "I would have been happy to deal with it all in exchange for true peace and an end to hunger, suffering, and disease. Traffic and crowds would have been a small price to pay."

"So why didn't you come?"

"Please, you've got to be kidding. It clearly wasn't happening. You said so yourself."

"No I didn't"

Shirah sighed. "Look, I'm not holding my breath. I'm not expecting it to ever really happen. It's a myth, but if I'm wrong, I'll be happy to eat my words and welcome him with open arms."

"Just don't go hugging him. I'm sure he'd be shomer negiyah."

Shirah laughed.

"Where's Andy?"

"He's still out shopping at the shuk."

"Where are the girls?" I asked.

"They went with him. Do you want to stay for dinner?" she inquired.

"I'd love to. Thanks. It will be good to spend more time with all of you. I'm pretty disappointed. Even though I knew it was a long shot."

"Why did you think it was a long shot?" she asked.

"People were so pessimistic and so sure that it wasn't the time and it wasn't for real. I had a sense that it wasn't going to happen because of that, not because Rabbi Yehoshua isn't or couldn't be the Messiah, but because no one was ready to accept it."

"You really think he is who he said he is?"

"He was completely sincere. Why would he have done this if he weren't certain? Aryeh thinks so too."

"And *who* is Aryeh, a new boyfriend?"

"No. He's the guy I was handing out flyers with today before the rally."

"And? Tell me more about him. He sounds interesting," Shirah said.

"It wasn't like that. He's a Chassid," I laughed. "Sorry if I gave you the wrong impression."

"Are you sure? There's something about the way you said his name."

"You're reading too much into it. I'll probably never see him again."

"But you'd like to."

"Shirah, don't be ridiculous. He's a Chassid, with peyot and a black hat, the whole deal."

"If you say so, but I have a good feeling about him," Shirah said. "Tell me more about the event. What exactly happened."

I told her all about my day and she asked more questions. "How did you get to the Knesset?"

"We took a bus."

"We?" She asked for clarification.

"Aryeh, a bunch of Chassidim who had gone with them to the Old City, and I."

"Were there any other women?"

"Some came to Zion Square, but not in our group. No other women met them beforehand, went to the Kotel, or went on to the Knesset with us."

"You're lucky they let you on the bus with them," Shirah said.

"It was a public bus. They couldn't stop me from going with them."

"Oh, I thought you meant it was a special bus they'd hired specifically for the event."

"No. I was surprised. I thought we'd walk there all together, but it seems the one I think could be the Messiah and Eliyahu didn't have the energy after the trip to the Old City. Plus they were running very late."

"So what did he look like?" Shirah asked.

"He looked like a pious old Chassid. A very tired but very sweet, old religious man, kind of like Santa Claus, only in a black suit, not a red one."

Shirah laughed.

"Just kidding," I said. "He looked like any of our grandparents from the old photos."

"Like Bubby Sarah?" Shirah teased.

"Very funny. You know what I mean."

"Was there anything special about him?"

"I didn't get to see him for very long. He was very tired by the time they got to Zion Square and even more so after he spoke at the Knesset. What he said was a little eerie."

"Eerie?"

"Scary, I can't explain it, like we're going to be collectively punished for not believing."

"But you did believe."

"I know, that's why I said collectively, like what will happen will effect Israel or the Jewish people."

"Like revenge?"

"No, more like his succeeding would have brought peace and stopped something terrible from happening to us, like another war or something. It looked like he knew something that we don't know and it scared him."

"Doo doo doo doo," Shirah sang the theme music for *The Twilight Zone.*

"Exactly, it was pretty spooky. It was the only time I'd met him, but Aryeh had met him before. He said he seemed very holy."

"This Aryeh seems to have made quite an impression, even if he is a Chassid. Was he cute?" she asked.

"*Cute?* He's a *Chassid*," I said.

"I know, you've already mentioned that, but there's something about the way you're talking about him, not like your average Chassid. Tell me about him."

"Really, Shirah, you're being ridiculous," I said.

"Am I? Humor me and answer the question. What was he like?" She bent to get a wok from a low cupboard and put the vegetables she'd chopped into it.

"He was tall, dark-haired, had *peyot*, a black hat, black suit, white shirt, your typical Chassid," I said.

"How old is he?" she asked, going to the fridge and taking out more vegetables for the stir-fry.

"About my age, I'd say. I'm not sure. He could be a year or two older or younger. Honestly, I didn't look at him that way, for goodness sake, *he's a Chassid.*"

"So you keep insisting," Shirah said. "I just get the feeling there was a really good connection between you and chemistry. I get the sense of mutual interests and mutual interest."

"Well, I did think he was nice. I enjoyed talking to him and working with him," I said. "He was one of the first people I met who were genuinely excited about the prospect of the Messiah coming and willing to do something to help. We felt this sense of urgency with only an hour or so left before the rally. The atmosphere was charged. We wanted to get the word out, to get as many people as we could to go to Zion Square. We weren't very successful, but we were in sync with each other. We got along well. I don't know if we'd get along well in any other setting. Plus, I'm probably never going to see him again,"

"You never know. Stranger things have happened," Shirah said.

I laughed. "Shirah, do you think I am so desperate that now you're trying to fix me up with a Chassid?"

"Arielle, sweetheart, I just get a really good feeling about him, crazy as it sounds. Of course I don't think you're desperate. You're beautiful. By the way, how was the Shabbat dinner? You told me that Jean Marc was going to be there."

"He was with his new girlfriend. This one is British and a gorgeous blonde."

"Don't worry, it won't last," Shirah said.

"Shirah, I don't want to get back together with him. It's fine with me if he winds up marrying her. Okay, not her, she's moving back to England and I'd hate for him to leave the country, but I'd be completely fine with him finding the woman of his dreams and living happily ever after."

"And you don't want that to be you anymore?" she asked. Picking up two carrot sticks, she took a bite of one and offered me the other.

I looked down at the carrot stick in my hand and answered, "I don't think so. Too much time has passed. He's a good friend, but I can't see us getting back together." I took a bite of the orange strip.

"But do you want to?"

"I don't think so. Sure, the spark is still there. I don't know if I'll ever stop being attracted to him, but there are a lot of guys I'm attracted to," I said.

"Like the Chassid."

"His name is Aryeh, and please stop. It's ludicrous. We have nothing in common, and I have no interest in becoming ultra-Orthodox. Can you imagine me in a wig? Please! It would never work. Besides, he didn't take my number, and I have no way of finding him, even if I wanted to."

"Whatever you say. Sounds like he was cute." Shirah gave me an I-told-you-so smile.

"Shirah, you're crazy," I said, shaking my head.

"Admit it. You liked him."

"Okay. I admit to thinking he was handsome; that under all that black clothing was a hunk of a guy. A bit pale, but definitely handsome. He had this amazing speaking voice, a deep, resonant baritone, with beautiful modulation, like an FM radio disc jockey, you know what I mean?"

"A bedroom voice," Shirah said. "Like late-night FM radio?"

"No, just the daytime FM DJs. He could probably pull off that late-night DJ voice, but that's not how he sounded."

"So you did notice him more than you wanted to admit."

"It doesn't matter. He lives in a different world." I shook my head, getting annoyed at her persistence.

"Okay, I'll drop it, but you know me. When I get these feelings, I'm rarely wrong," Shirah said.

"You're often right, but I don't know if you're rarely wrong," I conceded after a moment, thinking about what she'd said.

"We'll see," Shirah said. "Was it hard to say good-bye?"

"Actually, it was. It seemed like we had a really good connection, like we were old friends saying good-bye. Like after a whole year on the one-year program or like at the end of the summer leaving sleep-away camp."

"I knew it. You just admitted it. There was a connection."

"Maybe there was, but it doesn't matter. Besides, I don't think he noticed me."

"In that outfit? He would have been blind not to notice you. Honey, you look gorgeous."

"Thanks, but you're biased. Anyway, it doesn't matter," I said. "Can we change the subject? I think we've exhausted this one."

"Sure. You want to help me cut up the rest of these vegetables for the stir-fry?"

"Of course."

Andy and the girls arrived while I was chopping onions, carrots, and potatoes.

"Arielle, good to see you. You're looking lovely today," Andy said.

"Thank you," I said, stopping what I was doing to give him a kiss and to give each of the girls a hug.

"How was the shuk? Did you get any special deals?" Shirah asked, rummaging through the bags he'd carried in with him and set down on the counter, as if looking for the prize hidden at the bottom of a Cracker Jack box.

"Just what was on the list you gave me. Sorry."

"What's this?" Shirah asked, pulling out a paper bag filled with pastries. "I don't remember this being on the list."

"It wasn't?" Andy asked, feigning innocence.

"No, it most certainly wasn't, but thank you! I was in the mood for something sweet. They're perfect," she said, pulling a chocolate croissantlike *rugalah* out of the bag and taking a bite.

"Save them for after dinner." Andy sounded the stern parent.

"After dinner? I need my strength to cook it," Shirah said as she took another bite.

"Would you like one?" she offered. She held out the bag of pastries, and I chose one, took a bite of it, and went back to chopping vegetables. Shirah put some brown rice in the pressure cooker and chopped up some tofu and broccoli, keeping them in separate piles to add each at the proper time to what was already cooking in the wok.

After dinner, we sat on the patio and had Turkish coffee and more of the pastries then watched the 8:00 p.m. news. There was no mention of the rally or any gathering outside the Knesset but a lot of talk about the economy and increasing tension in the territories.

That night after the girls went to bed, Andy and Shirah asked me to stay and watch a movie with them.

"Another time. I really need to get back to campus at a decent hour. I've still got studying to do. I have tests coming up and papers to write."

"But you're coming for dinner on Shabbat, aren't you?" Shirah asked.

"Sure. If I can stay over?"

"Of course, anytime."

"Just making sure, you know it means the world to me," I said.

"It means a lot to us too. You're family."

"I don't know what I'd do without you." I gave her a fierce hug, grateful for her love and making me feel so at home no matter what.

"G'd willing, you'll never have to find out," Shirah said.

"*Tfoo, Tfoo, Tfoo,*" I said, and she joined me in warding off the evil eye.

"Amen to that!" Andy laughed. He was used to our family superstitions.

"Okay, I'll see you Friday, if not before," I said and gave them each a hug and kissed them on each cheek before setting out for the bus stop. Everything looked the same, but I felt different after the day's events—or nonevents. I thought about the paper I would write as I rode the bus back to campus.

*   *   *

By the time I got to the dorms, my sadness had returned. I felt sadder than I expected I'd feel if it didn't work out. Linda was already at our apartment, having finished her classes for the day. I'd missed mine, but I'd been "on assignment," I justified.

"So how did it go today?" Linda asked.

"How do you think it went?" I asked.

"From the looks of it, I'd say not good. What happened when you went this morning?"

I told her all about what had happened, and she gave me a hug. "Come on, you knew it was a long shot," she said. "You said it yourself. I know you're disappointed, but at least you got a great project out of it. Too bad you didn't find a video camera but think of all the experience you've gained interviewing people."

"I would give up all the experience I got, if only he had succeeded," I said.

"I know, but at least you got something out of it, so it's not a total loss."

"True. I'm glad I was there, I'm glad I got to witness it. When the guy I'd been talking to people with, Aryeh, suggested that we get more publicity out and try again in the future, he told us that this was the only chance he'd have and we'd have to wait another generation for the next potential Messiah to reveal himself. He's old and frail and very weak. He just got out of the hospital."

"But if he's sick, what would happen if he revealed himself and died soon after? He wouldn't have been able to fulfill the prophecies anyway. Would an old, sickly man be able to bring peace to the world?" Linda said skeptically, humoring me since I knew she didn't believe in the first place.

"I don't know. You could be right, but as the saying goes, *lo aleicha hamelacha ligmor* . . . [It's not up to you to finish the work, but neither are you allowed to desist from it.] You have to do all you can, even if you can't finish what you start. Maybe that was his thought. Or that Hashem would heal him so he could do what he came to do. Who knows? It's moot at this point," I said.

"True," Linda concurred. "If all the sick would be healed, surely it could have included him . . . how about some ice cream?" she asked in an effort to cheer me up.

"Thanks. Have you ever known me to turn down ice cream?" I went to the cabinet and took out the bowls and got spoons from the drawer as she took the containers of chocolate and coffee ice cream out of the freezer. We filled our bowls and toasted "*l'chaim*," clinking spoons together.

All I have to show for the last few weeks are the stories for my screenwriting and journalism classes. It made a good story, but I wish it wasn't just a story. I began to wonder even more what it would take for people to believe. Would it ever happen? Would the Messiah ever succeed, or were people just too jaded and too skeptical to accept anyone claiming to be the Messiah? I realized that my project wasn't over. A new project was unfolding, one I'll probably work on for the rest of my life if I have to—or until the Messiah comes. May it be soon! I plan to educate people about the Messiah so that they'll be ready the next time he comes, in the next generation; G'd willing, they'll be willing to accept him with open arms and to change their lives, if that's what it takes, to be worthy that he succeed the next time.

*   *   *

Chapter 4

The world will be filled with the knowledge of G'd, as the waters cover the sea.

—Isaiah 11:9

David
Jerusalem, June 14, 1987

When we left the Knesset, I rode back to the hotel with Uncle Yehoshua and Eliyahu, helped them pack everything up, and put Eliyahu in a cab. He was going to stay with his daughter in Bnei Brak, at least temporarily. I didn't know what he'd decide to do now that it was over, whether he'd stay in Israel or go back to the States. It was too soon to ask him. He'd had it all figured out, but with the failure of today's events, all his plans would have to change.

I took Yehoshua to stay with my Uncle Manny, one of his nephews who hadn't excommunicated him. My father's younger brother, Manny, hadn't come today or to any of the planning meetings, but he was willing to let Uncle Yehoshua stay with him and his family in Sanhedria.

Once he was settled in, I kissed Uncle Yehoshua good-bye, promised to visit him soon, and headed home, to the *Asbestonim*, graduate dorms on Mt. Scopus, which were built to solve a campus housing shortage before the dangers of asbestos were discovered. I tried not to think of the dangers and kept my windows open as much as possible, and figured I wasn't home much. I was grateful to have my own room instead of sharing with a roommate and spent as much time as I could outside, enjoying the grass, flowers, and trees around each building. There were moments that I could forget that it was situated between a cemetery, a hospital, and high-rise dorm buildings. It felt like being out in the country.

Too exhausted and sad to work, I lay down on my narrow, single bed and looked up at the ceiling. Despite the odds and all the evidence to the contrary, I really believed it would happen. What can I say? I believe my Uncle Yehoshua and Eliyahu. Even if we didn't succeed, I believe that was his role in life, that he has or had that potential. I don't know what it will take for someone to succeed. I pray that it happens in my lifetime.

Why didn't I tell more people? I chided myself. Why didn't I speak to them in a more certain manner? Did my own doubts and insecurity come through? If only I was more charismatic, more of a leader, maybe then people would have come. *What ifs* and *if onlys* went through my mind. What makes one person able to influence large numbers of people while others can't? It's not the message itself. I see that time and again. It's something intangible, that magnetism some people have. Are they born with it, or can it be cultivated? If it can't, we're out of luck. Why is it that when some people talk, people listen—like E. F. Hutton—while when other people talk, no one pays attention to what they have to say? I wish I knew these secrets. If I did, I could have passed them on to Uncle Yehoshua, and the world would be a different place right now.

"Hello, my love, Mazel Tov, Mazel Tov, she had a boy!" Miri called out as she walked through the open entrance.

"That's great news," I said. Enfolding her in my arms, I kissed her deeply. Her lips were a soothing balm. "That's good news. I needed some after the day I've had," I said, then kissed the column of her neck.

"Oh no, I was praying for it to go well. I guess it didn't, huh? Tell me all about it." She too was disappointed, but didn't sound surprised.

I related the events of the day, sitting down as I spoke and pulling her onto my lap. Her arms went around my shoulders, and I played with her hair.

"Stop feeling so guilty. You did what you could," she said, resting her cheek on my chest.

I squeezed her to me. "Thanks for saying that but no, I didn't do enough. I should have gotten them all to come."

"Woulda, shoulda, coulda's never change anything. Even if his relatives had come, it wouldn't have been enough for him to succeed."

"If they had believed all along and helped out it might have."

"Possibly, but they didn't. There's nothing you could have done to change that. We need to look to the future, not beat ourselves up over the past."

"But we need to learn from the past and our past mistakes," I reminded her.

"Of course. So some of what you're doing now is productive, but most of it isn't. That's just beating yourself up and accomplishes nothing." She hugged me. "Now if you want to do something productive? Let's make dinner." She laughed, climbing out of my lap. She kissed the tip of my nose and pulled me to my feet.

"I have something I'd rather do." I pulled her to me again and nuzzled her neck. She laughed.

"First dinner. I'm hungry."

"I'm hungry too," I said, continuing the path down her shoulder.

"Food. Right now I need food."

"If you insist," I let her go and rummaged through the refrigerator. She told me all about her day—the labor and delivery as we put together a light supper of omelets, toast, fresh salad followed by coffee and ice cream for dessert. "I wish you could stay," I said as I kissed her goodnight sometime later.

"So do I, but it won't be long now. You're coming for Shabbat, aren't you?"

"Of course. Tell me, why did we plan the wedding for November? We should have made it June," I complained.

"June? But we only got engaged on Purim. There wasn't enough time to plan a wedding for June."

"Sure there was. My family does it all the time. That's how all the ultra-Orthodox do it. Three months is plenty of time," I said.

"Doesn't sound like enough to me—not with my full schedule or yours."

"We should have asked my mother to help us. She would have been able to do it. She's done it for each of my sisters."

"Maybe, but they weren't thousands of miles away. Besides, I like being engaged. I don't want to rush things. This is a wonderful phase of our lives."

"I'm ready to move on to the next phase—marriage."

"Thank G'd for that! I'm glad you're impatient and excited to marry me. Now I've got to go or I'll miss the last bus," she said.

"You could always stay here," I suggested. She playfully punched my arm. "Do you want me to come with you?"

"No, then you'll have to take a taxi back."

"Or I could stay over . . ."

She giggled. "You're persistent tonight. What's gotten into you? You know my roommates are all there. Plus, we agreed. You are not staying in my room until after the wedding."

"Of course I know. I'm not planning to, but I could stay on the sofa."

"My housemates would freak out if they woke up to find you on the sofa," Miri said. "What if they weren't dressed properly when they came downstairs? No. You can't."

"It's a far walk from the bus stop. I don't like you walking home so late at night. I'm coming with you. I have money to take a cab back. Don't worry," I insisted as we walked to the bus stop. I rode the bus with her and walked her from the bus stop to her apartment on Shimshon Street, then came in for a while before calling a taxi to take me home.

*   *   *

In the days that followed, my Uncle Yehoshua was re-hospitalized. I went to visit him regularly, spending hours by his side as he lay mostly unconscious in his bed. Eliyahu was often there as well. He'd decided to stay in Israel indefinitely. I spent a lot of time contemplating Uncle Yehoshua's aborted attempt to reveal himself as the Messiah to the point where I became almost obsessed with it. I went over all the details again and again in my mind, wondering what would have made a difference. What could we have done? What will need to be done in the future to ensure the success of the next potential Messiah to bring salvation? I talked about it with Miri incessantly and started to imagine scenarios of what might have happened in past generations, wondering how many times Hashem had been ready and even tried to send a redeemer, but the people wouldn't accept him. It's hard to describe the way I *imagined* the scenarios. Sometimes I just thought about them, but at other times I *saw* them. The scenes filled my dreams as well as my waking hours. Some might call what I saw *visions*, but I'm not sure what they were or where they came from. Some of them seemed so real, like they'd really happened, but they might have all stemmed from my imagination.

Were these the kinds of visions Uncle Yehoshua had? Were these types of visions the reason he thought he was the Messiah and the same reason others thought him crazy? I could understand the confusion. They seemed real to me, but how could I be sure? How could I be sure where they stemmed from? I had to understand them better. And what of Eliyahu's experiences? He always seemed so certain. Were they both sick—delusional as the rebbe claimed? In all other matters they seemed normal, perfectly rational, and stable. Wouldn't there be other indications of mental illness if they really had it? And what, I needed to understand, was happening to me? "Please G'd, I beg you. What are you trying to show me? What are you trying to tell me? I beg you, G'd, in either case, please take it away. I am not worthy. I am not deserving to take on such a role, and I need your help to know I'm not going insane."

At first I didn't tell a soul, but then I knew that I had to tell Miri; that it wasn't fair to keep it from her. If she decided to call off the wedding, I'd understand.

"I think you should see a doctor," she suggested. I was amazed at how calm she was. "There's a neurologist I know of, Dr. Federman. I think he's pretty liberal and open-minded," she said. I made an appointment and met with Dr. Federman. He asked me a lot of questions then ran some tests. The results didn't reveal any organic problem. He said, "Don't worry. You have a vivid imagination, and there's nothing wrong with that. There's nothing to worry about, unless you're hearing voices. You're not, are you?"

"No. No voices, just images," I assured him, "but they're different than my imagination or the imagination I've always had. I never *saw* things in my mind's eye like this before."

"You seem like a very stable young man. I don't think it's anything to be concerned about," Dr. Federman dismissed my fears with a wave of his hand.

"That's good to know," Miri said, then suggested I go see a healer she had studied with who had psychic abilities. "Yonit is wonderful. You'll love her. She's a psychotherapist as well as a powerful healer. Wouldn't it be amazing if they were truly visions?"

Yonit, a dark haired American immigrant in her late forties, was dressed in a teal-colored moo moo. She suggested that I keep a journal and write down what I'd been seeing and describe my dreams and visions as thoroughly as I could. In addition, she recommended that I write *about* them and the feelings they evoked, and anything else I wanted to write about. She encouraged me to draw the images I saw as well if I could. I kept the notebook next to my bed so I could write things down as soon as I woke up from a dream. It was difficult at first, but the longer I did it, the more I enjoyed it. It felt like a gift to myself in the present and a record I would be grateful for in the future, though I didn't yet know why.

Along with Yonit, Miri introduced me to other guides and teachers known for their wisdom and psychics known for their accuracy—those whom people came to see from all over the country for answers to their questions and problems. Miri was determined to help me develop the *gift* I'd been given, as she called it, and get me to appreciate, not dread, it. We started attending Saturday evening *salons* with Colette, an expert who did groundbreaking work with guided imagery. Colette was considered a pioneer who'd influenced the work of psychologists and shaped the field of creative visualization and psychoneuroimmunology. I started taking classes with both Yonit and Colette and, much to my surprise, found it all fascinating. Yonit helped me develop my psychic senses for healing and said I was a natural. I didn't know what I was doing much of the time, but I started to get a sense of what was going on with people and what they needed in our classroom trial sessions and in our student-run clinic. Miri had already been through the training and said she used a lot of these techniques in her work as a midwife.

Even if nothing else came of it, I'm glad I took the classes. They helped me understand Miri more completely and will help me to be a better rabbi and teacher. Yonit's main teachings were about sending universal, unconditionally loving energy, not our own personal energy, to clients. This energy comes from the *or ein sof* (Infinite Light, a Kabbalistic term for G'd). Using our personal energy will deplete us whereas using the Infinite Light will bring healing to us as well as the people we treat, if we need it. She taught us about always asking for permission before we did our healing work, even from a distance. I found distant healing to be akin to prayer and found myself taking my prayers for the sick more seriously. I came to understand there are many rituals in Judaism that are a type of energy transfer, like *smicha*, laying on of hands of a rabbi to ordain another person and bring them into the rabbinate; and of course the priestly blessing the *Cohanim* bestow on the congregation is an energy transfer. Parents placing their hands on their children's heads on Friday nights and saying those same words of *Cohanim* is also a transfer of energy.

All of this enhanced our relationship and brought Miri and me closer than ever. The visions of past Messiahs stopped, or maybe I'd seen everything I needed to see. I'm not sure, but I was relieved, and working with experts in the paranormal who were also highly educated psychologists made it feel safe for me to explore these realms and other dimensions and to stay focused and grounded in the world, for which I will be eternally grateful.

*   *   *

Chapter 5

Each one of us has the power to change the world. Simply seeking the welfare of one's neighbor, near and far, inspires transformation. And who knows where this process ends.

—*Rabbi Labl Wolf*

Arielle
September 1987

Searching the crowd waiting outside the airport, I spotted Shirah waving her arms overhead and smiled. I pushed my cart through the line, happy to have her there to welcome me home. After a month visiting friends and family in the States, I was ready to get back to my life again. We hugged and laughed together as she helped me schlep my suitcases to the *sherut* taxi stand. The people around us probably thought it had been years since we'd seen each other, based on our greeting. "Thanks for coming to meet me. It really wasn't necessary," I thanked her.

"Are you kidding, and let you face that crowd alone with no one to greet you? That would be too sad. I wish I had a car at times like these, but the *sherut* is great. I see you didn't get to do much shopping this time," she said in jest. As usual on our trips back from the States, I had reached the limit of how much baggage I could bring into the country, two bags of a maximum of fifty pounds each, filled with some lovely new outfits, presents for friends and family who hadn't had the opportunity to travel abroad this summer, and products that were hard to attain or much more expensive in Israel, like albacore solid white tuna, aluminum foil, shampoo, and American toothpaste.

"I got almost everything on your list, plus a present for each of you, but you'll have to wait until the next time I come to visit you, unless you want to come up with me to Idelson instead of having the driver take you straight home," I said.

"Aren't you a sweetheart? Sure, I'll be happy to come up with you to your apartment. So, *nu,* how was your trip?" Shirah asked.

"It was great—wonderful to see my parents and my brother, amazing to see my friends, and a relief to come back to Israel. I missed it so much."

"Of course. How are your parents?"

"They're doing well, as are yours. I saw them at the wedding," I said. "Of course they asked all about you and the girls, so I told them even though I know you talk with them every week or two."

"That's right. I wish we could have gone, but with four of us, we couldn't swing it. So, *nu,* tell me about the wedding," Shirah urged.

"The wedding was beautiful. Everyone asked about you and sent their love. It was in their yard, with a big white tent, not what you'd expect with Uncle Manny, but Sarah insisted. Uncle Manny went all out over the food. You know how he is." All he talks about is the food at any wedding or bar mitzvah he goes to. "The smorgasbord was phenomenal. I think he must have fasted for a week, not his usual two days, so he'd be hungry enough to fully enjoy it and do it justice. You know, he bases his impression of how good any *simcha* is on the food. My father's not much better, but he doesn't go on for hours about it. Sarah looked gorgeous, as always. She was a completely radiant bride, and Mark was very handsome and dapper in his tux. They are so in love, you should have seen the way he looked at her," I said.

"I'm so happy for her. Little Sarah, married. I wish we could have been there. Were you okay with it?" Shirah asked, referring to the fact that my little cousin Sarah is two years my junior.

"Of course. Though it was a bit tiring and annoying to hear all the guests asking if I was involved with anyone or getting married anytime soon. Everyone had someone to fix me up with. I got so many blessings, especially from our relatives, saying '*Im yirtzeh Hashem* by you.'"

"Oh, yes, that wonderful Yiddish expression, 'If it's G'd's will, may it happen to you.' I prefer the Hebrew '*B'karov etzlech,*'" Shirah sympathized.

"So do I," I said. "The best was not at the wedding, but when we visited my aunt Chana and all Mom's side of the family blessed me to marry a *talmid chacham*,"

"That must have been lovely. It would have scared the living daylights out of me when I was your age." Shirah laughed.

"I know they mean well, but it's not like I'm an old maid. I'm only twenty-four. And when will I ever wear a sleeveless peach organza bridesmaid's dress again? Please!"

"You never know. They could become all the rage."

"I left it at my parents' house. There's no way I'd have a place to wear it here. It's so *fru-fru* and over the top. Tell me about your summer," I said. "How have you been since I've been gone? How's Andy? How are the girls?"

"We're all fine. We've had a great time going to the beach on Shabbat, we took a trip up to the Galilee, went to Rosh Hanikra, and the girls have been in day camp when Andy and I are at work. Not much more to tell than that. We saw your cousin Shaina and her husband and the baby. He's beautiful. They dropped by one day. I didn't know if they'd eat anything in my house, so I served them everything on paper plates, fresh fruit, uncut, and all store-bought cookies and cakes I had in closed packages, so they could check all the hechshers for themselves. Shaina can't wait to see you, of course. She said she missed you when you came to Far Rockaway to see her family. They were busy with some event in her husband's family, a wedding or a bar mitzvah of one of his siblings."

"Yeah, it was a bar mitzvah, I think. It was a shame that I missed them. I feel bad I didn't fly back for their wedding last year, but I would have missed school, and I don't think I could ever afford to fly back for every wedding in that family, though Shaina is the closest to my age, and I've always been closest to her of all the cousins on my mother's side of the family."

"Did you meet anyone while you were gone? Take any of those well-wishers up on their offers to fix you up with a Prince Charming?" Shirah asked.

"No. What would be the point, unless he was committed to living in Israel?"

"Having some fun while you're footloose and fancy free," Shirah said.

"Footloose and fancy free? That's not how I'd describe myself."

"Well, young, beautiful, and unattached."

"Thank you. With my luck, I'd fall in love with someone and be torn about coming back."

"A *talmid chacham*, they said? What about that guy you met in June? The one I told you I had a good feeling about? I think there's something more there. I don't think it's over."

"What guy? I didn't meet anyone."

"You must remember, in June. That day . . ."

"Oh, you mean from the rally? Aryeh?"

"That's the one."

"I did have a strange feeling when they all blessed me to marry a wise Torah scholar that they were interceding in my future," I admitted. "It felt weird, like something was affected cosmically."

"Interesting. Tell me more about the wedding."

"What can I say? It was great to see everyone," I said. "The music was great, and the band was fabulous," I said.

"Did they let you sing?"

"Yes, I sang *We've Only Just Begun* by the Carpenters for Sarah and 'Proud Mary' for Uncle Manny and then some Hebrew songs—whatever the band knew, which wasn't very much. It wasn't Sarah and Mark's priority when choosing a band. They knew more than the Hora, but not much more."

"Was there dancing?"

"Lots. They rented a dance floor and extended the patio, so actually, it was quite large. Lots of rock and roll and some Jewish favorites, and the old big band sound Uncle Manny loves so much."

"And Sheila? How is she?"

"Aunt Sheila seems to be doing well. We talked a lot at the shower. At the wedding she stayed with her side of the family and her guests. She was annoyed to walk down the aisle with Uncle Manny but looked extremely happy, happier than I've seen her in years, and why not? It was her youngest daughter's wedding. All her children are now safely taken care of, she's done her job—married her daughters off to a nice, Jewish medical student, law student, and now an MBA."

"Every Jewish mother's dream," Shirah agreed. "Want to come for dinner or are you too tired?"

"Thanks, I'd love to come, but don't be offended if I call it an early night."

"You know what I always say, 'You do what you gotta do and then you go,'" Shirah said in an accent imitating a New York gangster. She did say it quite often, as did Andy. There was a story behind it. Before making aliyah they'd overheard a rather large man saying those words to his companians, and started speculating on what they were up to. They never found out but thought the words, in all their simplicity, expressed our purpose in life better than any others and Andy claimed they were the words he wanted on his tombstone someday.

*   *   *

I raced across campus, late again to meet Linda and Stacey. From the distance, I saw someone waving in my direction. I turned to make sure it was me he was waving at, but there was no one behind me. As I drew closer, I recognized Jean Marc.

"Arielle," he said. "How are you?" He smiled, opened his arms, and I walked into his expectant embrace. He kissed me on each cheek. "It's so good to see you, as always, *cherie*. You look lovely. What a beautiful dress. That color blue is perfect with your complexion." He held me at arm's length to get a good look at me.

"Hmm." I cleared my throat in an attempt to get his eyes to move back to my face. "You're looking pretty handsome yourself. How's life? Are you still seeing Leslie?" I asked.

"Life is fine. Leslie? Oh, that British girl I brought to dinner last June?" He made a typically French facial expression indicating that he didn't know how she was, a cross between a pout and a pursing of his lips, while lifting an eyebrow. "No. It's over."

"Another heart broken?"

"Why do you think I'm the one who ended it? You knew she was going back to England."

"That's right. So she ended it?" I asked, incredulous.

"Not exactly. It was just one of those things. It was mutual. What can you do? We wanted different things in life," he said. He put his hand on my back, pulled two trays off a stack, and guided me through the cafeteria line. He took a salad and asked for couscous with a topping of beef and vegetables. I had an Israeli salad and a vegetable version of the stew filled with chickpeas, pumpkin, carrots, and zucchini. The golden yellow tint to the mixture was probably from turmeric, not real saffron or a full curry. "Want to share a dessert?" he asked.

"You're assuming I'm joining you? Thank you for the invitation." I laughed. "How do you know I haven't made plans to meet someone else here?"

"Pardon me. You're right, of course. I was so happy to see you, I was hoping for your company."

I smiled. He was always so charming, always knew the right thing to say. "Actually, I'm meeting Stacey and Linda, but you can join us," I invited, hoping my girlfriends wouldn't mind. I felt myself torn between the bubble of joyful exuberance starting to fill me just being around him, and cautious resistance to his charm. I knew Linda would warn me of the folly of getting any closer to him again while Stacey would be happy and excited for me.

"Great. How about dessert? Chocolate mousse or a torte?" he asked.

"Anything chocolate," I said. "You choose."

He chose the mousse and added it to his tray. We each paid for our choices. "Arielle, it has been too long," Jean Marc said as we walked to a small round table where Linda was already seated with Elliot. "I can't believe it's already been, what—three months. How is it possible?"

"Three or four."

He clicked his tongue. "No, impossible." We reached the table and put down our trays. Stacey had not arrived yet. Linda raised her eyebrows at me. I'm sure I blushed.

"Jean Marc, it's good to see you. I think it's been a while; since that dinner at our place. Where have you been hiding?" Linda asked.

"Me? Hiding? No, I haven't been hiding, just busy working, and I had a long stint in *miluim* on the Lebanese border. More than the border actually, but let's not talk about that unpleasantness. How about you? You are looking lovely. And you, Elliot, how has life been treating you?" Jean Marc asked.

Before he could answer, Stacey joined us. Jean Marc got up, let her take his seat, and pulled over an empty chair from a nearby table. More pleasantries were exchanged, and we fell into silence for a while, focusing on our meals.

"How was your summer?" Stacey asked no one in particular, but it must have been directed toward Jean Marc or Elliot since she saw Linda and me regularly.

Jean Marc was the first to respond. "It was a lovely summer, other than the exams and reserve duty. I got to visit my family in Paris and to travel a bit through France and Italy. The countryside of both countries is so verdant. We spent time in Lyon and Nice, traveled through the Champagne and Bordeaux regions."

"I bet you had some great wine," Elliot said.

"Not a lot, only when we could get kosher wine. We went to the Rashi winery, an appropriate name for kosher French wine, wouldn't you say?" (Rashi, the famous rabbi lived in the eleventh and twelfth centuries in Troyes, France, and wrote a commentary on the Torah, founded a yeshiva, and made his living primarily as a vintner.)

"Only kosher wine? What a waste," said Elliot.

"Even kosher wine in France is good. And in Italy. I loved Italy," I said.

"That's right, you were there in 1982, after the one-year program, while I was in Operation Peace for the Galilee—great name for a war, wouldn't you say? War with Lebanon would have been more appropriate. And we're still there! I can attest to that, unfortunately. Tyre is very hot in July. Have you been?" Jean Marc asked Elliot.

"I don't think I've been there in July, but yes, many times," replied the Englishman. "Whatever happened to that knockout blonde you were with when we saw you last? Ow!" Elliot said when Linda punched him in the arm at his last question.

"Leslie? She went back to London."

"That's right, she said she couldn't live so far away from her family long-term. And not even you could entice her to stay?" I asked, now remembering the reason for the breakup and feeling bad that it had happened to him again.

"No, *cherie*. She wanted me to leave Israel for her, but of course that's preposterous. I wouldn't leave for her or any woman. There are enough fabulous women who want to live here." He gave me a knowing smile. Was it my imagination, or was Jean Marc coming on to me? Of course, he always flirted, but this seemed like more. *Wait a minute*, I reminded myself. *You don't even know if he's still single or if he's already involved with someone else. And you promised yourself you'd stay away. Remember?* Of course I remember, but it's been so long since I've dated anyone. *Have faith*, I told myself. *Someone will come along, when you least expect it.* "So what happened that day at Zion Square? I assume nothing since we haven't heard anything about the Messiah being here. Or is he?" Jean Marc asked.

"It was a nonevent, as you suspected. It depends who you ask, whether the Messiah came. If it was him, he didn't succeed, of course, but from the look of him, he might have been. I only saw him for an hour or so, and he was a very pious old Chassid. I'm sure he believed he was the Messiah and had been told to come forward. He didn't look or seem crazy, nor did Eliyahu."

"Eliyahu?" Jean Marc asked.

"Yes, the man helping to publicize the rally. His name was Eliyahu."

"That is too strange a coincidence."

"Yes, it struck me as meaningful at the time, more than just a coincidence."

"But he failed. Another false Messiah."

"Or a failed attempt of the Messiah of a generation to bring about the redemption," I said. Jean Marc made that face again; his nostrils flared.

"You think he has come before?" he asked.

"I'm sure he's tried," I said.

"Not this again," Linda complained. "Jean Marc, don't get her started."

"I think it's too late," Elliot said.

"Sorry, I'll be good," I replied. "I've said my piece."

When the others had left for class, Jean Marc and I remained at the table. "You really think the Messiah has come in the past and failed?" he asked.

"Yes. Don't you?"

"I never really thought about it. Why do you think that?"

"It says that the Messiah will reveal a new Torah, the Torah of the Messiah, but then, whatever people have come out claiming to be the Messiah, or who others say might be the Messiah, have been cut down for any teachings that they put forth that are contrary to the Torah. That's always been used as proof that the person claiming to be the Messiah is a phony, but what if they're not? How can we be sure? There have been a number of them in the past, from Jesus to Bar Kochva to Shabbtai Tzvi. How do we know that none of them were truly meant to be the Messiah but either didn't finish the job or weren't accepted by the Jewish people for some reason? Maybe it was for the new Torah that they tried to teach?"

"This is heretical. You know that, don't you?"

"Is it? I think there are a lot of people out there who would agree or at least wonder. Maybe we missed our chance," I speculated. "Maybe we messed up on a number of occasions."

"Maybe. But I don't think he's come yet."

"We're all entitled to our own opinions. You said something earlier that's been on my mind. I never asked you how it was for you that summer," I apologized. "I felt horrible leaving at the time. It was so hard to go, but what good would it have done to stay?" I asked.

Jean Marc shrugged. "It's all water under the bridge, as you Americans say, but if you really want to know, I would have loved for you to have stayed. It would have felt supportive to me and to the country."

"We'd already decided it was over before the war started," I said, remembering back to the time we'd been dating before I was to go back to America at the end of the one-year program to finish my degree.

"That's an interesting perspective. We agreed, yes, but it hadn't ended. We'd decided it would end when you left; that we wouldn't continue our relationship long distance, but that didn't mean you had to leave when you'd planned. Other soldiers had their families and their girlfriends sending them packages, waiting to see them when they came home on leave, but as a *chayal boded,* all I had was memories of you and my imagination of you traipsing through Europe on your way home. I thought you'd never be back." This was the most serious I ever remembered him being, the most I realized he'd ever felt for me.

"I know you thought that, but I always said I'd be back when I graduated. Why didn't you say anything?" I asked, touching the back of his hand.

"What was I supposed to say? How could I have asked you to stay? You had to finish college, as you said."

"You knew I wanted to stay. You knew how much I loved you, how much I dreaded leaving."

"Did I? You said you loved me, but I didn't know for sure, especially when you insisted on leaving." He shrugged.

"I didn't want to go. I wanted to stay forever, I just had to go back to finish school. It seemed like staying longer would have just put off the inevitable. I didn't want to let Stacey down. We already had our tickets, I couldn't leave her in a lurch." I defended my behavior, but had I really done the right thing? At the time, I'd been torn. I wanted to stay. I would have preferred to stay actually, but Stacey got so freaked out about it and then gave me such a guilt trip. I just couldn't bail on her.

"I knew all that. Maybe it wasn't rational," he said with a shrug, "I don't know that I even thought it all out. I don't think I realized how much I cared for you or would miss you until you were gone," he said. "This isn't the place for this conversation. What are you doing now? Let's go for a walk."

"I have class in a few minutes. How about tonight?"

"I'd love to. I'm working until late, but I could come by around midnight."

"Um. I don't think that's a good idea," I said, as tempting as it sounded. "How about tomorrow night?"

"I'll be working again, but could come by around the same time." His voice had grown huskier and so did mine.

"No, that won't work," I said.

"Then it's the weekend, and I'll be away. How about if I come by next week? I'm not working Monday."

"Sure. Stop by when you can. If I'm there, we'll talk, if not, you can try again another time."

We walked on in silence, suddenly not knowing what else to say. When we got to my classroom, he took my hand and pulled me around a corner, behind a column, looked into my eyes and smiled. He brought his face slowly toward mine, giving me a chance to stop him if I wished, but I didn't wish, and I didn't stop him. Finally, his lips met and parted mine in a kiss filled with passion and promises. "Okay, my sweet, I'll see you next week."

"I'm looking forward to it," I agreed. He drew me back to him and kissed me on each cheek in the French fashion of greeting and parting. When I expected him to let me go, he pulled me in closer, and brought his lips back to mine.

"This is to tide me over until next week."

It felt wonderful to kiss Jean Marc again after so many years. I'd always loved the way he kissed. We would kiss for hours, reveling in the sensuous pleasure, exploring each others mouths, our tongues intertwining—sometimes playfully, more often urgently.

As if coming back from a long distance, I suddenly registered the sounds of people walking and talking nearby. "Class is about to start. I'd better go," I said, reluctant to let him go. Jean Marc caught his breath before he spoke. "Are you sure you're not free tonight? I'm not sure I can wait till next week to see you again."

"Sorry but I'm sure I can't tonight. But maybe we can find a time sooner than next week," I coaxed, while disengaging from his arms.

"I'll see if I can get off work early one night."

"Great . . . If you can." I smiled and backed away from him, turned the corner, and entered the lecture hall for my Mass Communications class.

*   *   *

"You're really going to see him again?" Linda asked. "Are you sure it's wise?"

"No," I said. "I'm not sure at all, but I know I have to do it. He deserves at least that, and the attraction is still there. If what he says is true, why not give him a chance?"

"Arielle, if he really wanted you, he would have come to see you or called you sooner. You don't hear from the guy for months at a time, then you bump into him by chance, and you're ready to start this whole thing up again? Have some pride. Don't do it. You make it too easy for him," Linda insisted.

"I don't know. That kiss felt like he really wants me. I wasn't planning to start seeing him again, I'm still not, but I want to hear what he has to say—to understand what it was like for him after I left. I always assumed he met someone else right away and started dating, just like Alain did on kibbutz, but maybe I'm wrong. Maybe I meant more to Jean Marc than I thought. We both knew when we started dating that it was a risk—that I was only here for the year, and it was already more than half over. After four months together, what could either of us expect?" I asked. "It wasn't realistic to ask each other to wait or have a long-distance relationship."

"Stacey and Amram did it."

"And that's great for them, but I'd tried it before, and it had been disastrous, and Jean Marc didn't want it either."

"Because he never took you seriously. He thought of it as a short-term fling in the first place."

"Maybe. You could be right. That's what I thought too, but it's not what he's saying now."

"How convenient. All right. Hear him out, but give it time. Think it through. Okay? Don't just jump into a relationship with him again."

"I won't. Why are you being so adamant about this?"

"I just don't want to see you get hurt. He's such a flirt. Can you trust him?" Linda demanded to know.

"You're right, but really, who else have you seen him flirt with?"

"Only you, but in front of every girl I've ever seen him with."

"I know, except Leslie. He didn't flirt with me in front of her."

"That's true. Maybe he's growing up."

"Maybe."

"That still doesn't mean he's right for you. Frenchmen are notorious for having affairs."

"I've heard that. But is it also true of religious Frenchmen?"

"I don't know. Are you willing to risk it?"

"Good point," I conceded. "I'll see how I feel when he comes to talk. If nothing else, I need closure."

*   *   *

But he didn't come to talk—not that night, or the next, not even the next week, or the week after that. In fact, Jean Marc didn't stop by, leave a message of any kind, nor did we even bump into each other for over a month. I didn't know whether to be relieved or disappointed. I went by his dorm several times and never found him in.

After a month I finally stopped trying. "What do you think happened?" I asked Linda one night around bedtime. "It's so strange. He really seemed sincere. It's hard to believe that it meant nothing to him."

"Who knows? You made the right decision. I told you he couldn't be trusted."

"I didn't really make a decision. Do you think something might have happened to him? Like he suddenly got called away on reserve duty?"

"Have you heard about anything like that happening with other people?"

"No, but it just seems strange. I haven't seen him anywhere. It's as if he vanished into thin air."

"I doubt that anything happened to him. It's just the way he is."

"I don't know. Maybe I should stop by again and leave a note. He said he'd see me within the week, but that was over a month ago. What do you think happened?"

"I think he didn't get what he wanted the moment he wanted it, and then he moved on. He has the attention span of a flea. That's what I think. You're lucky you didn't get taken in by him again."

"Almost," I admitted. "It was hard not to."

"Well, you did the right thing."

"The right thing? I didn't do anything."

"Enough about that. What are you doing this weekend?"

"Going to my cousins," I informed her.

"Oh. I thought you could come with me to my cousins in Ra'anana."

"Sorry, but as I said, I have plans. This time I'm going to my religious cousins in Arzei HaBirah, the ones who just got here a few months ago. I told you about them. Actually, I don't know why I'm going to them for Shabbat. Don't get me wrong. I'm thrilled that Shaina and Yossi are here for the year. I adore Shaina, but I really don't enjoy being in an ultra-Orthodox environment for Shabbat, especially not here, where there are so many wonderful options. I could stay on campus and hang out with my friends. I could go to services at Hillel, to the synagogue overlooking the Old City, or to the Conservative synagogue on French Hill. It's not such a far walk, and I really like it. I could go to Shirah and Andy, like usual, or I could have gone with you, you've been inviting me forever . . . so why am I going to Arzei HaBirah when it's so not my scene, especially not on Shabbat. I can take it for a few hours, but a whole weekend?" I went on. "I just couldn't avoid it any longer. I've been making excuses since they arrived, through the High Holidays, Succot and Simchat Torah, but I can't keep putting them off. Besides, as I said, Shaina's great. Yossi seems really nice too. How bad could it be?"

Linda just shook her head. "You're a braver woman than I! Good luck."

I've been going to dinner at their apartment in the middle of the week every couple of weeks since they arrived in Jerusalem in August. In fact, I've seen them much more since they've been here than I did when I lived in the States. In the States, I'd see Shaina two or three times a year, if that. I'm sure it will be fun. Just what do I have in common with Shaina anymore, though?

"We were so close when we were little, but it's been years. Funny, I started dating way before she did, and now she's married and has a baby. I can't even imagine having a serious boyfriend. I'd love one, but . . . anyway, I don't know if we have anything in common anymore, if we ever really did. It's funny, when I started dating is when we really drifted apart. I guess it was natural. I lived on Long Island, her family was in Far Rockaway, not that far geographically, but worlds apart in *hashkafa.* You know what I mean?"

Linda grunted. "Um hum."

"Despite the difference in their ages, our mothers were always really close. My mother was six when Shaina's mother was born, but her mother, my aunt Chana, is already a grandmother at thirty-eight. I love Aunt Chana and her whole family and loved to spend weekends and holidays with them when I was young. I liked going into that different world, sort of like an anthropologist. Maybe that's when my interest in studying other cultures and making documentaries started.

"Shaina and I loved playing together when we were little. When it was just the two of us, playing with dolls, coloring, painting, going for walks, jumping rope, playing cards or board games with all our siblings, there was never any problem. It was just when we grew out of those pastimes that we lost the common ground we'd shared. Shabbat was nice together until I was about eleven or twelve when my uncle asked me not to sing at the table. There were men present who were not my blood relatives, including him, and they shouldn't hear my voice. For some people, this might not have been a big deal, but asking me not to sing was like asking me not to breathe. I love to sing, especially Shabbat zemiroth. My grandfather insisted that I be allowed to sing in his home, but he was the only one, so I sang when I was in my grandparents' house, which was just down the block. Then I realized that I should also keep my voice down in shul when I was there, even though the women's section was separated from the men by a thick partition.

"The differences didn't seem like such a big deal when we were young, and, of course, I'd always be on my best behavior when we were there so that they wouldn't be offended or mortified to know that we weren't that observant. My parents both grew up Orthodox and raised us to be basically *shomrei Shabbat,* but not like that, not like they are. Even going primarily to a Lubavitch shul in our town, we were nowhere near as observant as Shaina's family. "It's just one weekend. It's not such a big deal, I keep telling myself."

"And me," Linda jumped in.

"And since it's almost winter," I said, "Shabbat ends early, and I can leave by six or seven Saturday night, unless we're having a really good time. You never know. Maybe I'll be pleasantly surprised. I hope so! I'm sure it will make our mothers happy. They'll be thrilled to know that we'd spent the weekend together. I know my parents worry about me being alone here."

"You've got me." Linda smiled.

"Thanks! I agree, we've got each other, but my parents don't really know you. To them a blood and genealogical link is what can be trusted," I explained.

"I'm not really alone, and this is where I want to be. Still, to my parents it's a big deal that I'm a single woman on my own in a foreign country. I try to explain to them that living in Israel isn't like living in, let's say, France. This is our home. We belong here. All Jews belong here. Most in the Diaspora either don't realize it, don't care, or are afraid to uproot their lives and their families and make a go of it here. This is what we dreamed of for two thousand years. To me it's absolutely crazy that they don't get it; that they want to stay in *galut* when they have the opportunity to get on a plane any day and come home. Now they're all in self-imposed exile. Not everyone, there are Jews in countries like the Soviet Union, Iran, and Syria, to name a few, who I'm sure would love to come. They'd give anything to come if they could; yet people who live in free countries, democracies like America, have no desire to come. It's too hard a life here, they say. What do I know, I'm just an idealistic kid, they tell me. I've heard it all. You're so lucky your parents don't feel that way."

"Are you kidding? Since their divorce, my parents are so involved in their own lives, I doubt they even notice I'm not around. Plus they have my little sister to worry about. She's still in college and giving them plenty to focus on. I'm sure they're concerned about my being so far away, and it being the Middle East, but I'm an adult."

"That's what I'm talking about, your parents consider you an adult. I don't think mine understand that concept. I'm still their baby."

"And always will be. Who knows, my parents might react similarly with Suzie. She's still their baby. We all consider her our baby," Linda said, referring to her three older brothers and herself. "Well, have fun. You've still got an open invitation to my cousins anytime I go. It will be great. You don't have to compromise your beliefs. We can leave the dancing for Saturday night and hang out at their house on Friday night. They're great. I know you'll love them." Linda changed the subject. "Gotta get a move on."

"Have a great time!" I said as she picked up her duffel bag and headed out the door.

I have a lot of relatives in Israel, but they're all either much more religious or less religious than I am. I try to keep in contact with them, but I also want to be true to myself and my beliefs and preferred observance, so I usually don't stay with them on Shabbat. I feel like Goldilocks—I never find the environment that's "just right." There's no shoe that fits, religiously speaking, in my family. Or if there is, I haven't found it yet, like Prince Charming searching for all the damsels in the kingdom until he finds his Cinderella. I guess I'm not meant to be a princess! If I am meant to be a princess, my prince hasn't found me yet either . . . but there's time. I'm young. Not so young according to my Orthodox relatives, but in my opinion, too young to get married. I thought I was ready years ago when I was living on kibbutz. Alain asked me to marry him, and I said yes, but I had to go back to the States to go to college. I was sure he was the love of my life and promised to transfer to a college in Israel and be back within the year. After six months of a long-distance relationship, I got a letter saying he was engaged to someone else. That's why I've been so wary with Jean Marc. I didn't want to put myself in that position again. I know they're different people. I shouldn't judge Jean Marc by what happened with Alain. Some long-distance relationships work out, and sometimes people can get back together and work things out after a breakup.

Time was getting away from me. I had to go soon if I was going to make it before the buses stopped running. I was looking forward to spending time with Shaina again. It had been years since we'd spent Shabbat together. In the next couple of hours, I needed to pack, go to the market, and find a gift to bring them with a *hechsher* they accept. Searching my closet, I found two outfits that were *tznius* enough to wear, grateful for that reason if for no other, that it was winter. I chose my blue turtleneck dress, which reached to midcalf. It looked elegant but was made of a comfortable thick cotton that felt like the material of a sweatshirt. I paired it with a wide black elastic belt, and wore my beaded lapis and gold necklace and earrings.

Chapter 6

Our G'd and G'd of our fathers, may there ascend, come and reach, be seen, accepted, and heard, recalled and remembered before You, the remembrance and recollection of us, the remembrance of our fathers, the remembrance of Moshiach the son of David Your servant, the remembrance of Jerusalem Your holy city, and the remembrance of all your people the House of Israel for deliverance, well-being, grace, kindness, mercy, good life and peace . . . Remember us on this day L-rd our G'd, for good, be mindful of us on this day for blessing help us on this day for good life. With the promise of deliverance and compassion, spare us and be gracious to us, have mercy upon us and deliver us for our eyes are directed to You, G'd, for You, G'd, are a gracious and merciful King.

—Ya'aleh V'yavo prayer

David
Bloomington, Indiana
May 1994

"It's so exciting that your students have asked you to officiate at their wedding. And to think, they met in your class. I'm so happy for them." Miri gushed one Thursday evening over a late dinner. I had just finished teaching for the day and she'd had a late meeting with a patient who could only see her after work.

"So am I," I said. "They're good kids."

"They are, aren't they? Well, it's all set, Jeannie's parents will stay with us for Shabbat, and they'll all be here for meals. I told them where I leave the key if they arrive before either of us gets home tomorrow. I hope I don't get called in for a delivery. It's not likely, but there is a chance."

"There's always a chance."

"True."

"I do my best not to play favorites, but I must admit, if I've ever had any, Jeannie Friedman and Adam Walker are way up there. It's been such an honor to be in part responsible for their getting together and to watch their relationship grow. You've been a wonderful mentor for Jeannie."

"And you've been great with both of them. You know, I've never really felt qualified to be a *rebbetzin*, but I'm very grateful to serve in that capacity when the opportunity arises. I've really enjoyed working with Jeannie. Thanks." More and more people had been turning to Miri for guidance and counsel of late. "I'm sorry I'm not a better *rebbetzin*, but you knew what you were getting yourself in to," Miri apologized.

"Honey, you're better at it than you give yourself credit for, and besides, I didn't marry you to make you a *rebbetzin*. I married you because I loved you—I love you."

"I know and I love you, but I feel bad that I don't do more for the students. You deserve to have a wife who's a real *rebbetzin*."

"Are you kidding? What you've been doing for Jeannie, the way you've been teaching her all she needs to know as a new bride, if I'd had any doubts before, which I didn't, they'd be completely gone now. You *are* a real *rebbetzin*. Besides, you are a terrific *balabusta*."

"When I'm here, but you can't count on it, can you?"

"That doesn't matter. You're great at whatever you do. It's wonderful when you're here, and everyone understands when you're called away. If it happens this weekend with Adam and Jeannie's families here, I can deal with it. I've dealt with it before. This won't be much different."

"I know. I just so want to be here. I've been planning it for weeks. The menu is all prepared, and I've started cooking early, just in case."

"And it all smells wonderful. Is there anything else you need me to get? I can go to the supermarket, or any other store you need. I have a light day tomorrow."

"No, I think we've got it covered." Both Jeannie's and Adam's parents were coming down for the weekend in order to meet each other before the wedding, which would be held a few weeks after graduation. They'd already spoken on the phone, discussed the wedding plans, and gotten to know each other a bit, but the parents had never met in person. We had agreed to host them all for Shabbat meals and offered for them to stay over with us in our home. Jeannie's parents, who observed the Sabbath, agreed, and Adam's parents would be staying at a hotel nearby.

"I've been so enjoying teaching Jeannie. She's such a special young woman. And they're making aliyah after graduate school. I'm so happy for them."

"I know. That's their plan. I hope they're able to see it through. It will be a few years before they're able to go," I reminded her. "Who knows if they'll still feel the same way? They'll also have a lot of school loans to pay back, unless they've gotten complete scholarships which they haven't told us about."

"That's true. Or unless their families offer to pay."

"Or they change their plans and go to graduate school in Israel."

"Do they have school loans to pay now, after finishing their undergraduate degrees?"

"I'm not sure, but they won't have as much trouble paying off that amount as they would with master's and MBA costs at top schools."

"It's amazing that they've both been accepted at schools in the same city."

"Boston has a lot of great schools."

"It does." Miri changed the subject. "I was so surprised when she asked me to teach her. I'm always surprised when people ask for my advice. They think that just because I'm married to a rabbi I have some special insight or know what's right for them. Sometimes I just want to laugh when I think about it. I don't know any more than they do."

"Don't be so modest. You do it very well," I assure her. "And they don't only come to you because you're married to a rabbi. You offer them your perspective and your perceptions, not to mention all the free health advice."

Miri laughed. "Thank you. You always know just what to say to make me feel better. With my job at the hospital, I know I'm far from the model Jewish homemaker a rabbi's wife is generally expected to be."

"It doesn't bother me that we don't have students or people from the community over for Shabbat meals as often as many rabbis and their families do. We do what we can. If I were a congregational rabbi, maybe it would be different, but it's not part of my job description," I said for what felt like the hundredth time. "I'm fine with it. I knew what I was getting into when I asked you to marry me."

She was given authorization by Rabbi Yehuda to drive to births on the Sabbath if the laboring woman would feel any sense of distress if she weren't there. He concluded that it is of primary importance that laboring women feel at ease and that anything that might make them more nervous or uncomfortable should be avoided. For this reason, though there are other midwives or doctors already at the hospital, Miri is allowed to drive or ride in a car on Shabbat if called, even if it means breaking the laws of Shabbat to get to the hospital. However, she is not permitted to drive home afterward, if it's still Shabbat, since there is no longer an emergency, and it's no longer a matter of life or death; fortunately, the hospital is only a thirty minute walk from our house, but she often stays till morning if a woman has given birth in the middle of the night, rather than walking home alone.

"You're always so understanding and you've been so good at dealing with being alone for such long periods at a time," she said.

We have guests most weekends anyway, and we let them know in advance that Miri might not be there or that she'll have to leave at a moment's notice. Most people understand, especially students, and, if anything, they respect and trust her as role model. It's not as expected of a rabbi who isn't the head of a synagogue to host people regularly, but there are so few rabbis here and so many Jewish students that we see it as part of the job. Besides, we enjoy it.

Our luck held out and Miri was able to be with us for all of what turned out to be a lovely Shabbat with the bride and groom and their parents. We attended a large gathering Saturday night at Adam's fraternity to which all of their friends had been invited. By the time Miri and I arrived, the party was in full swing, and it appeared that Jeannie and Adam's parents were relieved to see some familiar faces.

"Thank you so much for all you've done for our kids," Mrs. Friedman said. "Jeannie has told me so much about you both. You being here helped keep her on the path."

"We really didn't see her that often the last couple of years; only on Shabbat and holidays," I said.

"Well, that's pretty often, and being your student, and just knowing you and your wife were here if she ever needed have been wonderful. I was so scared that she'd stop being observant like so many kids do when they go away to school. It's a real relief that her faith has if anything strengthened since she's been at college."

"She's a very special young woman. We both think the world of her."

"And it's very mutual," she said.

"We're going to miss her," Miri chimed in. "We'll miss them both. Adam is a wonderful young man, and he loves her so much. It's beautiful to see the way he looks at her and the way he treats her."

"Thank you. That's so good to know. We've only met him a couple of times, so it's very good to hear from people who know him better—from *adults* who know him better."

"I'll vouch for him," I assured her. "He's one of the good ones."

"Call us any time if you have questions or if there's anything we can do for you before the wedding. Most of the planning has fallen on you, hasn't it? I love the synagogue you've chosen. It's so beautiful," Miri said.

"You've been there?" asked Mr. Friedman. "What a small world."

"I grew up not far from there, on Long Island. My parents still live there, so we'll get the chance to see them."

"You don't get back often?" Mrs. Friedman asked.

"What's often?" Miri asked. "We go back at least once a year, usually in the summer and sometimes for holidays or when there's a break from classes, but we have to split our time between both families."

"You know it's going to be a small wedding," Mrs. Friedman continued.

"Yes. Jeannie told me. That's why they're having this party tonight, so that they didn't have to invite all their friends from school and have their friends go through the expense of flying to New York regardless of where they're from, or feeling bad that they missed the wedding."

"I'm very proud of them for making some tough decisions, like finding positions that they can start right away, instead of taking an expensive honeymoon or an extended trip abroad as some of their friends are doing, and working as much as they can while they're in school."

"They're very pragmatic and practical," I joined in.

Mrs. Friedman laughed. "That's Adam's influence, unless Jeannie has changed completely from the girl I raised. I used to plead with her to be practical, but it never seemed to have an effect."

"Maybe it sank in."

"With Adam's help. Thank G'd!"

"It's great that you like him so much."

"What's not to like?" She asked rhetorically. "He's a nice Jewish boy from a good family with a degree in engineering. I just hope her sisters will be as lucky."

"May all your daughters be blessed to find wonderful husbands who love them, and build good Jewish homes like the one they grew up in," I said.

"Thank you," Mrs. Friedman said, growing emotional.

"Amen," Miri answered then gave Mrs. Friedman a hug.

*   *   *

We stayed longer at the party than we'd planned because we wanted to make sure that nothing got out of hand after some young men from another fraternity notorious for their unruly behavior crashed the party. After making sure that everyone who needed a ride home got one, we drove the Walkers to their hotel and then home with the Friedmans.

"We're exhausted. It's been a long day," Mr. Friedman said. "Thanks for everything. That was quite a party."

"I thought it would never end," Mrs. Friedman added. "I'm sure I won't have any trouble falling asleep tonight."

"We'll see you in the morning," Miri said as she started to clean the kitchen from any residual Shabbat mess.

"Do you really want to do that now? I'll help you in the morning."

"You know how I hate to leave a mess. Go, get ready for bed. I'll be right up."

"That's okay. I know how you hate to leave things until morning. I'll help you now," I said, turning on the faucet to wash the dishes. We worked together for a while in companionable silence. "Thanks. You were wonderful tonight." I started to serenade her with one of her favorite songs. I dried the dish I was holding, then my hands and came up behind her. "You're wonderful because I see the love-light in your eyes . . ." I sang. She joined in, laughing with tears in her eyes. She really is a wonder.

"You're so good to me. What did I do to deserve you?" she asked.

"What did *you* do? What did *I* do to deserve *you*? You're the one who made the sacrifices to be with me."

"What choice did I have? I couldn't imagine living without you," she said.

"And I am grateful everyday that you made that decision. I wish you didn't have to give up on your dream."

"We'll get there eventually. G'd willing."

"G'd willing. You're very emotional tonight. Did you drink more than I thought you did?"

"No. It's just having the Friedmans here and some of the conversations we've had this weekend. How they've accepted Adam as part of the family already, and then I've been thinking about having to say good-bye to them tomorrow, and to all of the seniors within the next week or so if they're not leaving immediately. I've grown to really love so many of them."

"I know. I'm sure we'll stay in touch with Jeannie and Adam."

"With Jeannie and Adam, sure, but not with everyone." My attempt to comfort her backfired. She let out a cry, bent forward holding her stomach, and crumpled into a ball.

I got down on my haunches and put my arms around her. "And there will be new students next year, and all the returning students who aren't graduating. You'll still get to see them." I gave it another try.

She shook her head as we rocked together, back and forth. "It's just—saying good-bye—I'm sick of it. It's so hard. Life moves on, people move on, we moved on and now this batch of seniors are moving on too."

"All true," I said. "It's the cycle of life."

Miri's sobbing intensified, wracking her body. I absorbed them as best I could, holding her close. "It's okay. It's natural to grow attached and not want to see them go."

"I know, it's just that . . . I've said good-bye to so many people I love, I don't want to do it anymore. It's too much. I miss them all. I miss my sisters, my parents, my nieces and nephews, but I live with it. I miss Nava, Chaim, and all of their children, Terry and Rob, Arielle, Aryeh, and all our old friends. I wasn't there when my grandparents died . . . I think it's a mistake, a terrible mistake. We're not supposed to live so far away from the people we love." My shirt had grown wet with her tears. I continued to hold her, stroking her hair, caressing her face, wiping away the flowing moisture with my hand. This wasn't like her. Miri loved meeting new people. She loved getting close to them and was always ready to include them in her life. She kept in touch with her family and friends all over the world, relishing each phone call and every letter. She especially loved the letters, which she could take out and read again, savoring their words, keeping track of everything going on in the lives of her friends and family as if distance didn't matter, nothing could diminish the love between them. I was at a loss for what else to say, so I just continued to hold and rock her, swaying from side to side.

After a while her tears subsided. "Feeling better?" I smiled down at her. "Come on, let's go to bed." I directed her toward the stairs, one arm still encircling her waist. Beside me, I heard her sniff several times, catching her breath, felt the movement of her hand as she brought it to her face to wipe her tears. This is why people used to carry handkerchiefs. For the first time I wished I had one to offer her. "Are you sure you want to go through this round of fertility treatments? The last two rounds have been . . ." I searched for just the right words, but if there were any, they alluded me, "emotional." I settled. "Maybe we should take a break, or start the adoption process like we've talked about. I hate that you're suffering."

"No. We can't stop now. Being more emotional is a small price to pay. I'm not suffering. Just because I'm a little more emotional doesn't mean we should stop trying. True, the last few rounds of treatments have been tougher; there have been some side effects, like my extreme emotions, and I've been so nauseous it's been difficult to work at times. I know you're ready to give up," she began to cry again, "but I'm not. What can I say? It might be a long shot, and I know we'll love a baby just as much if we adopt him or her—I just have this feeling that we're supposed to have a baby, that I'm supposed to give birth. I don't know why. It used to be that I wanted to have a baby; but it was just that, a sense of wanting. Now it's become something else. It's like a compulsion. It's like I have to bring a child into the world for a purpose. Call it what you want. I think it's an intuitive knowing. I can't explain it, but I have to keep trying."

"If that's what you want, fine. We'll see what the doctor says and do another round if we need to," I said. "What are a few months after all these years of trying? But why don't we start the adoption process at the same time? I love you, whether or not we have a child together biologically, raise children together that we adopt, or foster, it doesn't matter to me. You'll be a great mother. I know how you've always had your mind set on having a baby, but I want you to know that it's okay with me if we stop trying."

"Fine, let's go forward with the adoption process, but I want to do at least one last round after this one. You know the story of my friend Robin's family. After trying to have a baby for seven years, and never conceiving, and waiting for several years to adopt, they finally got a baby, and then she found out she was three months pregnant, so they kept the baby and then six months later had their own child, after which they wound up having two more children. There are so many stories of people waiting for years and years and not conceiving and finally, somehow, having a baby. Remember my friend Marina? She underwent fertility treatments for two years and then stopped, took a break, and wound up conceiving naturally. You never know, even if we adopt, it doesn't mean we're giving up on the possibility of my ever conceiving."

"Glad that's settled. Come here," I said, reaching for her as I turned out the light.

Chapter 7

The time of Moshiach corresponds to the Shabbat day. We will no longer be involved in refining the world, instead we will use the world to help us know G'd.
—From Sichot of the Rebbe, R. Menachem Mendel Schneerson

Arielle
Jerusalem, November 1987

Mahne Yehuda was filled with shoppers just hours before Shabbat. I bought a beautiful bouquet with birds-of-paradise to bring to Shaina and Yossi from a vendor promising to have the best merchandise. I continued shopping for treats to bring and got some hot, fresh nuts, and a box of rich, creamy, parve chocolate truffles. I'd never seen a whole box of them before, and smiled when I thought about all the boxes of chocolates I'd shared with Shaina over the years, and how we'd make sure that we each got at least one of the precious confections. Shaina and I had always loved the pyramid-shaped truffles best. We'd make sure we were the ones who got them, not her brothers and sisters or mine. With only an hour to spare, I made my way to their apartment.

I was looking forward to getting to know Yossi. I don't really know much about him. He's always quiet around me and hasn't talked to me much directly. I've only met him five or six times now. He seems very nice, and like Shaina, seems happy and generally cheerful. That's one of the things I've always admired about Shaina, her upbeat, positive disposition. She's always been that way. What a blessing. I don't know if she works at it or if it's just her natural state of being.

It's only a few minute bus ride from Mount Scopus to Arzei HaBirah, but it feels like entering a different world. The bus was crowded going up Rechov Yaffo, through the center of town, on Friday afternoon. Lots of people were on their way home before the siren sounded the start of Shabbat.

I rang the bell signaling to the driver that I needed to get off at the next stop. Loaded down as I was with my purse over my shoulder, bouquet and my suitcase in one hand, a shopping bag filled with the nuts and candies in the other, it was hard to maneuver my way through the crowd to get off the bus. As I eased my way through, I felt as if some men were squeezing closer to me, instead of allowing me to get through. Was it my imagination or were they after a quick, cheap thrill? Unfortunately, it wouldn't have been the first time. It might not have been all three of them intentionally doing it, and I should give whoever it was the benefit of the doubt, I know, but it really felt like it was intentional, like I wasn't just imagining their bodies pressing too intimately against mine. I could feel myself getting upset and annoyed and had to remember not to judge them all on the behavior of a few. They were probably born into this religious life and didn't choose it. They wore the garb because it was all they'd ever known and didn't always live up to the standards that one would expect of them.

The walk to Shaina and Yossi's apartment took a few minutes from the bus stop. I had already bathed and dressed for Shabbat. As I approached their multistoried building, I heard the sounds of babies crying, children laughing, and mothers calling to them to finish their preparations for Shabbat. Shaina greeted me with a broad smile and a warm welcoming hug. "Great to see you again. Thanks for having me," I said, as I handed her the tokens I brought for them.

"Thank you. I'm so glad you're spending Shabbes with us. Let me show you to your room." They'd taken the crib out of the baby's bedroom to give me some privacy, but it was still clearly the nursery with shelves filled with stuffed animals and picture books, and colorful wall hangings of Noah's Ark and Psalms for protection in hand-written calligraphy.

After putting my overnight bag in the room, I headed back out to the living room to see if I could help Shaina with the final preparations for Shabbat. "Just relax, I have everything under control, or," she said, relenting, "you can come in the kitchen and keep me company." I chose to keep her company and without asking got another knife from the parve drawer and started chopping vegetables alongside her.

After Shaina and I lit candles, Shaina suggested I go to shul with Yossi, even though she was staying home with the baby. Upon walking to shul, Yossi talked about his impressions of Israel and what they'd gotten to see of the country since their arrival. He liked the yeshiva and the neighborhood and told me they'd invited some young men he studied with to come for dinner. The synagogue was modern, with white walls, a domed ceiling, and beautiful woodwork including an intricately carved partition. The lower five and a half feet of it were a dark brown solid wood, and it was then covered with curtains of an opaque beige material, impossible to see through or over. The curtains rose above my head, so the only way to see anything that was going on was to look through one of the thin slats between the wooden partitions. All the action was occurring in the men's section. There were only two other women present, an elderly matron dressed in black and a young girl of about five or six, who ran off to play with her brothers and the other boys who'd come with their fathers. The women's section was larger and more airy than in many synagogues I'd attended, and somehow managed not to feel too oppressive.

I enjoyed the short service welcoming the Sabbath bride. The mens' fervor was tangible as they sang *Lecha Dodi* and other hymns. After the service, I found Yossi outside, standing with two young men about our age. He introduced them as Asher and Aryeh, students at his yeshiva who were also from New York. Surprisingly, Aryeh looked familiar. I tried to place him and noticed from his quizzical expression that he was trying to place me too. Suddenly it clicked, and a satisfied smile lit his face, as if he'd solved an interesting puzzle.

"*Gut Shabbes,*" he said, and upon hearing just those two words, I instantly knew. I'd recognize that deep resonant voice anywhere. This was the same Aryeh I had met last June, the young Chassid whom I'd handed out flyers with during that fateful failed attempt of the Messiah. It was no wonder I hadn't recognized him. Aryeh had changed. Whereas before he had a crew cut, his dark brown hair had grown and his thick, curly locks now reached almost to his collar. He no longer had *peyot*, only long sideburns that extended a bit below his jawline, longer than was fashionable among anyone but the Orthodox; he was wearing a regular black suit jacket with a white button-down shirt and tie instead of the longer-style Chassidic suit jacket he had worn when I first met him. He didn't wear a *gartel*, the rope belt worn by many Chassidim around their waists.

"Good to see you again," he said, still smiling.

"Good to see you too." I smiled back.

"Do you live around here?"

"I live on *Har Hatsofim*," I said, using the Hebrew name for Mount Scopus. "I'm staying with Yossi and Shaina for Shabbat," I answered, surprised to see him and curious about the changes I saw in him.

"How do you know Yossi and Shaina?"

"Shaina's my cousin," I replied. "Didn't you go to a yeshiva in Geulah?" I asked.

"I changed yeshivas."

"Really?" I said. "It looks like you've changed more than yeshivas."

"It all goes together. I haven't seen you here before."

"I don't generally come for Shabbat. We usually get together during the week. This is a little much for me."

"A little much?" There was a question in his voice. "In what way?"

"Well, I'm sure you noticed that I'm not *that* religious."

"Actually, no. I didn't notice. You looked quite observant to me. Not that I was looking. But you were dressed in a perfectly appropriate fashion, more colorfully than the women I was used to seeing, as I remember, but quite appropriate."

"So you couldn't tell I'm not ultra-Orthodox?"

"I can't say I really thought about it much. At the time, I don't know that I could tell the difference between what you consider Orthodox or ultra-Orthodox," he said, "Chassidic and non-Chassidic Orthodox, yes, ultra- or non-ultra-Orthodox, no."

"Well, I don't really consider myself Orthodox either. Not completely, but please don't tell."

"Your secret is safe with me."

"Thanks."

"Primarily, that day I was very focused on getting the message out, on getting people to believe he was really here."

"I know. It was so exciting . . . and frustrating . . . and disappointing . . ."

"Quite devastating . . ." Aryeh continued.

"Really? That bad?" I asked.

"For me it was."

"What are you two talking about?" Yossi broke in on our conversation.

"Nothing much," Aryeh said.

"We've met before," I said simultaneously.

"Really. So you know each other." Yossi smiled.

"Not really," I said, as Aryeh said, "A little."

Yossi looked back and forth between us, confused, but didn't press the issue.

*　　*　　*

The air had grown even more chilled as evening descended. After our initial conversation outside the synagogue, the men walked together, talking to each other with familiarity. I walked behind for the four blocks between the synagogue and Yossi and Shaina's apartment. There wasn't enough room on the sidewalk for us to all walk together. I would have liked to speak with Aryeh more, but it might have seemed inappropriate for him to walk beside me when we hardly knew each other. We'd only met that once, though it's a day etched in my memory. He'd changed so much since then. I wondered if I looked different too. With him you could tell on the outside that something had changed, and it clearly reflected changes he'd been going through internally. I'd wondered about him these last months—what his life has been like since the Messiah didn't come—or didn't succeed. While I felt certain by the end of the day that it had been real, Aryeh has been far more certain all along and seemed even more disappointed than I'd been. Disappointed and disillusioned was my guess, based on the changes he'd been making. I wondered why he'd gone from Chassidic to *chareidi*, if the Messiah had been a Chassid. I hoped I'd get the chance to ask him about it. I must admit he intrigued me. Shirah was right about that. Though I barely knew him, I felt a special connection to him based on what we'd shared that day.

All the wonderful Shabbat aromas wafted toward us as we entered the building and grew stronger as we climbed the stairs to Yossi and Shaina's apartment. I could smell freshly baked *challot*, chicken soup, gefilte fish, garlic and onions, roasted potatoes, and sweet baked desserts. I could hear Kiddush being said in the apartment directly opposite theirs as we reached the landing. As we entered the apartment, we took off our coats and hung them in the closet. The dining table was set with a beautiful white linen tablecloth and real china, silver and lovely crystal water goblets, not what one would expect of a young couple living abroad for one year, and a glass vase filled with red, yellow, and pink rosebuds and cascading white baby's breath. Shaina explained that she had splurged and bought the china and water goblets since they were so much less expensive than they would have cost in New York, and she planned to ship them home when the year ended. It was funny to see her beautiful table since her mother, my aunt Chana, always used paper goods and plasticware, though the wine cups for Kiddush are all made of silver. I guess there's a difference in having to wash dishes for four to five people per meal instead of fifteen to twenty as they have in her family, including all her brothers and sisters and the guests they often invite. Also, paper goods in Israel are so much more expensive. The cost would be exorbitant to use disposable goods every week. I think that Shaina might also hope that if all works out, they'll stay in Israel for at least one more year, (like me, she's very Zionistic). When we were young, she'd talked about living in Israel someday. It had been one of her conditions when dating—to marry someone who would like to live in Israel.

We gathered around the table and sang *Shalom Aleichem* and *Eishet Chayil*, then Yossi put his hands on the baby's head and blessed him. I sang softly hoping that this was enough of a concession to the laws of *kol isha*, knowing it would be safer to not sing at all, but not willing to go that far, to keep to the strictest understanding of the centuries-old rabbinic prohibition against men listening to a woman's voice. There are opinions among Orthodox Jews that it isn't an issue in the modern world, which is what I follow; and others that if the woman is singing with others, not alone, it's permissible; and still others say only an unamplified natural voice of a woman singing alone is prohibited, and that hearing a woman's voice through a microphone or on a recording is allowed.

Such is the nature of Jewish law. There's a saying, "three rabbis, four opinions." The saying the law comes from is "*kol isha erva.*" There are differing interpretations of the word *erva*—one is that it means "alluring"; the other is that it is "her nakedness." So the original prohibition was for men not to hear women's voices when reciting the *Sh'ma* prayer, when full-focused attention and conviction—*kavanah*—is required. From that they drew all kinds of stringent ways to keep this law. It's a sore point with me, one that keeps me from considering myself Orthodox as I refuse to adhere to this rule. I figure if they have a problem with it, they won't invite me back again; or if they ask me not to sing, I can decide for myself whether I want to ever stay with them again. It might sound harsh, but singing is that important to me. Singing softly is not nearly as satisfying as singing out in full voice. What can I say? It's how I like to pray. Anything less feels like I haven't fully expressed my feelings to G'd. Whether it's my love, gratitude, praise, or yearning, it doesn't feel complete or real when I have to hold myself back when I sing or refrain from singing at all.

After each of the men made Kiddush, we all filed into the small kitchen to wash our hands with the silver washing cup—twice on the right hand and twice on the left. I saw that Aryeh poured the water out three times on each hand and wondered if that was a different custom from his Chassidic upbringing. I wondered how he'd gotten to the same yeshiva with Yossi, a Litvish *chareidi* yeshiva. It's known that Litvish and Chassidim have separate schools, especially men's yeshivas and *kollels*. In some communities, girls of different backgrounds would study together if there wasn't a big enough community of either Litvish or Chassidic girls, but in Jerusalem, there must be enough yeshivas for young men to study among their own sect.

All was silent until the last of us returned from the kitchen after washing our hands in preparation for the bread we were about to eat. Shaina put the baby in his high chair, and Yossi sat, lifted the challot still under the challah cover, and said hamotzi. There were two smaller challot each at Aryeh and Asher's places for them to make hamotzi as well. One concession to being in Jerusalem with a young baby was that Shaina did not bake her own challah every week, but this week she had—the same outstanding recipe her mother used that my mother always said tasted like cake. It made me nostalgic for those days when, as a child, we would spend Shabbat together. Even when my mother got the recipe and tried to make it, it never came out quite as good. No one made challah like Aunt Chana except, apparently, Shaina. What a treat!

We passed around the plate of sweet gefilte fish, each slice garnished with a slice of carrot, another of her mother's wonderful recipes, served with red horseradish, followed by chicken soup, Israeli salads, and a main course of honey mustard chicken, rice, noodle kugel, and squash. Between courses, we sang zemiroth. I noticed that Shaina wasn't singing, but she didn't seem to mind my singing softly, and no one said a word or gave me cross looks, as sometimes happens when I sing in certain religious settings; as softly as I could, I joined the men in singing all the traditional Friday night melodies, *Menucha V'Simcha, Kah Ribbon Olam, Tzur Mishelo,* and others. For dessert, Shaina set out a variety of homemade parve cookies and pastries, a big bowl of fruit salad, and the parve chocolates I had brought. I was stuffed by the time the meal ended, having eaten more than usual because it all tasted so delicious. Before the Grace After Meals, Yossi gave a *d'var Torah* about the weekly Torah portion; then we discussed it.

Being a winter evening, even with all the singing and discussions, it was still early when we finished the meal. Shaina put the baby to bed and invited Asher and Aryeh to stay for as long as they liked. Yossi took out a Gemara, and they all started learning. I went to my room and got one of the books I'd brought with me. After I'd read only a couple of pages, Shaina returned to the living room, walked over to Yossi, and whispered something in his ear. Yossi closed the Gemara, said something to the men, and they joined us around the sofas.

Aryeh came and sat in an armchair next to the sofa facing me. "I was surprised to see you again. I still can't get over it."

"I was surprised to see you too," I replied. "It's the first time I've seen anyone from that day."

"Really? I've actually seen a couple of people. So you're still here," he stated the obvious.

"Apparently." I laughed. "And so are you."

"Yes, I am. I thought you were on a year program."

"I thought the same about you. I made aliyah a year and a half ago. I'm in my second year of my master's program at Hebrew University."

"Studying communications."

"That's right. You remembered."

"It would be hard to forget. You were taking notes most of the time for your article. Whatever happened with that?" he asked.

"Nothing. Since it was a nonevent. I didn't even try to get it published.

"That's a shame."

"It is, but not a total loss. It all went into my screenplay."

"You wrote a screenplay. Wow! I'd love to read it. What are you going to do with it?"

"I wrote it for my screenwriting class, it's a documentary. I got an A- in the class."

"That's impressive," Aryeh said.

"Thanks! And you? How long have you lived here?" I asked.

"It's my fifth year studying here."

"Really. You've been here a long time. You look so different. It took me a minute to recognize you. If Yossi hadn't said your name was Aryeh, I might not have put it together," I told him. "So why did you decide to move to your current yeshiva?"

"My outlook's changed, and this works better for me now."

"How so?" I asked.

"Well, I wanted to go to university, which is something that my former yeshiva frowned upon. They wouldn't allow me to do both simultaneously, and most of the students there stay in *kollel* without getting ordained until they get married and have children. Sometimes they stay for years after until the rabbis agree to ordain them. I found out that I could get two years of college credit from Rockland Community College for my yeshiva studies up to this point and that I could take courses through their distant learning program with professors here. In addition, the *rosh yeshiva* at Arzei HaBirah thinks that I should be able to finish learning what I need to in order to get *smicha* by the end of the academic year. Then I'll concentrate on finishing the requirements for my bachelor's, start my master's, and eventually, G'd willing, I'll do a doctorate."

"Sounds like you have it all planned out. I admire that. Good luck."

"Thanks. I'm going to need it. It should take about two more years to finish my bachelor's degree, two or three for the master's, and I have no idea how long it will take to do my doctorate afterwards."

"It's a long process. I doubt I'll continue after my master's. I want to make movies, not do academic research or teach. So I'm curious. I hope you don't mind my asking. Have you become a *mitnaged*, or are you still a Chassid? How does that work?" I asked.

"Neither, exactly. I'm grateful for my upbringing. I have a rich background in *Chassidut*, which will always be important to me. I plan to utilize it in my life as well as in my teaching someday, G'd willing. I still keep a lot of the customs, I love the stories and the piety of the great rebbes, but I can't see myself living that lifestyle anymore. I have too many questions that they weren't willing, or maybe they just weren't able, to answer," he said.

"Such as?"

"Such as why they have to be so closed off from the rest of the world and so fearful," he said. "Why women have to be kept from studying Talmud and other higher levels of learning. Why we have to have so many children even when we can't afford it and wind up living in poverty, or on welfare, or both."

"Those are serious points of contention. I've often wondered about those things myself." I liked that he was for women learning; that he was an advocate of progress and had the courage to follow his own beliefs and not perpetuate a situation he wanted to see change. "You said before that it was devastating for you when the Moshiach wasn't successful that day, or since then. Did that have anything to do with these changes?"

"It was the catalyst. Everyone thought I was crazy for believing, and they were pretty nasty about it. They were so sure that they would have known if Moshiach was really coming, and I was sure Rabbi Shapiro really was *him*. Crazy as it may sound, I'm still sure. I tried to find them again afterwards, but they were gone. They'd checked out of the hotel and seemed to disappear into thin air. It wasn't till a couple of months later that I met someone who'd been there and found out Rabbi Shapiro was in the hospital so I went to visit him."

"So you got to meet him? Did you get to talk to him?"

"I did. I met him before the event."

"That's right. Please, tell me, what he was like."

Aryeh closed his eyes and started swaying, looking like he was transported to another realm. When he finally spoke, it was with quiet reverence. "He was *mamash, really,* the holiest looking person I'd ever seen. The purest. The most radiant being I'd ever encountered. I never thought I'd see someone that holy in my lifetime. I didn't think they existed anymore." He shook his head as he said this and opened his eyes. "The first time I saw him, there was a light around him, a glow, like they say holy people have, like it's written shined from Moshe *rabeinu*. I've never seen anything like it." He shook his head again, slowly, from side to side. It was as if he was transported back to the encounter. "He was a holy man, with a sweet smile, like he loved me, even though he'd just met me . . . like he loved everyone. He was so full of love; I could feel it. It opened my heart. It changed me somehow. He changed me. He barely spoke, just smiled, thanked me for all my help and hummed a nigun as we worked. He asked me about myself, and he really listened. He asked what I was studying in yeshiva, what kind of Chassid I was, where I'd grown up . . . I don't remember all the questions, but he didn't tell me much about himself or pass on any profound teachings, just nodded his head and smiled and radiated love from his soft blue eyes." He shrugged.

As I listened to him speak, it was as if I were experiencing it as well. There was a vibration of holiness. "I felt something like that when I spoke with Eliyahu at the hotel. Maybe not to the same extent, but I'd never experienced holiness like that before. That's what convinced me they were for real." How strange, I thought. Just listening to Aryeh describe his experiences with Rabbi Shapiro, I was somehow able to see and feel it.

"The nigun he sang was an old one I'd heard before. It goes through my head sometimes still and I find myself singing it out loud or in my mind."

"Does it have a name?"

"If it does, I don't know it."

"Can you sing it for me?"

"I'm not a good singer but I'll try." Aryeh started to hum.

I love nigunim and listened intently. The others looked over at us curiously. It was a complex melody with several parts. "That's beautiful," I said when he finished. "Thank you for sharing it with me."

"You're welcome. Um . . . would you like to go for a walk?"

"Do you think it's okay?"

"Yes. I do, but if you prefer to be chaperoned, we can ask the others if anyone would like to join us," he said.

"It's not for my sake that I'm asking. I don't want to sully your reputation."

"Too late. I've already done that myself," he joked.

"I'm sure that's not true. We could invite them along," I said half as a question.

"We could. Would you prefer that we do?"

"Would you?"

"If that had been my preference, I would have suggested it to everyone in the first place, but as I said, I'm happy to invite them to join us if you'd feel more comfortable," he said in a quiet decisive tone, making his desire clear but open to my needs. I loved listening to him speak. He had such a beautiful, sexy voice.

"I feel comfortable with you. Where I'm from, it's no big deal for a man and woman to go for a walk alone. I just don't want to offend anyone or get you in trouble."

"It won't get me in trouble," he said with a twinkle in his eye.

"If you're sure. That would be nice. Let me just tell Shaina and Yossi that we're going out and get my coat."

To say that Shaina and Yossi were surprised to hear that Aryeh and I were going for a walk would be an understatement, but they didn't object or suggest that anyone join us. "Have fun," was all they said.

*   *   *

"It's such an unexpected surprise to see you again," I said as we walked through the quiet streets of Arzei HaBirah. I pulled my coat tighter around me to fend off the chill. "I can't get over it. It's brought back a lot of memories from that period. It's great to talk to you about all this. There's been no one for me to talk to about it at all."

"I know. Strange, isn't it?" he agreed. "I know we only spent a few hours together that day, but I feel so comfortable with you, like I really know you. I've thought about you quite a few times since that day."

"You have? I've thought about you too. I've wondered what it was like for you when you got back to your yeshiva? You were much more invested in it all than I was."

"It was lousy, actually," he said. "Shimmie, the guy I'd brought with me, was just embarrassed and wanted to forget all about it. He didn't want to think about the possibility that the Moshiach had really been there with us. He got angry when I tried to talk about it with him. I looked all around me, and I couldn't relate to the other students or the teachers. I didn't feel like I belonged there. It might not seem to make any sense, but I just felt like we'd gotten off-track somewhere, the Jewish people I mean, the ultra-Orthodox in particular, and that this *chareidi* lifestyle wasn't the way Hashem wants us to live; that we have to live in the world, not shut ourselves off from it. I continued to study at that yeshiva through the end of the semester, but during summer vacation, I started looking for a place that would suit me better. The *ba'alei teshuvah* yeshivas didn't know what to do with me, and the modern Orthodox yeshivas had nothing for someone in my position—older, having done a lot of learning, but without having gone to college. They were either for boys straight out of high school or for guys who'd finished their bachelor's degrees."

"So now you're in Yossi's yeshiva and studying in college. That must keep you busy," I said. We kept walking as we spoke. The streets were deserted.

"Yes, but I'm glad to be busy. I feel in some ways like I'm experiencing life for the first time. Initially, I thought of leaving yeshiva completely, of enrolling in university or getting a job. Then I found this yeshiva, and it seemed like the perfect solution."

"And you haven't told anyone there what happened?"

"No." He paused, seeming to drift away in thought. "I don't know what the guys here would think if they knew. I've spoken with them about the Moshiach, of course. It's one of those topics that come up all the time in the yeshiva world. People say they believe, but none of them were there that day . . . who knows if they'd heard about it."

"Yossi wasn't even in the country yet when it happened. They just arrived in August," I reminded him.

"That's true. Asher wasn't here yet either. And you? Have you told anyone?"

"Well, I wrote an article about it, and my documentary, so I didn't keep it a secret, but as I mentioned, there's really no one I can talk about it with who understands. I didn't get the article published or the screenplay filmed, but the professors read them, of course, and everyone in my classes had the chance to read them if they wanted to. They said that I did a good job, but who knows if any of them believed. What we do know is that none of them came either, and I'd told all of them about it in advance and practically begged them to come . . . but none of them did. Any of them could have been there."

"And outside of your classes, have you talked with anyone about it?"

"Beforehand, I did. I interviewed my cousins, my roommates, friends, and anyone who'd answer my questions. Then after the event, I spoke with my cousins about it and my roommates. I told them all how disappointed I was that so few people came and that I'd really hoped it would happen. It's hard for me to believe that other people don't have the same desire for the Messiah to come. I thought everyone wanted it, that we were all waiting for it—maybe not the assimilated Jews, Jews in America, but certainly Israelis. I still don't understand how they weren't even curious," I said. "How could they not have been curious?" I turned to face him.

"You got me," he said. "I don't know either." We had the street to ourselves. No one was out walking yet on this chilly Shabbat evening. Soon people who'd been invited for meals with friends or family would be leaving their hosts' apartments to go home.

"It's awfully quiet," I observed.

"I was just noticing that too. There are usually more people out on Friday nights after dinner. I'm trying to figure out if we're too early or if they've already been out and gone home."

"You know the neighborhood better than I do."

"Not much. I've only been here a couple of months."

"Is it that much different than Geulah?"

"Yes, very."

"How so?"

"Well, the streets themselves are different, the streets here are wider, there's more open space, and it's newer and cleaner, there aren't as many stores all around, it's more residential. The streetlights are different, not so glaring, and there are some lovely parks, and a lot more trees. I know those are all external features, but it's like the Torah, that's the *p'shat,* but if you look more deeply, you see that there are many layers to it."

I laughed. Though I wasn't a Torah scholar by any stretch of the imagination, I knew about the concepts of the *pardes,* the four levels on which teaching could be interpreted, the simple, hinted, allegorical, and mystical, and the "seventy faces of the Torah"—the many different levels at which one can understand scripture.

"I'm serious," he said, his face mirroring his words. His deep-set brown eyes drew me in further and further, as if casting a spell. We stood like that for a long moment, gazing into each other's eyes, silent, and then I responded.

"I know you are, and I believe you. It's just the way you said it, I could see into at least some of what you were implying without you having to explicitly state it."

"It's better that way," he assured me. He smiled, just a slight curling at the corners of his lips.

"I'd like to learn how to do that," I said.

"I'll be happy to teach you," Aryeh said.

"That's very kind of you."

"Not so kind, it would give me an excuse to see you again. Honestly, I'd like to see you again. Do you have plans tomorrow night?"

He surprised me with his question. He didn't apologize or seem bothered to be asking me at the last minute; though I'd heard it advocated many times that women should decline invitations that are given after Wednesday, I gladly accepted, excited at the prospect of seeing him again.

"I didn't make any plans," I said. "I'd love to get together, that would be lovely."

As we walked back to Yossi and Shaina's apartment, coordinating some of the details for our date, I remembered my conversation with Shirah back in June and all the blessings I'd gotten over the summer. How odd that we were here together and that he had asked me out on a date. Never in a million years would I have believed last June that we'd see each other again or that he'd be open to dating someone like me, and vice versa. When we got to Yossi and Shaina's apartment, Asher was waiting with his coat on, ready to leave. Aryeh thanked Shaina and Yossi for dinner, said good night, and went back out the door with Asher.

*   *   *

When Shabbat ended, I went back to the dorms to get ready. I had a wonderful time at Shaina and Yossi's and could hardly believe it—I had a date. What a surprise! It was bizarre to think of myself going out with a guy in Yossi's yeshiva, a guy who wears a black hat, but I really like Aryeh. There's so much more to him than I would have imagined. He's intelligent, interesting, passionate about his beliefs, warm, and funny. We're so different, I can't imagine this working out, but I have to give it a chance.

Coming off the bus, I ran into Linda. "How was your Shabbat?" I asked.

"Great. We went out to dinner in Tel Aviv and then to a great club last night. We must have danced till 2:00 a.m., if not later. How was yours?"

"Actually, I had a great time with my cousins," I said, laughing at how different her Shabbat had been from mine.

"That's great! I know you were worried it would be hard to be in that environment for twenty-five hours," she reminded me. "I don't think I'd be able to do it." She laughed.

"It was much easier than I'd expected. My cousin Shaina is so down to earth. It's easy to talk to her, even if we don't have much in common anymore. And her husband is *so* nice. I got to know him a little better," I said.

"Well, good. I'm glad to hear it."

"Where's Elliot?" I asked. "I thought he was going with you to your cousins."

"He did, but he had something to do in town, so he'll come by when he's finished. How about you, any plans tonight?"

"Yes, actually. I have a date."

"A date? That's exciting. Have you been holding out on me? I didn't know you were dating anyone. Is he anyone I know? Not that cute southern guy you used to date who's in the army? Is he in town?"

"No. It's not Brian. I don't know if he's in town. I haven't seen him in months."

"Oh. So who is it? Please tell me it's not Jean Marc?" Linda gasped.

"No. It's not Jean Marc. His name is Aryeh."

"And *nu*?" she prompted.

"I met him briefly last June. We worked together on that project I did for my screenwriting class, and it turns out he's a friend of Yossi's—my cousin's husband. He came for Shabbat dinner, and we hit it off."

"A friend of your cousin? So how religious is this guy?" Linda asked, looking worried.

"Very," I admitted. "If you're around when he comes to pick me up, you'll see."

"He's coming to pick you up? You're not just meeting him in town? Interesting."

"He insisted. He's coming to pick me up, even though it's in the other direction."

"I like it. Sounds like he's got class."

"I think he does, but it's also part of his upbringing and culture."

"Whatever you say." Linda gave me a knowing look. "What are you going to wear?" she asked as we arrived back at our apartment.

"That's a good question," I said. "I've been thinking about it, and I don't know. Would it be better for me to wear a dress or a skirt and sweater that are completely *tznius*, in keeping with his expectations, or something that's a bit more my style, a little less modest than he's probably used to but still in the realm of the world he comes from, or should I wear a nice pair of slacks and see how he reacts? What do you think? I should have asked him how he feels about women wearing pants," I rambled nervously.

"I'm not a good person to ask. You know me, I'd go for the shock factor and see how he reacts, but that's me, get it all out there in the open . . . but you're different than I am. If you really like this guy, it's probably best to go with something basically in keeping with what he's used to, at least until you have a chance to talk with him about it," Linda reasoned.

"That's what I figured. It's a shame it's so cold out. Most of my skirts are lightweight, and my winter dresses are all formal Shabbat clothes, or they're low-cut."

"Yes, I've noticed your wonderful décolleté. If you really want to thrill him, wear that burgundy and gold Gunny Sack style. You look stunning in it! If not, the dress you're wearing right now is perfect," she said, referring to my blue turtleneck with the wide black belt. "You look great. If you change the belt and add one of your gorgeous scarves or shawls, you'll look fabulous, and he won't even realize you've been wearing it all day."

"That's a good idea, but I'll see if I have anything else to wear," I said. After showering, I looked through my closet and found an outfit that would work: a simple black skirt with a lilac velour cowl-neck sweater. It was elegant but comfortable, and that was important since I didn't know where we'd be going or what we'd be doing.

The buzzer rang precisely at 9:00 p.m. I answered the door to find Aryeh dressed casually in navy slacks and a blue crew neck sweater over a white button-down shirt. He had exchanged the black fedora I was used to seeing him wear for a black velvet *kippah*. I guess "used to" is an exaggeration as we've only seen each other three times, if you count the few minutes we talked after shul ended this morning. I was glad he was prompt. That was a good sign. Even though I tend to be late, it was good to know that he could be on time. I invited him in, and he looked around our small apartment. "Would you like something to drink?" I asked.

"No. I'm fine," he said.

"Then I'll get my coat."

"That's a lovely outfit you're wearing."

"Thank you. You look quite nice yourself."

"Not what you were expecting?"

"No. But I'm pleasantly surprised, I must admit. I assumed you'd be wearing a suit."

"Don't you like suits?" he teased.

"Suits are fine. They're very nice," I stammered.

He laughed. "This is a new look for me. What do you think?" He opened his arms, allowing me a chance to openly study his appearance.

"I think it works," I said, approvingly.

"Thanks. I'm glad you think so."

"Would it matter if I didn't?"

Linda came out just then, wearing jeans and a sweatshirt. "Hi," she said.

"This is my roommate, Linda."

"Nice to meet you," Aryeh said.

"Likewise." She looked him over from head to toe then raised her eyebrow in silent approval.

"Well," I stammered, hoping Aryeh didn't feel too embarrassed or offended. "I guess we'll be going."

"Have a great time," she said.

"You too. Tell Elliot I say *hi*." I got my coat, and we headed out the door and down to the bus stop.

"Have you eaten?" he asked as we waited for the bus.

"Just a bit for *seudah shlishit*. And you?"

"Same here. Are you hungry?"

"Not really, but I could eat something," I said. It's crazy how so much of our dating and socializing revolves around food. I wonder if it's the same everywhere.

"Have you been to Jan's Tea House?"

"Yes. That's a great idea. Have you been there?"

"No. This will be my first time."

"You're going to love it."

The bus was practically empty when it arrived. I suddenly felt unsure as to whether I should sit down first or wait for him to sit. If I sat first, would he sit next to me? Thank G'd for the seats with two benches facing one another. I chose to sit in one of those, thinking that he could choose to sit across from me if he didn't want to sit next to me, or he could still sit beside me if he preferred. He sat across from me and smiled. I felt relieved that I'd made the right decision. Or had I? If I had chosen a regular seat, would he have sat next to me? Did I want him to? When we went for our walk, we hadn't touched in any way. He hadn't taken my hand, and we hadn't sat down anywhere. Should I ask him about it or just assume that he is completely *shomer negiyah*? I chose to remain curious. If we got to that point, we'd talk about it. There was no reason to rush things. I didn't want him to worry that I wanted a physical relationship when I barely knew him. I wondered if he'd ever kissed someone before, I mean *really* kissed someone.

How strange to be in this position, I thought, to be dating someone who's never kissed and probably never even held hands with a woman. For someone new to this world, he seemed completely at ease. "Have you dated before?" I asked.

"I've been on a number of *shidduch* dates in the past. There was even a girl that I went out with several times, but we weren't right for each other."

"How could you be sure so quickly? Is it okay that I'm asking you these questions?"

"Of course, Arielle. You can ask me anything you'd like. I have nothing to hide. It's hard to explain how I knew. She was pretty and seemed smart, we just didn't have much to talk about."

"Do you think she wanted to continue dating you?"

"I don't know, but it doesn't really matter—it all turned out for the best. If I'd kept seeing her, we would have been engaged by the time that I had my epiphany, then one of three things would have happened: We would have either one, broken off the engagement, two, she'd have been drawn into quite a different life than she ever anticipated, or three, I'd have been stuck in one that I no longer wanted," he said pragmatically. "I'm sure she'll meet someone who's much better for her."

"It sounds like it really was for the best, as you said. And since then, have you dated at all?"

"No."

"Oh."

"I'm sure it seems odd to you," he said, after a slightly awkward silence.

"No," I hesitated. It did freak me out a bit to know that he'd only been on *shidduch* dates before, but I didn't want him to feel any more self-conscious or uncomfortable. I wanted to appear accepting and cool about it. "I have a lot of family like Shaina who are ultra-Orthodox and meet through *shidduchim*."

"How does it feel to know that you're the first girl I've ever asked out on a date who wasn't a *shidduch*?" he asked.

"Honestly, it feels a bit strange, but nice. It's very different for me."

"I'm sure it is," he said. "Have you dated a lot?"

"I've had my fair share of relationships." I shrugged. "I'm twenty-four. I went on my first date when I was twelve, but I didn't date anyone seriously until I was sixteen."

"So you've had serious relationships?"

"A couple," I said. "Does that bother you?"

"No." He shook his head. "If I had lived in that world, I probably would have dated too. Who knows? I know you didn't grow up *chareidi*. I didn't expect or hope that you'd be different than you are. I want you to feel free to be yourself."

"Even if that means wearing pants? You wouldn't care?"

"No, I wouldn't care. Is it important to you to wear pants?"

"Important? I wouldn't say it's important, but I like wearing pants. They're comfortable. I like wearing clothes that are comfortable. To me, pants seem just as modest as skirts and dresses, sometimes even more so, depending on the cut and the fit of the garment. And for some activities, they're far more appropriate, and safer."

"Safer?"

"Yes, like riding a horse or a bicycle. Can you imagine riding a bicycle in a skirt? It can get caught in the chains. Or doing gymnastics in a dress?"

"Personally, I can't imagine doing anything in a skirt or dress, but the girls I grew up with all seemed to manage," he said. "Though I can see your point."

"Have you ever gone mixed swimming?" I couldn't help asking.

"No, I haven't. At least not yet. I honestly don't know if I ever will. Does that bother you?"

"It doesn't bother me. It intrigues me. As you've said, we're from different worlds. You've left the one you grew up in, landed in another that is still a different type of society than the one I live in, maybe a little more modern and moderate, but still ultra-Orthodox. For you the changes must seem tremendous, to me they're still . . . a world apart. This is just a first date. You're not asking me to change, I'm assuming, and you can tell me if I'm wrong; that you haven't exactly *landed* in that world either, it's part of a progression or a process. You're exploring, evolving, and trying to figure out where you fit. Otherwise, you wouldn't have asked me to go for a walk or asked me out on a date. You would have approached this very differently."

"In what way?"

"You know in what way. You would have asked Shaina or Yossi if they could set us up, and you would have looked into my background. They would have called me up and asked me if I wanted to meet you, and they would have looked into your background, to find out all they could about you, even though they know you . . ."

He interupted. "But we'd already met."

"I know, but that doesn't matter. I know how things are done in the *chareidi* world. As I said, I have ultra-Orthodox relatives. You obviously don't really consider yourself ultra-Orthodox anymore."

"I still consider myself *halachically* observant, but . . . you're probably right. As I've admitted, this is a first for me." He shrugged.

Looking out the window, I noticed that we'd arrived downtown. "I think we need to get off here or at one of the next stops if we want to change buses," I said. "If we get off later, we'll need to walk from there."

"Do you have a preference?"

"I love to walk. It's not too cold. Walking would be nice."

"Great. Let's walk then."

We rode till the bus reached the corner of Keren Hayesod and Keren Kayemet streets. "I think we should get off here," I suggested. We walked in silence for a while. "I hope I haven't offended you."

"Not at all. You're very honest and forthright. I like that. I'm not used to it, but I like it! Honestly, I'm not very used to speaking with women, except relatives, and they're all Chassidic. As you can imagine, I haven't spoken to any of them in a while."

"Have you become estranged from your family?"

"Not at all. Actually, they don't know yet that anything's really changed."

"They don't know?" I asked, incredulous.

"They don't know the extent of it."

"How have you kept it from them?"

"I'm here, they're in New York. I haven't been home since Pesach, which was before anything had changed."

"But you talk to them, don't you? They know you've transferred to a different yeshiva?"

"Sure. I speak to them every few weeks. They know I've transferred, and they know I'm enrolled in college. Fortunately, I got a scholarship for college, so it hasn't caused them any financial strain, and at this point, I will pay my own way through school."

"It's great that you got a scholarship. So it's not an issue."

"It would still be an issue, but I think it's best not to tell them at this point."

"Will you tell them that you went out on a date?"

"Most likely, though I'll probably leave out how we met. If it comes up, I'll tell them that you're my *chevruta's* cousin by marriage."

"Perfectly acceptable." I laughed.

"I don't have to tell them that it wasn't a *shidduch*," he said, defensively.

"That's true. You're a big boy. You can make your own decisions."

"That's right, and who knows, maybe Eliyahu wanted us to meet. Maybe it was all planned . . ." he speculated.

"That's a nice thought. It did seem odd that he sent us off together, don't you think?"

"Yes. I thought so too at the time. It was unexpected."

"And a bit awkward."

"Definitely. It was strange that he sent us out alone together, but the urgency of the occasion made it seem perfectly reasonable."

"Or else you never would have agreed."

"Probably." He laughed. We walked on in silence for a moment, our pace well matched.

"So how was it to ask a girl out on a date for the first time?"

"It wasn't the first time."

"It was the first time that you faced the possibility of rejection by someone you'd already met."

"Not really. When I asked Bracha out on our second date, that was the first time I faced the possibility of rejection."

"Hmm, that's true."

"Nonetheless, it was exhilarating."

"Really?"

"Really. I felt pretty sure you'd say yes after we'd gone on our walk . . . some would call that our first date."

"And you? Do you consider that our first date?"

"No, although I asked you to go for a walk, I consider *this* our first date," he said.

"Are you sure it's a date and not just two new friends getting together?"

"Is that what you think this is?" he asked. He stopped walking and turned to face me.

I laughed. "Well, no. I thought that you meant for it to be a date. I was surprised, given where you come from and where you're living, but it seemed like you were asking me out, not just to get together as friends."

"And now?"

"And now?" I repeated. "I'm glad it's a date."

"So am I."

"I'm glad that's settled," I said.

"So am I. Can we talk about something else?" He faced forward and started walking again.

"What would you like to talk about?"

"Tell me about yourself. Where did you grow up? What was it like? What made you want to live in Israel? What are your hopes and aspirations? Tell me about your studies, whatever you'd like. There's so much I'd like to learn about you."

*   *   *

"It's a good thing you've been here before," Aryeh said as I directed him to the entrance of Jan's Tea House. "I never would have found this place."

There was a long line going out the door, but we didn't mind waiting. Aryeh asked question after question; I in turn asked him about his family, his upbringing, and about his plans for the future beyond what he'd already told me. I learned that he was also twenty-four, born seventh out of twelve children, and that his siblings ranged in age from fourteen to thirty-two. He had over thirty nieces and nephews already, and one of his younger sisters was already married with two children and another on the way. I told him that I had an older brother who was married and didn't have any children yet. We talked about our families, how hard it was to live so far away from them, and the importance of Israel to each of us. We had more in common than I would have expected, or maybe I was just looking for common ground. Our feelings about Israel were something we had in common, too, as were our love of the Jewish people, our hopes for Moshiach, and our desire for world peace.

He seemed surprised and intrigued when he saw the interior of the teahouse. Two distinct styles commingled, Eastern and Western. Ornate wooden tables and chairs that might have been at home in provincial France made up about a third of the seating, and the rest of the room was decorated in small round metal tables on wooden stands or long wooden tables sitting low to the ground surrounded by cushions and low velvet-covered plush ottomans that looked as if they could have furnished a Turkish palace. The strains of a Baroque concerto and a multitude of sweet and savory aromas filled the air. There were elegant European paintings next to long cloth wall coverings and embroidered tapestries. Some people I knew from Hebrew University invited us to join their table, but we declined, preferring to wait for our own. When it was finally our turn to be seated, there was a small table available surrounded by cushions.

"Is this okay?" I asked.

"It's fine," he said with a smile. Many couples lounged together on cushions, their arms around one another, holding hands or caressing each other in some way. Other groupings included eight to ten people huddled around tables, deep in conversation.

Aryeh's eyes grew wide as he took it all in. He took a seat on an ottoman, and I sat down on another, next to his. The waitress brought our menus, and we took some time to look them over. I couldn't decide whether to get a chocolate crepe or a cheese and onion quiche. I figured I'd wait to see what Aryeh ordered.

"What would you like?" he asked, surprising me.

"I'm not sure whether to get a meal-type dish or dessert."

"You can get both."

"Thanks, but I'm not that hungry, and they're *so* fattening."

"We could get one of each and share them, if you'd like."

"That's a great idea. I love to share. In my family, we always share when we go out to restaurants. I'm so glad you suggested it. So tell me, what would you like?"

"Whatever you'd like will be fine." He smiled, his eyes twinkling.

"Are you sure? This place isn't *mehadrin*, by the way."

"Arielle, I'm sure." His face grew serious again. "Don't worry. You're not corrupting me. I can take care of myself."

"All right. As long as you're sure. I don't want to be a bad influence."

"You're not. I'm at that yeshiva because it's a place that would accept all my previous learning and experience, where it wouldn't take years and years for me to be ordained, and I could go to college and continue to get credit for my yeshiva studies to apply toward my degree. It wasn't about wanting to be *yeshivish,* or Litvish, or *chareidi.* I chose it for practical purposes."

"But will your chances of being ordained be affected if the rabbis find out that you're not adhering to their rules?"

"I've spoken to the dean, and he understands that I'm still Orthodox, though I'm no longer . . . whatever I was . . . and he doesn't expect me to become some other brand of *chareidi.* If it's a problem, I'll find someplace else that will give me *smicha.* And if I don't, that will be fine too. I don't have to be a rabbi. I'm not even sure I want to be one anymore. I won't let my fear of people's opinions force me to act according to their beliefs and constraints. I'm not hiding from anyone or pretending to be something or someone I'm not."

"But you haven't told your parents yet."

"I will. When the time is right. I haven't really *landed yet,* as you've aptly described it. When I feel more certain of my *derech,* when I've explored and come to the place that feels right for me, more settled, I'll tell them."

"What if you never do?"

"Never do what?"

"Never come to the place that feels right for you, never feel settled?"

"I'm sure I will. I know my bottom line."

"And what's that?"

"Living according to Halacha, minus the *chumrot,* and the fences and the fences around fences."

"And you know what's Halacha and what are *chumrot?*"

"Yes. That's something I've learned through the years and am still learning."

"Most ultra-Orthodox don't seem to differentiate between them, at least from what I've seen."

"I'm not like the *chareidim* you've seen." He sounded annoyed. I was a bit taken aback.

"I'm sorry. I'm not trying to make you defensive."

"I'm not. I'm just explaining to you where I stand. I never dreamed you would be so concerned about my soul. You have nothing to feel guilty about. My choices are my own. It's not like I'm about to eat pork!"

"Okay. I'll stop trying to protect you or reminding you of where you come from. You're a grown man. As you've said, you can make your own choices. I'm sorry."

"It's okay. It's been sweet of you and kind of cute."

"Cute?"

"Yeah, in a slightly exasperating sort of way."

"Oh. Sorry."

The waitress came and took our order. When she left, Aryeh turned to face me and looked into my eyes. "Are you okay?" he asked. "Listen, I'm sorry I got upset. I know all this is pretty intense. I bet you've never been on a date like this before."

"That's for sure." I smiled.

"Look, I like you. It's still early in the evening, but I can already tell you that I'd like to see you again and maybe keep seeing you. There will be a lot of firsts for me. Sometimes, there will be things that you know I haven't done before, and other times, they might not be, like eating milk with a regular *hechsher* and not a super-duper one. Those are the fences around fences I was talking about. Got it?"

"Got it."

"Good. So if I ask you to go to a movie sometime, it won't be the first time I've ever gone to a movie. I've done that already. I've been to several. And I've watched television and heard women sing. In fact, I went to a concert with women singing, and I loved it. By the way, you have a beautiful voice."

"Thank you," I said, feeling my cheeks heat up. "So my singing didn't bother you?"

"Not at all. I loved it." He reached over and took my hand in his, looked down at it and traced the bones on the back of my palm.

"And is this the first time . . . ?" I asked.

"Yes. It is. And since you know that, you don't have to ask me again. Anything that happens between us physically will be a new experience for me."

My heart started racing, and my breathing grew shallow. I grew even more flushed, I'm sure. I haven't been so aroused just holding someone's hand since . . . possibly ever. I looked up and saw him still concentrating intently on my hand. From this angle, I could see that he had long dark eyelashes and full lips—lips that had never been kissed. He looked up and caught me staring at them. My heart raced even faster. I hope he couldn't hear it. I couldn't stop thinking about kissing him. I wanted to kiss him, for him to kiss me, but I didn't want to make the first move. I didn't want to rush him or push him to cross a boundary he might not want to cross.

"I know a thing or two about palm reading," I said, changing the subject to cover up the direction of my thoughts.

"You do? What can you tell me?" His voice sounded even deeper than usual.

It was my turn to explore his hand. I turned it over in mine. "This line shows you have a strong intellect," I said, tracing a line toward the top of his palm. "And this line shows that you'll have a long life and that in your early twenties your life will change drastically."

"You're making this up." He laughed.

"No, I promise. Do you see this line here?" I asked, tracing his lifeline. It felt like an electric current was going through me from the point of contact.

"Yes," he said. I wondered if he felt it too.

"You see how it's broken, and it moves off a bit to the side and then continues?"

"Mm-hmm," he said, looking at our joined hands.

"That shows that there's going to be a big change. It can either be a move—which you've already had—or a lifestyle change, or an illness that you overcome that alters your life as you knew it."

"Hmm. What do you know? There's something to it after all," he said. "Where did you learn this?"

"I'm interested in this kind of thing, the spiritual, the mystical, what they call the paranormal and parapsychological, psychic phenomenon, the possibility of levitation and healing with one's thoughts or hands, precognition, telepathy."

"Can you tell what I'm thinking?" he asked, and I hoped he couldn't tell what I was thinking, unless he was thinking the same.

"I said I'm interested in it, not that I can do it."

"How did you get into all this?"

"My mother is very intuitive. She always knew who was calling when the phone rang and would announce it before picking up the phone. She knew when my father's train was delayed coming home from work in the city or when someone was in trouble. She taught me some of what she knew. She had very strong dreams and somehow knew how to interpret them. They often came true, and sometimes she saw things, or people, like when her grandmother died, she said she saw her in her bedroom at the moment it was recorded that she'd passed. She was in a nursing home. My mother comes by it naturally. I've had to work to develop mine through books and through practicing whenever and however I can. I bought lots of books on these subjects and borrowed others from the library. I've gone to lectures, and still do, when I get the chance. It's what I want to do."

"I thought you wanted to be a writer or filmmaker," he said, puzzled.

"I do, but *these* topics, and people with these abilities are what I want to write and make films about. I want to prove that psychic phenomenon, spiritual experiences, and metaphysics are real, that there are people out there who can really do these things, that people have been doing them for centuries, that they're not all a bunch of quacks and charlatans."

"Of course there are people who can do these things. There have been prophets and healers since the beginning of time, and great rabbis through the centuries who have had those abilities. Some performed miracles, in fact there are still some who do."

"Well, Aryeh, in much of the modern world, people don't believe in any of this anymore. Most people have a rational, logical view of the universe. A mechanistic view, it's called. They don't even believe in G'd. If you can't prove something empirically, they don't believe it's true."

"And thus your interest in the Moshiach coming?"

"That and more—so much more. I really want the Messiah to come. When I realized that not every Jew believes or really wants him to come, I was shocked. It's why I'm here in Israel, to facilitate the process of redemption. We shouldn't just wait for the Messiah, we have to do all we can to bring him. If we're already gathered, already back in Israel, that's one less job he'll have to do, and one less obstacle to his success."

"I agree with you completely. That's a big part of why I came too and why I've stayed. Also to live in a Jewish country, in the land of the Torah."

"Of course. That too," I concurred. "I want to live in a place where being a Jew is natural, where I'm part of the majority, where the holidays fit in with the seasons. In other parts of the world, it rains in every season, here it really only starts to rain at about the time that we add in the prayer "*mashiv haru'ach umorid hagashem . . .*"

"And the rains end around Pesach, when we stop saying it. What you've expressed is exactly how I feel. It's amazing," Aryeh said excitedly.

"Here people can do what they want on Shabbat, and it's still a day of rest." I continued. "I love that even if people go to the beach and not to synagogue, or shopping, or out to a restaurant, it's still their day or rest and they call it Shabbat. I want to live where standardized tests are not given on my Sabbath or holidays, and my children won't feel like freaks for having to take the tests on Sundays with a small group of observant Jews and justify to everyone else why they need *special treatment*. Do you know, one of the New York State Regents exams was given on Shavuot when I was in tenth grade? We're not talking Iowa or Alabama here; we're talking New York state.

"There are as many Jews in New York as there are in Israel, and they didn't take a holiday like Shavuot into consideration when planning a critical statewide exam. It blew my mind. It proved to me yet again that we don't belong there—it's not our country. At first I would get upset about these things and rail against them trying to change things, like our choir taking us on a tour over Pesach and the Jewish choir director expecting us all, including about forty Jewish kids, to travel on Yom Tov and to eat in our hosts' nonkosher homes. It never bothered them to stay in homes that weren't kosher on other tours, and they often traveled on Shabbat, so why would this be any different? But it was, and over forty Jewish students wanted homes that were kosher for Pesach, but there were only four available in Newton, Massachusetts. The choir director called me a troublemaker for bringing it to people's attention and told me he'd kick me out if I missed any performances.

"Then I realized that though it's based on religious freedom, America is not a Jewish country. Even if it was built on the idea of religious freedom, it's up to each person to practice their religion around what's been created, but not for the society to take everyone's beliefs into account when planning things. They can't force me to take an exam on Shabbat or Shavuot, but they don't have to make arrangements for the test to only be given on days when Jews are permitted to write, or drive and don't *have to* be in synagogue. If the majority of Jews don't care enough to protest it or to take the tests on Sunday, that's just the way it is and the way it will continue to be. If I want something different for my life and my children's lives, G'd willing, I need to live in a Jewish country. I want to live in a place where Jews have sovereignty, where we make the laws."

"And all those laws foisted by the religious parties on the rest of the people don't bother you?" Aryeh asked.

"They do, but I'm a citizen, and I can protest and work to change it. Here I feel I have that right. It's not just about the religious laws. When Jews living in other countries protest Israeli policy, I feel it's wrong and makes Israel look bad. We need to present a united front. If I want to have a say in it, I have to put my fate with Israel. My life and my family's lives have to be on the line for me to have a say. I don't think that a lot of people put themselves in the shoes of the Israelis when they speak out against Israeli policy from abroad. They need to take it into consideration when they talk about what they think Israel should do regarding the treatment of Palestinians and whether there should be a Palestinian state."

"I see you've thought a lot about this."

"You could say that. And you, what do you think?"

Aryeh grew pensive. He was silent for a moment then spoke in a quiet voice. "I agree with all of what you said, though my experiences have been quite different," he said. "I was more sheltered from the outside world and never expected American values or laws to be similar to my way of life. We were so different; living in our community was as divorced from the society around us as possible. We mostly shopped in our own shops, went to our own schools, lived together in enclaves. The only non-Jews I knew were some people who lived in the neighborhood or worked in Jewish stores or cleaned our houses. I didn't have close contact or associations with any. No non-Jewish friends. We lived in our own world, the goyim and nonreligious Jews didn't really affect us. The yeshiva I went to didn't offer a Regents track, and anyone who took the SATs, though I don't think there were many of us, did so on Sunday. Politically, we went along with whatever our rebbe and the heads of the Agudah, said.

"Last summer I was so distraught, after that day we met," Aryeh continued. "I was so troubled that one night I went to the Kotel and prayed until the sun came up. I was so focused on my prayers that I didn't even realize it was already morning and time for shaharith. I thought about going back to my yeshiva to attend classes, but couldn't bring myself to leave the Wall. I saw a group of men gathering for shaharith. They were an interesting looking group, some wore suits, some wore tie-dyed T-shirts, and some were all dressed in white." I smiled, picturing the diverse group he described gathering on the men's side of the Wall.

"It was Rosh Chodesh Elul," he continued. "The group was led by an older man with a long flowing beard and a mustache. He wore a long-sleeved white kaftan with slits on both sides and *tzitzit* with real *techelet* strings hanging at each of the four corners over white cotton pants, and a very large white crocheted yarmulke. He had a rich baritone voice and led us in the most spectacular *Hallel*. Everyone sang or hummed along, but what made it even more special was that they played instruments. Sure, I've heard musicians play some of the *Tehillim* before, and I've sung along with them, but never during a prayer service." He described the service in detail and the feelings it evoked, told me about the beautiful apartment they went to for a meal in the Old City, and about meeting a rabbi named David and his fiancé. Aryeh told me about how friendly and welcoming they all were, and about how their camaraderie moved him.

"Rabbi Yehuda and the group's singing were so beautiful. The songs they sang moved me deeply. As soon as I caught on to each one I joined in. The women sang as well, and hearing women singing was something I wasn't used to, but instead of distracting or enticing me, I felt it enhanced the experience. The beautiful harmonies people were creating on the spot, the openness, love, and acceptance toward

everyone were all spectacular. And the stories were wonderful, even
the ones I'd heard before he told with different insights, so it was like
hearing them for the first time, in a deeper way. He opened my eyes
to a new world I hadn't known existed, a place that was still filled with
reverence and in which people followed the commandments but were
open to all people and all paths."

"It sounds amazing."

"It was."

"Yet you chose to go to Yossi's yeshiva."

"It wasn't my first choice, believe me. I asked if Rabbi Yehuda had
a yeshiva, but he doesn't. Not yet, anyway. It's something his followers
want to start. They have a number of different minyanim where they
daven in this style around the country, and there's a community that he
founded with some of his Chassidim," he told me. "I'd love to take you
there. I think you'd like it."

"You've been there?"

"Yes, several times now. It's like nothing I'd ever experienced."

"I'd love to go with you sometime."

"That will be great. I'll see if I can arrange it for this Shabbat, if
that's not too soon for you," he said, a question in his voice.

"No, I'd like that very much."

He smiled. "I'm glad that I'll be seeing you again, and that I didn't
scare you off."

"Not at all. It's been fascinating listening to you," I answered,
smiling back.

"We'd better be going if we want to make the last bus."

Looking at my watch, I realized we'd barely make it. We put on our
coats. He paid the bill then held the door for me to precede him into
the frigid Jerusalem night air.

We walked to the bus and waited at the stop. It had gotten colder as
the night progressed and seemed to be getting even colder with every
minute we waited. With no one else at the stop, I wasn't sure if we'd
missed the last bus back to Mount Scopus. We took the first bus that
came and transferred in town. Aryeh insisted on taking me all the way
back to campus, but I insisted it wasn't necessary. Our first argument
ensued with each of us standing our ground. He said he'd take a taxi
back to his dorm if there were no other bus after he dropped me off,
but I was adamant I'd be fine on my own.

"I really don't want you to walk alone from the bus stop so late at
night," he said.

"Thank you for your concern, but I'm sure there will be people on the bus whom I know. I come home this late on my own all the time." He relented when we transferred buses and saw that the bus was filled with students coming back to campus after a Saturday night in town. I greeted some friends, smiled, and nodded toward them. "They live in my building," I assured Aryeh. "They'll be getting off at my stop and we can walk together."

"If you're sure, okay." He agreed. "At the yeshiva, we study till late most nights. I don't know what your schedule is like, but I don't have a phone and don't want to leave things without knowing when I'll see you again."

"I'm usually back at my apartment by seven or so. Sometimes I go to the library, sometimes I go into town to see friends or family. My schedule varies."

"Are you free Thursday night?"

"I think so."

"Is there a way I can leave you a message somewhere?" he asked.

"I don't have a phone, but there's an office in the dorms that will take messages for people, and you can come up to visit anytime. If I'm not there, leave me a note. A lot of people do that."

"Okay. I'd like to let you know before Thursday night if we'll be able to go to Kehillat Kol Rina this weekend," he explained, "That's the community I was telling you about."

"Thank you. That's very thoughtful of you."

"If I can't arrange for us to spend Shabbat at *Kol Rina*, maybe we can stay with that family I told you about in the Old City, or with Rabbi David and his fiancé, Miri, in Baka. They have guests all the time."

"I don't have any classes on Friday, so if we go out of town, there's plenty of time to get there. We can leave anytime you'd like."

"I do have classes on Fridays, but only in the morning, so we could leave by about noon. We're coming to my stop. Are you sure you don't want me to take you all the way home? I'd be happy to. Really." He tried one last time to convince me.

I shook my head. "Don't be silly, I'll be fine."

He squeezed my hand and said, "I'd like to walk you home, but if you're sure you don't want me to . . ."

"It doesn't make sense. I don't want you to have to take a cab."

"Okay, I'll pick you up at about 9:00 p.m. on Thursday. Does that work for you?"

"That will be fine. It will give me a chance to study."

"Have a great week."

"You too."

"See you Thursday." He gave my hand a final squeeze, released it gently, then stood up to go.

"See you," I called after him as he exited from the back stairs of the bus.

*   *   *

Chapter 8

The world was created solely for the Messiah.

—Sanhedrin 98b

Miri
Bloomington Indiana
May 1994

The doctors were certain there was almost no chance of my conceiving. We contacted adoption agencies and were going through the process when one night I had a dream. In it, a rich baritone voice called out, "Continue the treatments for three more months. Do not give up. Your intuition has been correct. You will have a baby, and your baby will have the *neshama* of the Moshiach."

"The *neshama* of the Messiah? What does that mean?"

"It means that he will be a reincarnation of the soul that has come in every generation as redeemer," the voice boomed.

"So you mean to tell me that I am going to give birth to the Moshiach?"

"The soul of the Moshiach who comes in every generation. In this generation, it will be your son's destiny. He will have the potential to fulfill the long-awaited prophecies."

"Who are you?"

"You know who I am. I Am."

"That's impossible. I don't know who you are."

"I am that I am. There is a doctor you must contact. He has the ability to help you. You have heard of him, he has helped your friend. He offers a different type of treatment. One that is more to your liking."

"Who is this doctor? Please, tell me. I need to be sure."

"Do the treatments for three months. Follow his directions to the letter. Both you and your husband must follow what he says. Do all that he recommends and you will succeed."

"But who is the doctor?"

"His name is Alkolai. Call him at once," the voice said and then was gone.

I woke up from the dream and laughed. *Could it be?* I knew Dr. Alkolai. I'd thought of calling him many times, but he was in Israel; we lived in Bloomington, Indiana, now. Was it my subconscious, or was the voice in my dream really G'd? It didn't feel like my subconscious. Who or whatever it was, I knew that I had to call Dr. Alkolai. My friend Ruti and her husband had gone to see him. They'd been trying to have a baby for years as well, and Dr. Alkolai worked with them with homeopathy and acupuncture. Ruti was sure that the acupuncture was what helped her; her husband, Gilad, was sure that it was the homeopathy that had made the difference for him. No one had ever suggested that David had a problem, so I was surprised to hear that he should also be treated or *follow* what Dr. Alkolai would tell him. It was the middle of the night, but I realized that in Jerusalem, it was already morning. How were we going to manage this? Either we would have to travel to Israel, or we'd have to bring him to us.

I called and was told that he was out. "Would you like to make an appointment?" the receptionist asked.

I laughed. "I'm calling from America. Can you tell me when Dr. Alkolai will be in or have him call me back?"

The nurse gave me his schedule and asked me some questions. When we hung up, I had trouble getting back to sleep. Nothing like this had ever happened to me before. I didn't know if I should wake David or wait until morning to tell him. I got out of bed, got a notepad, and wrote down all the details of my dream that I could remember. Finally, when I was through, I went back to bed.

*   *   *

I must have fallen back to sleep because when I woke up, I was alone and the sun had risen. The aroma of fresh-brewed coffee greeted me as I padded downstairs and found David in the living room praying. He was wearing his green crew neck sweater and beige chinos. His *tallit* was around his shoulders, and his *tefillin* were wrapped around his arm and his head. I watched him sway back and forth for a moment. His eyes fixed on his prayer book, he was unaware of my presence. I always love to watch him pray. Something about his devotion and love for G'd is a greater aphrodisiac for me than a candlelight dinner or strawberries and champagne. It touches my heart in a deep, permanent way; not like the momentary pleasure of the scent of his cologne or a box of Godiva chocolates or even a bouquet of long-stemmed red roses.

After silently watching him for a minute or two, and thanking G'd for having blessed me with such a wonderful husband, I went to the kitchen and started making breakfast. I had a cup of decaf and got to work squeezing oranges, took out two whole wheat English muffins to put in the toaster, cut up some vegetables, and cracked some eggs for omelets, checking each for blood spots.

"Something smells good," David said as he entered the kitchen a few minutes later. He had already taken off his *tallit* and *tefillin*. He came over and gave me a kiss. "Thanks for making breakfast."

"You're welcome," I said as I poured him a cup of coffee and set the English muffins on the table. He sat down at the table and added milk to his cup, took half a toasted muffin, and slathered it with butter and raspberry preserves. I brought the omelets to the table and sat down across from him. "How did you sleep?"

"Well. And you?"

"I slept well. I had an idea I need to talk to you about, actually, it came to me in a dream."

"A dream? Dream analysis isn't really my forte, but shoot."

"I don't know that there's much that needs analyzing. It was pretty straightforward," I said and proceeded to share my dream with him.

"And you think that it was really G'd that came to you in your dream?"

"That's what he said."

"O . . . kay."

"Look, Dave. It doesn't matter if it was G'd or my subconscious. I think it was G'd, but even if it wasn't, I think we should explore this."

"Miri, Dr. Alkolai is in Jerusalem. What do you propose we do?"

"I don't know exactly. I called his office, and his receptionist took my number and said she'd have him call me back. If he doesn't call, I'll call him again. Who knows, maybe we can spend the summer in Israel. You're not teaching any classes, and we didn't really have plans except to visit our families for a week each before and after Jeannie and Adam's wedding. We could still spend a week in New York and see our families on the way there or on the way back."

"Can you miss that much work? Ten extra weeks vacation is a long time."

"I'll ask for a short leave of absence without pay."

"I don't have three months off either. I'll have to leave after nine weeks in Israel at most."

"So I'll stay a couple of weeks longer if I have to, and we'll spend less time in New York. We have some money saved. We can afford it if that's your hesitation. David, honey, we need to do this" I insisted.

"You're really sure about this aren't you? Well, okay then. We'll go. It's a little late to be getting tickets now, but we can do it. We already have the tickets to New York. Maybe we can get our return flights changed so we won't have to spend extra for that. It's just a matter of getting the logistics worked out . . . Okay. I'm psyched. It will be fun. We haven't done anything this spontaneous in a long time.

"It will be great to be in Israel again and to see everyone. It might be hard to rent a place at this time of the season. Where will we stay?" He didn't question my wanting to follow my dream, but I don't think he believed it was prophetic.

"We'll figure it out," I said. "If we can't find an apartment, I'm sure we can stay with Devorah. They'd be thrilled to have us, or we could go back and forth between your family members if we need to be closer to Dr. Alkolai."

"Devorah's house would be a bit crowded and the rest just a bit awkward, don't you think? I'll leave the details to you. Is your passport valid?"

"Yes. How about yours?"

"I have to check. These eggs are great, by the way."

"Thanks. I'm glad you like them." We chatted for a while longer, then David helped me clear off the table and wash the dishes.

"I've got to get ready for work. I have a long shift at the hospital today," I said. "I won't be home for dinner."

"I know. It's my late night at the university. My last class doesn't get out till nine. I'll grab something to eat, don't worry about it."

"I'll try him again later, if I don't hear from him."

"Maybe there's some way we can do this from here. Maybe there's someone he can recommend."

"Maybe, but I doubt it. If there were, wouldn't I have gotten that message?" I speculated.

"I don't know. It's worth finding out."

*   *   *

After several attempts, I finally got hold of Dr. Alkolai. There were a number of people he said we could see in the States, but there was no one who he would work with directly to oversee our case. The people he knew were in New York and California anyway, so it seems *bashert* that we go to Israel to work with him. He agreed to see me and scheduled my first appointment for the first week in June.

"Bring all your medical records when you come," he said.

"Thank you. I will. I look forward to seeing you."

"Have a safe trip."

"Thank you."

After we hung up, I turned to David. "It's so strange, when I lived in Israel, I sent so many patients to see Dr. Alkolai after hearing about him and witnessing the miracles he was able to bring about. Why did it take me seven years to come to him?"

"Honey, it didn't really take you seven years. The first year we were married we weren't trying to have a baby. Then we were only trying for a few months when I got the job offer and we moved back to the States. The doctors said to give it a year of actively trying before we did anything, and we were in Bloomington by then. It makes perfect sense that you wouldn't have thought to come back to Israel or call Israel to consult with Dr. Alkolai. You had the doctors and midwives you were working with here. It's not like you only went the conventional medicine route, you took herbs and supplements, you went to energy healers and reflexologists, you worked on yourself, you did hypnosis and guided imagery, you did everything you possibly could."

"I know. I've taken so many courses in most of those fields. I always thought that with all my knowledge, and with help from my teachers and mentors, something would work. I never imagined it would take so long or that I would be *barren* after all these years. G'd, I hate that word."

"You don't have to use the word if you hate it."

"It's just a mystery why I never called him before, is all I'm saying. I was open to him and what he does. Why didn't I ever look to work with someone like him or someone he'd recommend?"

"Sweetheart, you worked with so many people, with your teachers and mentors, as you just said, why should you have thought to call Dr. Alkolai?"

"Because I knew how successful he was with fertility issues."

"So were Yonit and Elana with the work they do. You were doing so many things, taking herbs and changing your diet, and then the hormone treatments and IVF . . ."

"I know. That's just the thing. Before we started the hormone treatments and the IVF, why didn't I think to contact him? You know how much I hated putting all those chemicals into my body and the toll all the drugs have taken on my health."

"Let it go. It's all in the past, spilled milk. Why look back with regrets? We're here now. G'd willing, he'll be able to help us," Dave said in an effort to comfort me.

"After years of doing those things with no results, I should have called him. I thought about him, but never in reference to my own case. I didn't think, 'If only we were in Israel, I could go see Dr. Alkolai.'"

"Well, honey, you'd never personally worked with him. He wasn't your doctor."

"Yes, but I sent so many people to him, and I knew what he could do," I insisted.

"Yes, but he was far away, and you can't change the past. Please, stop beating yourself up about it. I hate when you do this. I hate to see you get so down on yourself. Somehow, somewhere deep inside your subconscious, you knew and you remembered. You had that dream, didn't you?"

"So you think it was just a message from my subconscious?"

"It doesn't matter."

"No. No. I want to know. Is that really what you think? That this is all from my subconscious?"

"Please, Miri, let's not get into this again. We're going, aren't we? I've agreed. We've changed our plans for the summer completely, and we'll be in Jerusalem for three months to work with Dr. Alkolai. I trust your intuition, or guidance, whatever it is, wherever it came from, and I'm willing to follow it."

"But you don't believe the message came from G'd?"

"I don't know where it came from exactly, just like that period when my imagination was so vivid. I still don't know where my visions came from. I had dreams back then too, remember? You were amazing—the way you helped me through it all, introducing me to your teachers, never doubting my sanity. Even when I was afraid I might be going crazy, you stood by me, we weren't married yet. You could have bailed on me, but you didn't, you were even willing to stay with me if the tests showed that I was psychotic. Now that's love! That experience and the way you handled it changed me forever. It brought us so much closer and made me realize your strength and the depth of your love and commitment. I believe that your dream came from a higher source—but what exactly that source is I'm not sure. It could have come from your higher self, your super-conscious, or you could have tapped into what Jung calls the collective unconscious, or . . . it could be from G'd."

"It *was* from G'd. He called himself I Am That I Am. What could be more clear?" I asked, exasperated.

"Sweetheart, calm down. There's no reason to get upset. You yourself said it might have been your subconscious giving you a message in your dream. Does it really matter?"

"To me it does. That dream was one of the most profound experiences of my life. Why is it so hard for you to believe that G'd spoke to me? He's come to other people throughout the ages. He spoke to your uncle."

"True. I believe he did, but look where that got him! Look, this is my field. Of course I know there are people who've spoken with G'd. Despite sources holding that prophecy ended with the destruction of the First Temple, I believe G'd speaks to people regularly. We can get into semantics about whether or not it's G'd, the Father, or *ru'ach hakodesh*, or a *bat kol*, but I think it's all the same. G'd is One. Jews seem to be the only ones who have trouble believing that G'd still talks to people directly. Christians talk about hearing G'd's will for them constantly. Quakers get up in meetings and *speak through*. There are many accounts in the Bible of G'd communicating with people. G'd spoke to Adam and to Noah, to Abraham and to Hagar."

"To Jacob and Joseph. And most clearly to Moses, the greatest prophet."

"Joseph got his messages in dreams or intuition."

"But Jacob spoke with G'd. The angel that he wrestled with many say was G'd."

"That's true. There are sources that say it was G'd, not just an angel of G'd, and in other places in the text it says that G'd talked to him. And yes, of course, Moses and Abraham did speak to G'd, according to the Torah."

"Eliyahu? And Ezekiel? You teach about his vision in your classes."

"I teach about mystical experiences and the interface between religion and psychology, transpersonal experiences and how they affect us. Ezekiel's vision started the whole *ma'aseh hamerkava*, branch of mysticism, many books have been written on it. It changed the way mystics look at the world and gave them a map, if you will, of the godhead and the levels of the divine realms. It's something to aspire to. Only the rarest of the rare succeed."

"Your point being?"

"I believe that G'd has spoken to people or they've had *ru'ach hakodesh* come through them, the patriarchs, the matriarchs, all the prophets, many rabbis, and *tzaddikim,* throughout history, but it's pretty rare, in my understanding of the world, for G'd to actually speak to people in words."

"So you don't believe me."

"I believe that you had a profound dream that has led us on a new course. *B'ezrat Hashem,* we'll be successful. I believe it's a form of *ru'ach hakodesh.* But I don't know that it matters exactly where it's from. We'll go, and we'll work with Dr. Alkolai. G'd willing, it will work. If not, we'll adopt, as we'd already planned."

"You'll see. It's going to work. It has to."

"I hope you're right. I don't want you to be disappointed."

"And as for the rest of the dream?"

"You've got to admit. It's hard to believe."

"I know it sounds crazy, but you are of Davidic descent; we both are, though I'm a woman, so I don't know if people would be ready to accept that on its own, but no matter. Why not us? You're the one who's always talking about the Messiah. You and your family have always believed the Moshiach would come. Why couldn't it be true?"

"Miri, you of all people know what he could go through. I wouldn't want our child to have to go through all that, but if it's true, I will be the happiest man on Earth. It won't be easy, but we'll do everything we can to make sure that he grows up as normal and well adjusted as possible. But if it's not the case, I would love our child just as much, whether you give birth to him or her or we adopt."

That stopped me in my tracks. "Well, okay then. That's all that really matters anyway."

"Exactly. Have you told anyone else about your dream?"

"No."

"Do you plan to?"

"I hadn't thought about it. What do you think?"

"I think it's probably best not to tell anyone the second part, but to tell people you had a dream about Dr. Alkolai that inspired us to call him and to go to Israel to work with him . . . why not?" David concluded. "I'm sure they'll all be thrilled to see us."

"It's been too long."

"I know. It *has* been a long time," David agreed. "I know how much you miss it."

*   *   *

Chapter 9

A Song with musical accompaniment for the Sabbath day (Psalms 92:1). This is a song for the time to come, for the day that is all Shabbat and tranquility for all eternity.

—*Talmud, Tamid 33b*

Arielle

Jerusalem, November 1987

I must have changed my outfit ten times by the time Aryeh arrived, finally settling on a pair of navy blue wool slacks and a royal blue cowl-necked velour sweater, with dangling, iridescent, mother-of-pearl earrings. I was both excited and nervous. Thoughts of Aryeh were with me often over the course of the week. I had hoped he'd stop by to visit as I'd suggested but had to be content with a note from the office that he'd called and the message: he'd found places for us to stay for Shabbat. I pray that all goes well tonight, considering we already have plans to spend the weekend together.

Aryeh arrived promptly at nine, and I invited him in. He was wearing a black suit and a white button-down shirt with the collar open and no tie under his long dark gray wool coat. "Sorry, I didn't have a chance to change after class. I didn't want to keep you waiting, and frankly, I couldn't wait to see you," he said as he entered. He looked even more handsome than I remembered. My flatmates had all gone out, so we were alone.

"Do you want some tea or coffee, or should I get my coat?" I asked.

"That depends what you'd like to do? There's a movie playing in town at nine forty-five, which should allow us to get back on time, or we can go to a restaurant or out for coffee. Have you eaten?"

"Yes. I had something earlier," I said.

"Do you have a preference? Would you like to see a movie?"

"Whatever you'd like," I said, feeling suddenly shy. At that Aryeh tilted his head and stepped closer to me. He took off his coat, dropping it on a nearby chair, and gently pulled me into his arms, surprising me with his boldness.

"I've missed you," he said. "I don't care what we do tonight. I'm just happy to be with you again."

"Me too."

"That's good to know, I couldn't stop think about you," he said, as he bent his head and pressed his lips to mine. Our first kiss. I felt like I'd come home; like this was where I belonged, in Aryeh's arms. I kissed him back, opening my lips, deepening the kiss, allowing him entry. When he didn't respond as I expected, I sought his tongue with mine. He caught on quickly, his tongue circling mine. He pulled me against him, fitting my body to his. I led him into my room, where we continued to kiss for several minutes until he pulled away slightly, putting me at arm's distance. "I think we should go somewhere. As much as I'd love to just stay here with you, I don't think we should. So tell me what you'd like to do."

"Other than this?"

He laughed. "Other than this."

"Well, if you insist, there's a *mo'adon* here on campus, or we could go for a walk to the amphitheater."

"How about we go for a walk and then to the *mo'adon*."

"Sounds great. I'll get my coat." I was glad he took my suggestion. The amphitheater overlooks the Judean Desert and is quite romantic. It was warmer tonight than it had been on Saturday, but I took a blanket to keep us warm when we sat on the cold stone seats of the outdoor stadium. We held hands as we walked and stopped periodically to kiss.

"How's your week been?" Aryeh asked as we walked through the rose garden. His arm was around my shoulder, and he lifted his hand to run his fingers through my hair, causing my scalp and then my whole body to tingle. There wasn't much to see in the dark, but the path was secluded and much nicer than walking along the straight main road of the university.

"It's been good. And yours?"

"Mine's been good too. Uneventful, but good. You got my note?"

"Yes. Thank you. I'm looking forward to going to Kol Rina," I said. "It sounds amazing."

"Great. There's a *melaveh malka* Saturday night, and we're invited, so if you don't need to rush back, we can stay for it. We can even stay overnight Saturday, or we can probably find a ride back to Jerusalem afterwards. A lot of people will be coming down from Jerusalem to attend," Aryeh enthused. "By the way, next Thursday there's a wedding, if you'd like to come with me."

"You're inviting me to a wedding? You know the bride and groom?"

"Yes. I've told you about them, it's Rabbi David's wedding, and that's just the way Kol Rina is. Everyone is invited, and you'll meet Miri, the bride, this Shabbat. She'll be there for her *Shabbat Kallah.* I'm sure you're going to love her. She's a midwife and is into so many of the same things you are. I'll introduce you this weekend."

"I'm sure she'll be busy. Sounds like there's a lot going on. Are you sure it's okay if I come?" I was excited at the prospect, but worried that it was too soon, and that it would be construed as improper by the people who lived there. I trusted Aryeh, but I still hardly knew him, though I already felt like I'd known him forever.

"I'm positive. I've become quite close with David and Miri; they've been a godsend to me, actually, since this summer. He's my advisor and one of my teachers."

"Shabbat sounds like it will be lovely," I said. "I'm not sure about the wedding. That reminds me of something though. Tell me, what's the most wild and crazy thing you've ever done?"

"Um, Arielle, a lot of people would think that everything I've done in the past five months has been crazy, but 'wild and crazy' in the context you mean, I don't know that I've ever done anything that you'd consider really *wild or crazy.* What does it remind you of?"

"Well, one of the really mischievous things I've ever done was to crash some events at a kosher catering hall in the next town over when I was in junior high and high school. We found that weddings were the easiest. Some friends and I would dress up and go see what event was going on. The first time we did it was during a bar mitzvah of one of our friends. It was just ending, and we were still in the mood to dance, so we went over to a party in one of the other halls and joined in. It was so easy, and no one seemed to notice. We just danced and danced. Something about it, I guess the risk of being caught, made it really exciting. We talked about it for months, then one of my friends dared us to do it again, so we all dressed up and went to see what was going on there. It was over the summer, and there was a wedding, so we just went and danced. Then, a couple of times we ate at the smorgasbord or had some of the *hors d'oeuvres* they pass around on platters. It was so much fun, and our town was so boring that a few months later, we decided to do it again. When anyone came over to us who wasn't part of our group, we'd ask them if they were on the bride's side or the groom's side before they had a chance to ask us. Then we'd say we were from the opposite side. We never got caught, but one time we came pretty close. My friend Adam dated a girl he met at one of those weddings. She thought it was hilarious when she found out. I don't know if she told the groom, who it turned out was her brother."

Aryeh laughed. "Going to a wedding that's open to everyone will be pretty tame compared to crashing a wedding. Even if you don't know the bride or groom, it won't be such a big deal for you," Aryeh said.

"It will be like old times, only better!" I said. "I hope I haven't shocked you."

"I think you wanted to shock me," Aryeh said knowingly.

I thought about that for a minute. "Maybe. You could be right about that."

"Interesting. Why do you want to shock me?"

I shook my head. "You've got me. If that's what I was doing, it was completely unconscious. Why do you think I might want to shock you?"

"I'm not sure. Either you're trying to scare me off, or you're just being honest."

"I don't want to scare you off, and I do like to be honest. My life is basically an open book."

"But you don't share everything with your religious relatives," Aryeh reminded me.

"That's true," I admitted.

"So you don't mind shocking me, but you don't want to shock them?"

"I don't want to shock you, but I also don't want to keep secrets from you or to be afraid of what you'd think of me if you were to know the truth."

"The truth?"

I shrugged. "Everything I've done in my life, all the relationships I've had . . . that sort of thing. I think this is pretty innocuous, so it's a good place to start."

"Your past is your own, Arielle. I'm happy to hear anything you want to tell me about, but it's up to you."

"Thank you. I appreciate that. There are things I would like to share with you, like my time on kibbutz. Before college, I lived on a kibbutz up north for a semester. I was on the kibbutz ulpan. We worked half a day and studied half a day. I dated a man who was a candidate for membership and fell in love with him. I loved living on kibbutz and didn't want to leave but was still planning to move back and start college. A month before I was supposed to leave, he asked me to marry him. He wanted me to stay on the kibbutz and become a member too. I said yes. I wanted to marry him, but I was only seventeen and wasn't ready to stay on kibbutz for the rest of my life.

"I applied to university here, but my parents wouldn't sign the application forms, and I needed their signature to be accepted. I didn't know at the time that according to the Law of Return, I could have made aliyah on my own, and as an unaccompanied minor, new immigrant, could have been accepted, and my tuition probably would have been covered. All I knew was that there was a line on the application that stated that anyone under eighteen needed their parents' signature.

"I wanted to stay on kibbutz and go to college once I didn't need their signature, but my parents had a fit when I told them I was staying and getting engaged," I went on. "They insisted I come back to the States to start college as planned.

"I'd already been accepted at a couple of schools and planned on going to university upstate. I agreed to come home for one semester and start if they would agree to sign the forms so that I could go back at that time. When I got back, they claimed they'd only sign for me to go for one year, not to transfer to university in Israel permanently."

"You must have been upset," Aryeh sympathized.

"Honestly, I felt betrayed, but it was nothing compared to how betrayed I felt when I got a letter from my fiancé saying that it was over between us, and he was marrying someone else. I couldn't believe it. I decided to come back to Israel anyway and do the one-year program. When I got here, I went to see him. I think I was hoping that when he saw me, he'd be so overcome with love that he'd realize his mistake and we'd get back together. His new fiancé had also gone back to the States to finish college, but she'd been a junior and only had one year to finish, not three.

"When he saw me, I could see that he was still attracted to me and thought he still had feelings for me, so during our break over the High Holidays and Succot, I went to work there for a month. He tried to avoid me, but I wouldn't let him. I guess you could say that I seduced him, but when I succeeded, I thought it was more than that. I thought we were getting back together, but when it was over, he paced back and forth berating himself and telling me how horrible he felt for betraying *her* and that he wished I'd never come back. I asked if he'd felt bad about betraying *me* when he started seeing her, and he said no, he never really believed I'd come back, so he didn't think of it as a betrayal. I felt devastated at the time. Like I'd been violated, but it was my own doing. I'd tried to win him back, but I'd failed, and the worst part was hearing him talk about how guilty he felt for betraying *her*. I guess it wasn't meant to be and I'm better off without him."

"Sounds like it," Aryeh agreed. "I'm sorry you had to go through that. It must have been painful."

"It was. Thanks."

"You gave your heart to someone. It's not your fault he hurt you." Aryeh put his arm around me and held me close. "Anything else you want to tell me about?"

"Nothing urgent or pressing."

"We've got time to get to know each other. I know you had a very different kind of life and upbringing than I did, and I'm okay with that. In fact, I like that you have experience and know what you want. I love that you're educated and that you want to have a career outside the home. I think all those things are great."

We'd gotten to the amphitheater and were looking out at the starry desert sky, wrapped in the blanket I'd brought with us.

"And I love that you love those things about me," I said, snuggling closer to him.

He put his other arm around me, and he hugged me tight. I hugged him back, and we sat in silence for a while until he turned to me and said, "I don't know that this place is so much safer than your apartment," as he lifted my face tenderly toward his, his gentle fingers caressing my cheek, and kissed my lips.

"Are you sure you don't have experience doing this? For someone who's just started kissing, you are exceptionally good at it."

"Why, thank you. I guess I'm a natural."

"I guess you are."

"And you're a great teacher. So not everyone has been a good kisser in your experience?"

"No."

"That's it, just no, no more explanation than that?"

"You don't really want to hear about my past experiences, do you?" I asked, scrunching my nose at him and pulling him back for another kiss. "I'd much rather kiss you than talk about all the frog kisses I've suffered."

"Frog kisses?"

"Have you ever heard the fairy tales about princes who have been put under a magic spell and turned into toads?"

"Sorry, I've had a fairy-tale-deprived childhood." He laughed.

"I guess you have. Well, the frog or toad can only turn back into a prince from the kiss of a woman who truly loves him, thus the saying, 'You have to kiss a lot of frogs before you find your handsome prince,' but some frogs are just frogs, and there are no magic spells that will ever turn them into princes."

"But one woman's frog could be another woman's prince," Aryeh speculated.

"Interesting perspective. I never thought of that before, but I'm sure you're right."

*   *   *

We never made it to the *mo'adon*. It was refreshing to spend hours under the stars talking and just kissing a man I really liked with no pressure for anything further. I found myself wanting more, but at the same time relieved to be taking it slow. The first blush of love was upon us. I felt warm and aglow just thinking about him. It was nice. I hadn't felt this way since high school, but in high school I didn't have the desires I now have, or the experience. It was exciting to be his first love. I hoped it would last; that we'd continue to see each other and that the relationship would develop, though it was still hard for me to see myself with him in the long run. He was going through so much; had changed so much in such a short time. I didn't know where he would land when all was said and done. I don't think he did either. Meanwhile, I was excited that we'd be spending the weekend together, albeit in separate houses, but seeing each other as much as we could.

*   *   *

Aryeh and I met at the bus station at noon Friday. We had forty-five minutes before the next bus to Kol Rina. He got the tickets, and then we went shopping at the stores just outside the bus station for gifts for our host families and a wedding present for the bride and groom for next week. We bought wine and chocolates for the families we'd be staying with and a hand-painted silk challah cover and an olive wood cutting board with the word Shabbat engraved in Hebrew for David and Miri.

"By the way, have you spoken with Shaina this week?" Aryeh asked as we left the store and walked back toward the Central Bus Station.

"I spoke with her a few days ago, on Monday or Tuesday. I thanked them for having me over for Shabbat and made plans to see her next week. Why? Is everything okay?"

"As far as I know, everything's fine. I was just wondering."

"You haven't told Yossi that we're dating and were wondering if he knows?" I guessed.

He nodded. "I haven't said anything. Have you?"

"I told Shaina on Shabbat, right after you asked me, that we were going to go out on Saturday night. She was a bit surprised but seemed happy for me. I think they were surprised when you asked me to go for a walk Friday night in the first place. So of course, I told her that I'd had a good time and that I was going to see you again on Thursday. I didn't give her any details or anything, but I told her. I'm sorry if you were trying to keep it a secret," I said.

"No, no, it's fine. I wasn't trying to keep it a secret, but you're right, I didn't say anything to Yossi."

"Oh."

"Does that bother you?"

I shrugged. "It's up to you who you tell. You're not obligated to talk to anyone for my sake. I'm just a little surprised. I guess it's different for guys, especially when you're balancing between the yeshiva world and your new personal lifestyle. Is there anyone you can talk to about these things? I know I'd go crazy if I couldn't talk to anyone about my feelings."

"You can talk to me."

"Thank you, and you can talk to me, but sometimes you need someone else to give you a different perspective, someone you can talk to about the person you're involved with."

"I don't really know about that. As I told you, I've only gone on *shidduch* dates before and didn't really feel a need to talk to anyone about them. Maybe if I'd dated any of those girls more than three times, I would have felt differently."

"And you haven't wanted to tell anybody about me?" I asked, surprised.

"I've wanted to tell everyone . . ." He smiled.

"But . . ."

"But I've only told a couple of people. When I called looking for places for us to stay at Kol Rina this weekend, I asked my friends Nava and Chaim if a friend of mine could stay with them, and they asked if I was coming as well and didn't I need a place to stay. I explained that the friend I was bringing was a woman, and they asked all about you. I've never brought anyone with me before, and they're excited to meet you. Then I called Baruch to see if I could stay with him and his family, and I told him about you too."

"Really?"

"Really. I'm sure you'll like them. They're terrific people. Everyone I've met at Kol Rina is great. I think you're going to love it there. I hope you will."

"I hope so too," I said. There was almost a frenzy around the bus station in anticipation of Shabbat. People hurried to and fro, talking excitedly. When we reached our bus stop, there was a crowd already waiting for the next bus. We could barely hear each other over the din from the other people waiting, their arms loaded down with satchels filled with wine, *challot*, fruits and vegetables, chickens, fish, bouquets of flowers, and the rest of their Shabbat purchases. There were no supermarkets there, no shuk or marketplace, only a little grocery store without a lot of variety, Aryeh explained. Many people work in Jerusalem and commute to Kol Rina or one of the nearby towns and villages along the old Jerusalem—Tel Aviv highway that the bus passes through.

"And your friends who are getting married, what are they like?"

"David and Miri? I told you about them, David is the first person I met that day at the Kotel. We've become very close. He's my mentor and teacher. He also comes from a Chassidic background and left it behind. He grew up in Brooklyn and was the first in his family to attend university." He explained that David got *smicha* from Yeshiva University and was finishing his doctorate in Jewish thought at Hebrew University. "He's in his late twenties. The bride, Miri, is about our age. She's also American. Her sister Devorah lives in the kehilla—that's what everyone calls Kol Rina. They're the ones who brought me there for the first time."

"And they'll be there for Shabbat?"

"Miri will. Devorah is making her *Shabbat Kallah* there, and she's invited some of her close girlfriends. Her family who are already here from the States will probably be there for the weekend as well. We're lucky to have found places to stay."

"Wow. This is really going to be a special Shabbat."

"I've been told that it's going to be, as they say, '*Mamash*, the highest, the deepest, most incredible experience of our lives to date.' So what do you think about that?"

"I think we're very lucky. I love Rabbi Yehuda's music, but I've never met him. Thank you for the opportunity."

"I'm just glad you wanted to come," he said, putting his arm around my shoulder.

*   *   *

"Amazing. It must be ten degrees warmer here than in Jerusalem," I said as we walked from the bus stop along the old highway and made the trek to our hosts' homes loaded down with all of our bags. Most of the houses we passed were small one-story dwellings, many adorned with beautiful landscaping of lavender, rose bushes, lilies, azaleas, peonies, and well-manicured shrubbery. Aryeh walked me to my hosts for Shabbat, the Tanzers, and stayed to introduce me to Nava, who ushered us in. Nava was dressed in a beautiful gauzy floral print dress. Her hair was covered with colorful matching scarves intertwined in an intricate manner to create a turbanlike head covering. "Come in, come in," she said. "The kids are out playing, and Chaim isn't home yet. Would you like something to drink? You must be thirsty. It's a long walk from the road. I'm sorry no one could come get you," she went on, moving like a whirlwind as she spoke. "How was your trip?"

"It was fine, *baruch Hashem*," Aryeh said. "It's so nice to see you again. This is Arielle. Arielle, Nava," he introduced.

"Lovely to meet you," I said, presenting her with the gift I'd brought for her and her family.

"And you," Nava said. "Thank you so much. It wasn't necessary to bring anything. That was so sweet of you. You're lucky, Rabbi Yehuda is here this weekend."

"Yes, we know. I heard he came for the wedding," Aryeh said.

"I'm really looking forward to it. Thank you so much for having me," I said.

"It's our pleasure," Nava said. "Will you be here for the wedding? It's next Thursday."

"I don't know if I'll be able to come back," I said.

"Oh, you definitely should. It will be beautiful."

"But I don't know the bride or groom."

"That doesn't matter. Everyone is invited," Nava insisted.

"We'll see," I said.

"I'll introduce you. We're invited to a special *seudah shlishit* for women, but you'll meet her before then. And you, Aryeh? Will you be here for the wedding?"

"I wouldn't miss it for the world. The first wedding I attended here was so special, and that wasn't even with Rabbi Yehuda officiating."

"It will be so high, so holy. It's such a blessing to be at a wedding, you know. There's a midrash that says that all the souls meant to be present at a wedding are planned in advance. It's predetermined before we're even born, when the *shidduch* is made. You'll see if you're meant to be here. If you are, it will work out," Nava said with conviction. "Sometimes the bride and the groom don't even know who's meant to be there. You're invited to stay over Thursday night after the wedding, if you'd like, but I'm sure we'll be able to find you a ride back to Jerusalem if you'd prefer. Or you can stay for Shabbat next week as well."

"Thank you. That's so sweet and generous of you," I said.

"You're invited anytime."

Nava left the room for a moment, and I turned to Aryeh. "You were right. She's amazing. I can't believe how gracious and welcoming she is. We just met, and she's already issuing me an open invitation. I've never met anyone like her. If, as you said, everyone here is like this—wow!"

He nodded. "They are, trust me. I haven't met anyone here who isn't like this. It's pretty incredible."

Nava returned with a tray containing a pitcher of grapefruit juice, another of water, and a plate of home-baked chocolate chip cookies. "Please have some. Make yourself at home. If you're hungry, take anything you'd like. The kitchen cupboards and drawers all have labels, so you'll know what to use for meat or dairy. I'll show you to the room you'll be staying in. I'm sorry you'll have to share it with my daughter, Dina," she apologized.

"That's fine. I really appreciate your having me," I told her.

"Thank you, Nava. I'm going to go check in with Baruch and Orly, drop my stuff off, and say hello. If you don't have much to do to get ready for Shabbat, we can go for a walk . . . if not, I'll meet you back here to go to shul," Aryeh suggested.

"Well, if Nava needs any help . . ."

"No, no, no, you go and have a good time. I don't need any help," Nava jumped in.

"Okay, if you're sure. I'll see you soon then, Aryeh," I said.

Nava showed me to the room I'd be sharing with her daughter, and I took a quick shower and dressed for Shabbat. "Nava, Can I help you at least till Aryeh comes back?" I asked when I'd finished.

"Thanks. Just keep me company. There's not much left to do. I'll be fine."

"I'm happy to help. Put me to work."

"If you're sure," she said and handed me some plates, glasses, and silverware to set the table.

"That was quick," I said when Aryeh returned what seemed like only moments after he'd left. He'd changed into a pair of white slacks and a white button-down shirt and white kippah for Shabbat.

"What can I say? I just couldn't stay away." He chuckled.

"Nice outfit. Is that how everyone dresses here on Shabbat? It's just like the men dressed on Shabbat on my kibbutz."

"Really?"

"Yes," I said. "It's like most modern Orthodox dress on Shabbat throughout Israel."

"Pretty dress. I forgot to tell you that the women mostly wear white on Shabbat too but looks like you were prepared."

"I had a feeling."

"A premonition?"

I laughed. "No, just a good guess or you could call it a logical assumption."

"There's so much I want to show you and so many people I want you to meet," Aryeh said as we set out from the Tanzers' house. We walked along a path past several rows of one-story cottages, past the common areas where the synagogue and *mo'adon* were located. We passed a chicken coop, an open lot, and a little grocery store; then we walked beside a treelined area for a stretch.

"It looks a lot like a kibbutz," I said.

"I've never been to a kibbutz," said Aryeh.

"From what I can tell so far, the houses are a little bigger, and the kitchens and dining areas in particular are larger than on a kibbutz. On many kibbutzim, there are children's houses where the children live together full-time as well as studying together. I spent a summer on one like that on the coast, but on religious kibbutzim like the one I lived on, the children live at home with their parents until they were sixteen, so there's a bedroom in each house for the children. Anyone with more than one child gets a house. Otherwise, they live in apartments. From what I could see, the Tanzers have at least two bedrooms for their children."

"Are you still in touch with people on the kibbutz?"

"Not many. It's my own fault really. After Alain and I broke up, it was too hard for me to go back to visit. Most of the people I was close to there knew me as part of a couple. I'm sure that some of them would be happy to see me, but I still feel a bit awkward and uncomfortable about going to visit."

"That's a shame."

"I know. But it's okay. I have my own family around the country who complain and make me feel guilty about not visiting enough."

Beneath all the conversation was an awareness of the attraction we felt for each other, of the fact that we were alone and spending Shabbat together in this environment away from the watchful eyes of our friends and families. We walked on for a while longer until we saw people dressed in their Shabbat finery headed toward the synagogue.

"Do you need to go back to the Tanzers for anything before we go to shul? I think there's a place set up for women to light candles," he said as he steered us toward the synagogue.

"Sounds perfect." I went into the women's section, lit candles, and found a seat, leaving Aryeh to join the men. I was surprised at how many women came to shul for *Kabbalat Shabbat*. I felt quite comfortable, though the only person I knew in the women's section was Nava. She came and sat beside me, accompanied by a girl of about twelve, whom I assumed must be her daughter, Dina. Nava had changed into a white dress, similar in style to the dress she'd worn that afternoon. A braided gold and white silk band sat like a crown atop her pristine white Shabbat scarf, framing her delicate, pixielike features. Most of the women as well as the men were dressed in white.

Another pleasant surprise was that unlike in many Orthodox congregations, most of the women sang along during the service. I sang along with whatever I could. I didn't know many of the tunes but began to catch on as they were repeated over and over again, first with the words of the prayers and then as wordless nigunim. After *Lecha Dodi* and *Mizmor L'David,* the men began to dance, circling the *bima,* while the women continued to stand at their places singing, many with eyes closed, and swaying, transported to another realm by the fervent prayers. I'd never been to a service like it. Aryeh was right. I could see how he'd fallen in love with this special place and found myself falling in love with it as well—with this community and their special way of praying, with these people, and their unique way of life. They'd created a warm, loving environment where anyone seemed welcome, just as Aryeh had described.

When the service ended, the women all rushed over to hug a thin woman with long auburn hair who looked to be in her early twenties, flanked by a group of other young women. As women approached and wished her mazel tov, she smiled and gave each one a blessing in return, bringing tears to many eyes. She and Nava hugged for a long time, swaying from side to side in each other's arms. Nava said something to her, and it was the young woman's turn to have tears in hers. I could feel the love between them and felt blessed to witness the exchange.

"Arielle, come, there's someone I want you to meet," Nava called out, motioning for me to join her. "This is Miri."

"Mazel tov! It's so nice to meet you," I said, coming over to stand beside Nava. "I've heard so much about you."

"Really? Well, Thank you," she said. "And may you be blessed to find your *bashert* and stand under the chuppah, together, and build a *bayit ne'eman b'yisrael.*"

"Thank you," I replied, touched and moved by her words.

"Arielle also lives in Jerusalem," Nava told her.

"You do? Where?" Miri asked.

"In the Idelson dorms, on Har Hatzofim," I said. "And you?"

"I live in Baka. Do you know it?"

"Yes. It's a lovely neighborhood."

"It is, isn't it? I love it there."

"Is that where you're going to live after you're married?"

"Yes, we'll be staying in the area, for at least the first couple of years, and I hope longer. I love the community there. As much as I like to think of myself as Israeli, it's nice to be in a neighborhood with a lot of Anglos. It suits me. And it's near the hospital."

"Which hospital is that?"

"Misgav Ladach."

"Miri is a midwife," Nava informed me.

"That's right. Aryeh told me. It sounds so interesting. I've heard it's a wonderful hospital for having a baby."

"So you're Aryeh's friend." Her smile broadened. "I heard he'd met someone. I'm so happy to meet you. We love Aryeh. Yes, Misgav Ladach is the best. It's very progressive compared with New York, where I'm from originally, in terms of natural childbirth and allowing women choices of the kind of birth they'd like. The doctors are great as well. We have some world-class specialists who take care of difficult pregnancies and deliveries, C-sections, and complications that come up, but for the most part, the nurse-midwives like myself attend the births. I work at other hospitals as well, for my private patients, but Misgav Ladach is by far my favorite."

"That's great." I looked and saw that people were gathered around us wanting to greet the bride. "Well, it's lovely meeting you. Mazel tov again, I'd love to talk with you more, but I don't want to keep you, there are so many people here who want to congratulate you." I smiled.

She smiled, threw her arms open wide, and drew me to her. "Thank you," she said softly for me alone to hear. "There will be plenty of time for us to talk and get to know each other better." She kissed my cheek.

"Is her fiancé here this Shabbat too?" I asked Nava as Miri moved on to talk with another woman.

"No, we're having the *Shabbat Kallah* here, the *Ufruf* is in Jerusalem. Rabbi David's family is all here for the wedding already, and he has aunts and uncles who live there."

Aryeh joined us with Nava's husband, Chaim, and sons, Koby and Melech, in tow. We all walked back to their house together. Aryeh stayed for dinner, a traditional Shabbat meal; and after *Birkat Hamazon*, we went for a walk. It was darker than the streets of Arzei HaBirah on a Friday night, but lots of people were out walking to an *Oneg Shabbat* at the *mo'adon*. Rabbi Yehuda was there, already telling the first of many stories I was to hear. I wish I could remember them all! Between stories we sang, most of which were songs written by Rabbi Yehuda. People said that he didn't so much write them as receive them fully formed. Some were famous, but many more were new to me. We stayed until everyone was leaving; then Aryeh walked me back to the Tanzers, and after a long kiss good night in the shadows, he went to the Shem Tov's to sleep. The house was quiet, and all the lights had gone out. They must have been set on timers. Only a nightlight remained to illuminate my path, coming from the kitchen. I tiptoed down the hall and into Dina's room. Finding her fast asleep, I got ready for bed as quietly as I could.

*   *   *

Sunlight streamed through the window, waking me early the next morning. Dina was still fast asleep, so I took out a book to read, not wanting to wake her, but visions of Aryeh kept intruding, making it difficult to concentrate on the pages. I closed my eyes and pictured him as he looked last night, remembering all his expressions, at times pensive, at others focused, intently listening while someone spoke, or smiling and laughing.

Hearing voices coming from the hallway, I got dressed then ventured out of the room to wash and brush my teeth. By the time I returned, Dina was awake. Nava joined us for a light breakfast; then we all walked to shul together.

"Everything is so beautiful here," I said, noticing the manicured lawns, and flower gardens most people had planted, combinations of rose bushes, cactus plants, and taller trees lined the walk. How long have you lived here?"

"We're part of the founding *garin*. We met Rabbi Yehuda when we were still in college. Our school was on his circuit, he came every year for at least one Shabbat and gave a concert."

"So you didn't grow up Orthodox?"

"Not at all," said Nava. "My family was very Reform. I loved Judaism but didn't find much spirituality in it. I found more spirituality in yoga and meditation than I did in my own religion. I guess you could say I was a seeker. I started to explore other religions, like many of my friends were doing. Then I met Rabbi Yehuda and learned that there was such a thing as Jewish meditation."

"What is his background, Rabbi Yehuda?" I asked. "How did he create this interesting blend?"

"Rabbi Yehuda survived the Holocaust as a young man, and like many survivors, he left religious observance behind him when he came to Israel. He started his own business and was opening new markets in different countries when he met an Indian businessman who invited him to visit. Spirituality permeated the air in India, and he felt a pull to stay and explore. He came back to Israel, sold his company, and went back to the Far East where he traveled and finally went to live in an ashram.

"After he reached a very high level of understanding, he had a dream and got a message to come home. At first he thought this only meant physically, and he balked at the idea, but when he told his guru, he agreed that it was best for Rabbi Yehuda to go back, not only to Israel, but to his own religion and to explore the mystical teachings it contained. The guru told him that the truth was available in all faiths and that all paths lead to the One, but that it is best for each of us to seek the truth in our own religion. The guru said that the religion a person is born to is the best path for their particular soul, since it's the religion of their ancestors, and because karmically, for some reason they were born to that religion, so there's a special connection to that path, so Rabbi Yehuda packed the few things he had taken with him, came to Israel and went to learn in a yeshiva in the Old City. He enjoyed learning, but found it very dry and hard to reconcile with the spirituality he'd found in the east, until he began to explore Kabbalistic teachings.

"He was still considered too young by most Kabbalists to take him on as a student, but he found one who would, and he began studying with him. The rabbi incorporated meditation as well as singing and dancing into their prayer services, and opened up the teaching of Kabbalah to people other than married men over the age of forty who had already learned the entire Talmud. After several years, the rabbi ordained him and told him that it was time for him to go out and spread the teachings; that he would form his own community. He didn't know where to start. He followed his rabbi's guidance and traveled to America where young people and students began to flock to him. People who had been disenchanted by observance bereft of spirituality started to follow him.

"At the time, most students were turned off to Judaism and searching for meaning in life through different paths, either drugs or Eastern religions, like Rabbi Yehuda had. He found a way to meld the two, keeping full prayer services, incorporating Chassidic tales and

Kabbalistic meditations and practices, chanting, singing and telling stories, while exploring how to deepen the role for women without breaking *halacha*. He took what he knew was available in Judaism that would turn students and spiritual seekers on in order to reach them and bring them back, creating a type of Judaism relevant and meaningful to spiritual seekers and intelligent thinkers who wanted to still be a part of the modern world. Then he went back to Israel, and some of his followers came with him and formed Kol Rina. He has a house here, but he is so in demand teaching and giving concerts all over the world that he seldom gets to stay for more than a few weeks at a time," Nava finished.

The congregation had reached the *Sh'ma* when we arrived. I looked over at the men's section and saw Aryeh in profile, his dark head slightly bent, as he concentrated on his prayers. I watched him a moment longer then opened my prayer book. The sky grew dark and it began to rain, but the downpour only lasted a few minutes. Nava turned to me as the Torah was placed on the reading table and said, "You're in for a treat, the *shamash* today brings down the holiest blessings." I didn't understand what she meant, but before I was able to ask, she was again focusing on her prayers. When the *shamash* offered the *Mi Shebeirach* prayers, it became clear. After each aliyah, in addition to the prescribed words written in the prayer book. He took a moment, closed his eyes, and tilted his head upward as if carefully listening. He then began to sway forward and back, as if by doing so the message he was receiving was becoming clearer. Then he spoke in hushed tones, making the perfect request on behalf of each person who had received an aliyah or read from the Torah. It was as if he received a message from another realm and brought it through for that person. Along with the requests, sometimes the solutions were contained in his words, or hints for the best course of action a person should take, whether it was regarding family matters or business, health or general good fortune. I wanted to speak to the man and learn how he did it.

"Can other people do that?" I asked Nava when the service ended.

"Others try, but Gavriel does it the best. He's a clear channel."

"It's amazing."

"I agree," Nava said, smiling proudly.

"That was incredible," I said to Aryeh when he joined us.

"It was, wasn't it? I don't think I'll ever stop feeling that way."

"We never do," Nava laughed. "We'll see you later. Have fun at the Shem Tovs."

"Thanks. Have a good lunch. We'll see you later," Aryeh said, and directed me toward the home of his hosts.

Baruch and Orly were warm and welcoming, as everyone I'd met on Kol Rina had been. Lunch was made up mostly of salads and cold foods other than a hot, spicy, Sefardic *chamin* with chick peas, rice, wheat berries, and hard boiled eggs, far different than the Ashkenazic *chulent* I was accustomed to. When we finished eating, Baruch gave a *dvar* Torah and sang a Yemenite song. Orly joined in, her high soprano harmonizing perfectly with his melodic tenor. The trills and embellishments that came naturally to Orly mystified me.

"That was beautiful," I said when they finished. "You both sing so beautifully. Hard as I've tried, I've never been able to get my vocal chords to cooperate and make those trills properly."

Baruch laughed. "It's proof that Orly is a great teacher. She never gave up on me. It took years for me to be able to sing that way."

"Well, it was worth it. You have a beautiful voice," I said. "You both do."

"Thank you. It's all from Hashem. I can't take credit. We love to sing. The children do too." One of the boys made a face, denying his mothers words. "Come on, sing with us." Orly began to sing *Dror Yikra* and the children joined in, proving her right. The rest of us joined in as well, and the children asked to be excused when we were finished. "First say *Birkat Hamazon,* then you can go." The children quickly said the Grace After Meals and ran out to play with the neighborhood children. Their lawn was adjacent to other lawns forming a large square, and we could watch all the children playing through the glass sliding door.

After the children left, I learned that Orly, who had told me she was a teacher was actually a professor at Bar Ilan University and had immigrated with her family from Yemen as a small child, and that Baruch was a doctor from Manhattan who had become a *ba'al teshuva* after he started attending Rabbi Yehuda's services regularly. "When I first became religious," Baruch told us, "I followed Rabbi Yehuda's customs. I didn't consider myself Sefardic or Ashkenazic. My family didn't really have any traditions they followed. My parents were born in America, and they didn't know much about their Jewish backgrounds. I could have gone back to the customs of my great-grandparents, but that seemed pointless when Orly comes from such a rich tradition and culture."

"Did you have a Yemenite wedding, and a *Henna?*"

"Yup. We did it all."

"I'd love to see pictures,"

Orly laughed and said. "I'd love to show them to you."

"You asked for it," Baruch said. "I should have warned you."

"I love looking at pictures," I assured him.

"Let's do it later. I'm sure the men will find it boring," Orly suggested. Baruch nodded.

Instead, we all went for a walk around the community. Aryeh introduced me to his friends, and Baruch and Orly introduced us to everyone else we passed along the way. When it was time for afternoon service we left the men off at the synagogue, and Orly and I walked to Miri's sister's home for the third meal.

During the celebration, I got the chance to get to know Miri a little better and met her sister Devorah, and Devorah's daughters, Keter, Bina, and Tiferet. Women and young girls took turns telling stories and blessing Miri; then some of the girls put on a skit about the Torah portion. When they were finished, we ate dessert and sang more songs, until it was time for the evening prayer service and havdalah.

At the concert Saturday evening, Rabbi Yehuda played many of my new favorites, as well as songs I'd never heard before, punctuating many with stories about the Chassidic masters and their students, and miraculous occurrences happening all around us that are clearly performed by the Divine.

"It's been amazing, just like you described it. Thank you so much for bringing me, Aryeh," I said when it was over. We got a ride back to Jerusalem with Miri's friend, Terry, who'd come for the Shabbat Kallah. She let us off near the Central Bus Station, and we took a bus to Mount Scopus. Aryeh insisted on taking me all the way home this time, even though it was pretty late and he risked missing the last bus. I invited him in for a minute, and we shared some more toe-curling kisses. Before he left, we finalized our plans for Thursday. I let Aryeh know that I would be happy to come with him to the wedding. I was excited about it now that I'd met Miri, and she'd issued me a personal invitation. I was so impressed with her and felt like I've known her for years. I loved talking with her about all she's studied and how she incorporates alternative medicine and natural healing into her work. It was hard to believe that she was my age, she was already a certified nurse-midwife working in a hospital, and that she'd trained in so many other modalities. So much of what she had studied, the healing methods, for instance, were subjects I wanted to write and make films about.

*   *   *

As soon as Aryeh left, I went to my room and got ready for bed. Too wound up to sleep, I took out my journal and started to write. A short while later, I heard the door open, and Linda entered the room we shared.

"Hi! Did you have a good weekend?" she asked.

"The best. And you?"

"Mine was pretty good too. I can't believe we have classes tomorrow. What a bummer. I miss lazy American Sundays!"

"I know what you mean. Sundays are one of the few things I miss about America, though part of the day would always be depressing, the thought of going back to school on Monday and starting a new week. I started dreading Monday morning around 4:00 or 5:00 p.m. on Sundays," I admitted.

"Not me. I loved Sundays. It would hit me around nine or ten o'clock, if at all."

"You're lucky."

"Yeah. I guess. I can't believe it's already Thanksgiving this Thursday."

"Wow, that's right. I'd forgotten all about it."

"Then I guess you haven't made any plans. How could you forget Thanksgiving? The fourth Thursday of November, every year."

"I don't celebrate Thanksgiving."

"What do you mean you don't celebrate Thanksgiving?"

"I stopped."

"Why?"

"If you hadn't noticed, we're not in America anymore. It's not a Jewish holiday. We're in Israel, and Thanksgiving is not a holiday here. I was glad to give it up. So you have plans then? Otherwise I'd say come with us to the wedding."

"The wedding at Kol Rina? You're really going to go when you don't even know the bride or groom?"

"I know the bride. We met this weekend."

"You met her this weekend, and you're going to her wedding," Linda said incredulously.

"Why not? We had a great talk all about alternative medicine. She even offered to let me interview her and to introduce me to anyone she knows. Besides, she invited me. I know it seems strange. Weddings cost a fortune, so you'd think they'd have to limit the number of people, but it's not like that at the kehilla. They're very warm and welcoming and very inclusive. Anyone who even hears about a wedding is invited, they said. I'm sure they wouldn't mind if you came."

Linda shook her head. "I can't see myself doing that."

"Okay. It's up to you. Maybe you'll come with me another time."

"We'll see," Linda said evasively. "I think I'm going to go to Ra'anana."

"Great. Enjoy your feast and your family. Will you be there all weekend?"

"Yes. There's no reason to come back for Shabbat if I'm already on the coast."

"That's great. I know how you love the beach."

"Don't you miss it? When was the last time you went to the beach?"

"Over the summer."

"Maybe you can come for the weekend, after the wedding. You could take a bus there Thursday night or Friday and join me there. My cousins would love to to meet you."

"I don't think so, but thanks. We've been invited to *sheva brachot*," I explained.

"You said we. All this is with Aryeh, I assume?"

"Yes." I'm sure I blushed.

"Sounds like it's getting serious."

"No. It's just been a couple of weeks."

"An intense couple of weeks," Linda prodded.

"Yes. It's been pretty intense," I admitted.

"You really like him?"

"Yeah. I do. He's very interesting."

"I'm sure he is. And pretty handsome."

"That too. But that's not the main thing."

"It never is." Linda laughed.

"So you think he's handsome?"

"If you like the tall, dark, and hungry type, definitely."

"He's not that thin. It's just the clothes he wears."

"If you say so, and those chiseled features. So you're going to stay for Shabbat?"

"I don't know. We were invited, and the *sheva brachot* will be at Kol Rina on Saturday night. There are *sheva brachot* in Jerusalem on Friday night, which we're also invited to."

"Could you walk there?"

"If I stay at Shaina and Yossi's again, I could walk there."

"Well, that should be fun. Sounds like you're really getting into the whole religious world." I could hear the cynicism in her voice.

"I don't know. We'll see. Aryeh and the people in the kehilla are different. The whole community is different. They're not oppressively religious."

"And the woman's role? That doesn't bother you?"

"It's still hard for me, but the way they do things is so much more liberal. It's very spiritual and loving. I felt really at home there, really comfortable."

"That's great. Look, I'm happy for you. I just don't want to see you get brainwashed or pushed into a lifestyle you don't want—that you wouldn't be happy living."

"I know. Don't worry. I'll be fine," I tried to reassure her.

"I hope so. So tell me more about the weekend."

"What can I say? It was great. The people were great. I loved Nava and Chaim and their kids—that's the family I stayed with. They're all so happy. Even though they struggle financially and live in a small house, they're really happy."

"Happy is good," Linda said with an exaggerated Brooklyn Jewish accent.

"Yes. Happy is very good. And the other people we met were really nice, very warm, and welcoming. No one is snobby or jappy, or cliquish. They're just warm and openhearted and truly seem to love everyone. It's amazing."

"Sounds incredible," Linda said, still sounding skeptical.

"I know it sounds too good to believe. You'll just have to come with me sometime and see for yourself. You could still come with me to the wedding. As I said, it's open. Oh, I forgot, you have other plans."

"Right, otherwise, I wouldn't miss it for the world." Linda laughed.

"You know, you really should keep an open mind. You might be surprised. You might like it."

"That would be a surprise."

"So why did you want to live in a religious apartment if it's something you're so opposed to?"

"I wanted a kosher kitchen, just like I grew up with. Can't imagine living in a place that's not kosher. Get it?"

"Got it."

"Good."

"We should really get to bed. When's your first class tomorrow?"

"At ten, and yours?"

"Not till the afternoon."

"You're lucky."

"I know, but I still need to study. I have lots of reading to do, and the Hebrew reading takes me forever."

"I can't even imagine. I don't know how you do it."

"Thank G'd, a lot of the reading is also in English, or available in English. That helps. Otherwise, I don't think I could do it. My cousin studied law here, and it was all in Hebrew, thousands and thousands of pages of Hebrew legalese. Can you imagine?"

"No. I shudder just to think about it. I'm going to get ready for bed then."

Still on a high from Shabbat at Kol Rina, I reached for my journal, wanting to capture my impressions and experiences while they were still fresh in my mind. I wrote:

Shabbat at Kol Rina was magical, like being in paradise. I had the sense of being enveloped in love and peace, what I imagine Olam Habah, the world to come, will be like. I've kept Shabbat every week of my life, but it was as if I'd never done so before. I'd heard stories about Rabbi Yehuda before, from his supporters and detractors, and frankly I hadn't known what to believe, but there was a holiness about him, and I chose to give him the benefit of the doubt. Hearing him pray, sing, tell stories, and teach, I found it hard to believe any of the rumors I'd heard. I overheard someone say, "His heart is as big and as wide as the whole world." From what I experienced, he truly seemed capable of loving everyone, every soul. His love was palpable. I felt it emanating from him.

Shabbat with Aryeh has taken our relationship to a new level. I feel so grateful to be getting to know him and for all we've shared. It's hard to believe it was only a week since our first date. Who would have thought that day in June that any of this would have happened? It blows my mind to remember what he was like back then. Of course, it's too early to know if we're right for each other for long term. I just know that the more time I spend with him, the more I like him, and the more time I want to spend with him.

*   *   *

Chapter 10

Sing to Hashem a new song, sing to Hashem—everyone on earth.
Sing to Hashem, bless His name; announce His salvation daily.
                                                          —Tehillim 96:1-2

Miri
Jerusalem and Bloomington
Summer 1994

Our plans fell into place as if we were driving down the road, and every light turned green as we approached. A colleague asked David if he knew of anyone interested in exchanging their home in Bloomington for an apartment in Jerusalem. We contacted the professor who was coming from Hebrew University for the summer and made all the arrangements, thrilled to learn that the apartment we'd be staying in was in our old neighborhood, only a few blocks from our old apartment. We changed our return airplane flight from New York, and got a reasonable deal for the tickets to Israel. We spent a few days before Adam and Jeannie's wedding with David's parents, then the weekend with mine, and flew out the day after the wedding. Both our families understood and accommodated our change of plans, and my parents took the opportunity to send presents to their grandchildren.

The plane ride was smooth and uneventful, and it was wonderful to hear Hebrew all around me again after so many years. Stepping on to the tarmac, I felt the same euphoric sense of coming home I remembered from the past. The thick summer air was filled with the scent of holiness. We got through customs easily. I presented my Israeli passport, and Dave gave the blue-uniformed clerk his American one. "*Bruchim haba'im*," she said, stamping our respective passports.

After collecting our luggage, we picked up our rental car and drove straight to Dr. Alkolai's Jerusalem office with our luggage still in the trunk. Originally from France, Dr. Alkolai was a *ba'al teshuvah* who had come back to the fold through Lubavitch after finishing his medical training in both allopathic and Oriental medicine. His long brown beard and mustache were flecked with gray, as was his short-cropped hair, which was covered with a large knit black *kippah*. He'd also trained as a classical homeopath and had been living in Jerusalem for about twenty years. The white walls of his office were filled with bookshelves containing medical reference books, a complete set of *Shas* and many other sacred tomes, along with large framed photographs of the Lubavitcher Rebbe and the Baba Sali, a great Sephardic rabbi also said to perform miracles.

I had first heard about Dr. Alkolai when he cured my niece of severe allergies. The results were so impressive that my sister and I started referring everyone we knew to him, including my former roommate, Ruti, who had been trying for three years to get pregnant to no avail. After Ruti's success, I started recommending Dr. Alkolai to any one I knew with fertility problems. During my time practicing midwifery in Jerusalem, I had seen many of them get pregnant, never expecting to need his services myself. Stories abounded of the miracles the Chassidic physician had performed using a combination of allopathic and complementary medical treatments.

In addition to taking blood work, listening to our heartbeats, and giving each of us a regular checkup, Dr. Alkolai checked our eyes, ears, tongues, and pulses, looking for a cause based on both Oriental and Western medicine. We answered long questionnaires to determine what homeopathic remedies might assist each of us and used a system called NAET, created by a female physician from India, to eliminate any allergies that might be interfering with our optimal health and ability to procreate. His soft-spoken, gentle manner, along with his heavy French accent made it difficult to understand his questions and instructions at times. We spoke solely in Hebrew, though I had heard that his English was fluent and far superior to his knowledge of Hebrew.

"So you've been trying to get pregnant for about seven years?" he asked, glancing back and forth between us.

"We've been married for seven years, but we weren't really trying to get pregnant the first year, so the doctors wanted us to actively try for a year before starting any methods of intervention," I explained.

"And you've spent the past five years doing fertility treatments. It looks like you've tried everything available, including IVF," Dr. Alkolai said, looking up from my file.

"Yes. We have," I said. He nodded as he looked me over from head to toe. His eyes darted around my face, spending time concentrating on each feature. He picked up his small flashlight and looked into my eyes again.

"I have an idea of where to start," he said. "There will be dietary changes and some allergy elimination treatments as well as homeopathic remedies for you. I also think that regular exercise is essential, walking in particular. We will try this first. Today we will eliminate the allergies to milk and eggs. You will need to avoid these foods for twenty-five hours. Do not even go into a store that contains them. No stores or restaurants. If they are in your home or hotel room, have your husband go in first and remove them when you are at least one hundred feet away at all times. I will give you a list of foods to avoid in the meantime until you have your NAET session for each particular food and substance. I will need to see you again in three days for the next session."

"Eggs and milk. I never knew I was allergic to either," I said.

"Have you ever noticed your problem with mucus and your sinuses?"

"Not really."

"When you get sick, do you have a lot of phlegm? It might not be a problem all the time, but when you are feeling run-down and your immune system is weakened, it becomes a problem?"

"Yes, but I thought that was normal."

"No. Many people think that, but it's not normal. You won't have that problem anymore after the treatment. It might take two sessions, then there are the strawberries and the pineapple. I will make you a list. There is also the mold and dust and, most important, your husband's seed."

"My husband's seed?"

"Yes. Your body is rejecting it. It's not as uncommon as you might think. A woman's body can have an allergy to her husband's essence. Like with all allergies, your body is responding in such a way because it believes it needs to be protected from a harmful substance. We will do that treatment soon, but first the milk and eggs."

"Is there anything else we need to do or know at this point?"

"After today's treatment, spend some time together in nature. And go to the Kotel. I will give you a list of *Tehillim* to say as well. Say them while there is still daylight. You can say them anywhere, but at the Kotel, it will be even stronger, yes?" He nodded. "We will start the treatment now. You can both be in the room for the treatment."

"And for me?" David asked. "Is there anything I need to do?"

"We will get to it, but not today," he said. "Fill out the questionnaires, and I will look them over. I need more information." Looking at David, he said, "Either there is no health problem or it is hidden. If it's hiding, we will uncover it."

The treatment took only about twenty minutes. I had to hold some vials in my hands which contained a homeopathic distillation of albumen and milk, while he used an electrical device along my spine that he said worked like acupuncture needles.

"*Zehu!* That's all for today," he said, removing the vials from my hand.

"Do you think this will really work within three months?" I asked. "We only have three months to be here."

"The Lord is great; His ways a mystery," he said. "I cannot make that determination. I am merely his servant."

"Thank you," I said, my eyes welling with tears. I looked up and saw that Dave also had tears in his. He shook Dr. Alkolai's hand, and the tall doctor smiled down at him then put an arm around his shoulder. "You have had a long journey. I am optimistic. With Hashem's help, I don't see why we would not succeed . . . as I said, I cannot promise you anything, but I will do all that I can."

"That's all we ask," Dave said as he stepped from Dr. Alkolai's embrace.

As we left the office, David put his arm around me. "Honey, I'm so glad we came. At first I thought this idea was crazy, but I'm beginning to believe it's really possible. Wherever your dream came from, we've been guided here," he said, his voice filled with tears.

"Yes. We have. Thank you for listening. I love you so much!" I gave him a squeeze around the waist.

* * *

We parked near the apartment where we'd be living and spent the rest of the afternoon strolling the streets of Jerusalem, making our way to the Haas Tayelet, where we walked along the limestone paths down the mountain overlooking Abu Tor and the Old City.

"Can you believe how much they've expanded this place since we left?" I asked, as we arrived at the end closest to Talpiot. "It's incredible. I remember standing on this hill when it was barren.

"They've built it up so much, it reaches way down the hill now and all the way to Abu Tor. Remember all those great Shabbat picnics we had here?"

"And all the romantic evenings we sat overlooking the Old City. We came here for *Eicha* every Tisha B'Av, it was so appropriate back when it was a desolate hill, so different once they started building."

"I can't even imagine what that would be like now, but we'll be here for it."

"Strange to look forward to a fast day, but it will be so special to be here for it again, then to walk to the Kotel."

"Like old times. Its so good to be back," David said.

"It is, isn't it? I've missed it so much," I cried, unable to hold back the tears.

"I know, honey. I've missed it too."

"Really? You've missed it?"

"Of course I've missed it. Didn't you know?" David shook his head, incredulous.

"No. Not really."

"Well, now you know. I do—I miss it every day."

"But you never talk about it," I said, letting the tears flow freely down my cheeks.

"Never talk about it? Honey, I talk about Israel all the time."

"But not about missing it." I sniffed.

"I thought that talking about it would only make it harder for you."

"But maybe I wouldn't have felt so alone in missing it, like no one understands me, not even you. I didn't realize you felt like you had to hold things back from me, to protect me. You can talk about anything with me."

"Honey, I'm sorry. I should have let you know how hard it was for me too. It wasn't fair of me to keep it from you, or to downplay it. Of course, I understand how you feel." David gathered me in his arms for a long hug. "I'd love nothing more than to live here."

"You would? Really? I just miss it so much." He gently rocked me as I sobbed.

"So do I," his voice was barely audible above my sobs.

"I know that if I'd stayed and not married you, I would have missed you more, and I wouldn't have been nearly as happy as I've been with you all these years."

"I'm grateful that you did. I can't imagine my life without you. I don't know what I would have done if you'd said no," Dave said, holding me tighter. He tilted my head up to his, wiped my tears, and smiled. "Have I told you recently how much I love you?"

"Not in the last few hours."

"Well I do. I love you very much. Sometimes I feel so guilty that I took you away from all this," he said, stroking my hair. "I know how much you wanted to stay. I just want you to know that I appreciate it. Every day of my life, I am thankful that you agreed to marry me. I'm grateful to be married to you, and I promise you, someday, we will move back, *b'ezrat Hashem.*"

"I'll hold you to it. It would be nice to come back for a while, for a year or even a semester when you get your sabbatical."

"That's a great idea. I'd love to do that. And G'd willing, we'll have a child with us when we come."

"A son."

"A son or a daughter, it doesn't matter."

"I know, but *He* said it would be a son."

"*He*, meaning the voice in your dream?"

"Yes."

"Well. We'll see about that, won't we?" David answered with a raise of his eyebrow.

All in all it was a magical day. We watched the sunset over the Old City, then headed to the Jewish Quarter, and walked down to the Kotel, taking note of the areas that had been excavated or developed since we'd left. At the Kotel we each read the chapters of *Tehillim* that Dr. Alkolai had prescribed. David found a minyan and davened Minchah; then we wandered the streets of the Old City and headed back to our apartment passing the artist's studios of Chutzot Hayotzer and the beautiful stone streets of Yemin Moshe, with their lovely gardens and houses. We stopped at the overlook where Moses Montefoire's original carriage was on display, next to Mishkenot She'ananim, one of the oldest neighborhoods outside the walls of the Old City. David went up to the apartment first with our suitcases and took out the products the landlord had kindly stocked the apartment with for us that Dr. Alkolai had warned me to stay away from. I explored the landscaping around the building, enjoying the tree filled garden until David came down again and told me the coast was clear. Then I went up and explored the spacious two bedroom apartment where we'd be spending the next two months, delighted to see it's simple, but elegant decor, and a large balcony that overlooked the trees, red shingled rooftops, and the garden below. There was a table and chairs, which we took advantage of right away. It was the perfect night for a romantic dinner *al fresco*.

*   *   *

That summer was an enchanted time. Even the treatments were part of it's magic. Dr. Alkolai found some minor issues to treat David for. He explained it would improve his overall health and might make it easier for me to conceive. While our visit revolved around our treatments with Dr. Alkolai every few days, most of our time was spent on *tiyulim*—hikes, car, and bus tours around the country. We explored the beaches along the coast, up to Acco and Rosh Hanikra, spending several days at Achziv Beach, where we had spent our honeymoon, then went up to Tiberias and Tsfat, exploring the artist's colony, visiting ancient and modern synagogues and praying at the graves of great rabbis and Kabbalists.

Free of all obligations, we had a wonderful opportunity that summer to open our home to guests the way we always wanted, but had rarely been able to do before. We visited friends and spent as much time with family as we could, especially with my sister Devorah and her family. I didn't know how I'd be able to say good-bye again. After ten weeks, we packed up the apartment, and David went back to Bloomington, and I rotated between the homes of friends and family members for my last two weeks of treatments.

Within a few months of returning home, I knew I was pregnant. I called and thanked Dr. Alkolai profusely and told him how grateful I was. "May it all go smoothly, and may the baby come at a good and fortuitous time," he said.

My pregnancy was relatively uneventful. It was easier than I'd expected, and I relished every change in my body, even the morning sickness. Being a nurse-midwife, I knew what to expect at every stage, though the experience of it was completely different than I'd imagined it would feel. I was so happy and excited, even though the hormones running through my body sometimes caused me to feel teary, insecure, and out of control. I was insecure about David's feelings for me and whether I was ready to be a mother. We took courses in the Bradley method, and though natural childbirth was still extremely painful, I was able to cope. David was a great help. He remained very loving and affectionate throughout the pregnancy and the birth, regardless of how I was behaving, which I know at times was highly irrational.

The night I gave birth, light filled the delivery room. The witnesses described the light as pouring out of me, permeating the room, and emanating from the baby. Looking into the baby's open eyes was like looking into the eyes of G'd; they were wise and loving. We felt that the Schechina was with us. The light stayed around the baby for days before it began to fade. The hospital staff worried and took the baby away to be tested. They asked if I'd been exposed to anything radioactive. The tests showed him to be perfectly normal and healthy. We took him home after two days, and by the time of the *brit*, the light around him had all but faded.

Chapter 11

May the Merciful One grant us the privilege of reaching the days of the Messiah and the life of the World to Come.

—from the Grace After Meals

Arielle
Jerusalem, November 1987

The line of people waiting to greet the bride stretched from the edge of the grass to the middle of the lush green lawn where Miri sat in a white satin-covered high-backed chair, outside the community clubhouse. Unlike most Israeli lines, this one was orderly, with everyone patiently waiting their turn. Miri greeted each guest in turn with a warm, radiant smile, giving them her full attention. I took my place in line, and Aryeh went to find the groom and join the *chatan's tisch*.

Nava came to stand with me and talk as I waited, and soon Orly joined us. No one behind us seemed to mind when they joined me. Not only did we wait to congratulate and bless the bride, I learned, we waited to receive her blessings as well. "On the wedding day," Nava explained, "the bride and groom have a special opportunity, a special ability, to bless people. They've been to the mikveh, given *tzedaka*, davened special prayers from the Yom Kippur service atoning for all their sins, and have been fasting all day, so they're like newborn babies with a clean slate. They're perfectly pure, like angels. In that state, the heavens are open to hear and answer their prayers more than at any other time."

"Really? I never heard that before."

"Not everyone knows. It's a secret from Kabbalah." Nava and Orly stood back when we reached the front of the line, giving me space for a private moment with the bride.

"Mazel Tov. You look so beautiful," I gushed, admiring Miri's simple but elegant satin and chiffon bridal gown and her crown of white rosebuds with baby's breath, when it was my turn. "It's such an honor to be here."

"Arielle, I'm so glad you came! I was afraid you wouldn't be able to make it. Mom, Mrs. Shapiro, this is the girl I was telling you about, my new friend, Arielle. She has the most beautiful voice. I hope you'll get to hear her sing. She's a journalism student at Hebrew University."

"Thank you, Miri. It's nice to meet you, Mrs. Roth, Mrs. Shapiro," I said, turning to each of them as they stood on either side of Miri, seated on her makeshift throne. Mrs. Shapiro looked out of place in her silver gray sequined evening gown and perfectly coiffed shoulder-length honey-brown wig. Mrs. Roth wore a calf-length flowing silver chiffon. "It's *bashert*." Miri gave me a tight hug and a peck on the cheek. "I have a feeling we're going to be good friends."

"I hope so." I smiled.

"I'm sure of it," Miri gushed. Miri held onto my hands and taking a deep breath closed her eyes. When she opened them she looked into my eyes and said, "May Hashem bless you with clarity and vision, with the confidence and steadfastness to follow your goals, and with the wisdom to know when it's best to let go and follow a new course." She paused then said, "May you have a long, happy, healthy life filled with love, and may you and your partner, whoever he may be, honor and respect each other in all ways, may you be a team, true helpmates for each other to achieve the greatest versions of yourselves possible in this lifetime."

"Thank you," I said, with tears in my eyes. "I won't keep you any longer, so many people are still waiting to wish you mazel tov. I'm so happy for you. It's such an honor to be here and share in your simcha. Thank you."

Musicians played quietly in the background until a cadre of men entered the clearing escorting the groom. Immediately, as if on cue, the band changed its tempo and played the popular wedding refrain, "*Od yeshama, b'arei yehuda, uvechutsot, uvechutsot, Yerushalayim. Kol sasson ve'kol simcha, kol chatan v'kol kallah . . .*" The men sang the verse over and over as they danced backward, preceding the groom, as they approached the bride.

When David reached Miri, they looked deeply into one another's eyes. It was a moving, intimate moment. All their love, hopes, and dreams for the future visible in those seconds before he covered her face with the veil then was escorted out again; his father and Miri's on either side of him and the dancing men preceding them as they receded back to another room. Miri sat, holding her mother's hand, and reading Psalms and a long list of prayer requests she'd compiled for anyone in need: prayers for healing the sick, for good health, financial success, for fertility, and for *shidduchim* for all the people she knew who needed them. She prayed for everyone, not just her own future, but for all of Israel and all the world.

The guests mingled, and day turned to night. The time came to head over to where the canopy would be placed in a different part of the lawn. We found Aryeh standing with Chaim and Baruch waiting for the ceremony to begin. Men and women stood together under the stars. There was a nip in the air. Everyone huddled as close as we could together to keep warm and to see and hear the ceremony once it started. The throng parted as Miri approached the chuppah, her mother and father on either side of her, carrying candles protected by teardrop-shaped glass holders. When she arrived under the chuppah, she circled David seven times, followed by her mother, holding up the long train of her satin wedding gown. The chuppah, made of a rainbow-colored *tallit*, was held high above their heads by four of the grooms close friends, each standing at one of its corners. Another *tallit*, this one pure white, a wedding gift from Miri to David, was draped around David's shoulders. He wore a white kittel, and a white crocheted *kippah*. A hush fell over the crowd as Miri finished the seventh circuit.

"*Baruch ha-bah b'shem adoshem,*" Rabbi Yehuda sang in welcome. He continued to sing the formal words that would bind the young couple in holy matrimony. When he finished, he gave a *d'var torah* and sang a song, inviting everyone to join in. It became a meditation as the few simple words of the chant were repeated over and over again. The bride's and groom's faces were radiant, their love palpable. I could feel something happening, as if there were some spiritual, otherworldly force binding them together. It had started when Miri circled David, and it grew stronger as the ceremony continued.

Rabbi Yehuda relayed the story of a Chassid in a little town in Europe who asked his rebbe if the Messiah had arrived. The rebbe opened the window, inhaled deeply, and said, "No. Not yet." The Chassid asked how one could know, what would the signs be, and the rebbe said "There will be a special scent in the air, and I didn't smell it this morning." No matter what time of year, the rebbe would leave the windows open at least a little crack. His students didn't understand why, and one very cold winter day, a student dared to ask why he always left the windows open, and he explained that he wanted to know the moment the first scent of the Messiah wafted through the air. Aryeh and I looked at each other and smiled as we listened to Rabbi Yehuda. He continued in a sing-song manner, blessing the bride and groom: "And my holy brother David and holy sister Miriam, may you always be ready, always waiting"—he swayed, his eyes closed as if bringing down the words and bestowing a blessing with them from on high—"for the scent of Moshiach, for the *geulah* to come and bring peace to all *am yisrael* and to all people everywhere. May you build a *bayit ne'eman b'yisrael,* an everlasting home, with the love between you always present, always growing, and may it fill your lives with the experience of the Garden of Eden in this world."

It felt so intimate, as if we were witnessing the holiest level of union possible. It was as if we were all blessed just by being there. The world around us seemed to disappear as I stood holding hands with Aryeh, our bodies pressed together, shoulder to shoulder, in the crowd. There were over two hundred people gathered; most were people I'd never met, but it was as if we were standing together at Mt. Sinai. The holiness of the moment like the giving of the Torah. Nava and Chaim stood on my other side with Dina and Melech. Koby was off with his friends. Tears were flowing down Nava's cheeks. I reached down and took her hand; and she put her arm around me, sniffed, and smiled.

The *ketubah* was read, then six rabbis and honored guests, each recited or sang one of the *sheva brachot*. The last blessing was left for Rabbi Yehuda. When the ceremony ended, another rabbi sang a prayer, and Aryeh translated. "I will betroth you to me forever. I will betroth you to me in righteousness, justice, in kindness, in mercy. I will betroth you to me in faithfulness, and you shall know the L'rd."

"My Hebrew is considered fluent, but some biblical and literary Hebrew still eludes me," I admitted. "I hope I'll understand it someday. What a beautiful prayer."

"It's actually said by men every morning as we put on our tefillin," Aryeh said.

"Really? I never knew that. It almost makes me wish I could wear tefillin."

"It's not a traditional part of the wedding service, but some people add it since it's such a beautiful prayer and the words are so fitting."

Something about being at a wedding together was very romantic. Our whispered conversation was interrupted by congratulatory shouts—mazel tov!—as David broke the glass, and the musicians broke into song.

A path was cleared, and David and Miri were ushered to a cabin not far away for some time alone together. While they were away, the band played, the photographer snapped pictures, the videographer filmed the event, and people found their tables, which were set up outside, leaving the clubhouse for dancing. At some weddings in the community, it was all held outside in a larger park clearing, but this was considered a relatively small wedding, and since it was November, they had opted for a partial indoor venue. We didn't linger over the meal. As soon as we finished each course, we raced to the crowded clubhouse, which had been transformed for the occasion with beautiful wall hangings, artwork, streamers, and colored lights. Though men and women sat together at the meal, there were separate circles for dancing, and several tables had been set aside for those who preferred separate seating, a concession to Dave's ultra-Orthodox relatives. Later in the evening, the groups joined in a more contemporary free-form type of dancing, still all to religious music. Rabbi Yehuda joined the musicians, playing guitar and singing when he chose, but he was not officially a part of the wedding band.

When Miri and David joined the party, the dancing was in full swing. The men swept David into their circle, and the women enfolded Miri into ours. Miri was pulled into the center to dance with her mother and sister; then she pulled in friends and family members to dance with one at a time while the rest of us continued to dance in a large circle around them. As more women joined in, one circle became two then three. An inner circle formed for a while with Miri, her mother, mother-in-law, sister, and David's sisters and sisters-in-law.

Nava told me that Devorah, Miri's sister, was her best friend. I'd wondered at the strong connection between Nava and Miri, and now it seemed clearer. The Roth girls grew up Conservative, but Devorah became a *ba'alat teshuvah* through Rabbi Yehuda and met her husband, Shimon, who was one of Rabbi Yehuda's followers, while in college. Miri, many years younger than Devorah, often came to stay with her sister at Kol Rina. Though not a member, she was loosely part of the kehilla, as his followers call themselves.

I lost track of Aryeh as I danced with the women. At one point, I saw him dancing with the men. At another, I saw him standing on the side, talking with a friend, and watching me dance. I smiled when I saw him. He smiled back and raised his hand in a slight wave. The man, a white-haired, bearded Chassid, was oddly familiar. It took a moment for me to place him, and then I realized Aryeh was speaking with Eliyahu.

I hadn't seen him since that day in June. I blinked and shook my head. I couldn't believe my eyes. He smiled broadly and nodded when he saw that I'd recognized him. I made my way toward them, my mind filled with questions.

"Eliyahu, it's so good to see you. How are you? I hope you're well. And Yehoshua? How's Yehoshua? Is he here?"

"Arielle! Such a sweet *maydel*. How are you? I didn't know you knew the bride and groom. They're a wonderful couple, don't you think?"

"Yes. They're fantastic. We just met recently, through Aryeh."

"Yes, Aryeh." He nodded and pinched Aryeh's cheek as if he were a little boy. "Don't let me keep you. You young people should enjoy the wedding. I'm going to go sit down."

"We'll join you. So, *nu*, how have you been? How is Yehoshua?" I asked.

"I'm doing well. Thank G'd. Yehoshua is back in the hospital. Honestly, I'm surprised to see you together, but happy to see it. Very happy. I think it will make Yehoshua happy too."

"But he didn't even meet me. He doesn't know me."

"Soon. Aryeh, why don't you bring her with you next time you come see him."

"Of course. I'd be happy to."

"You've gone to see him? Why didn't you tell me?"

Aryeh shrugged. "I guess it didn't come up."

"What do you mean 'it didn't come up'? I'm sure you realized I'd be interested."

"What good would it have done? It's over," he said in a hushed tone.

"It's not over. They're still here. I had no idea where to find them."

"I didn't know if he'd want other visitors, especially since, as you said, you didn't really know him."

"I'm sure Yehoshua would be happy for Arielle to come see him. Please don't fight about it," Eliyahu said. "You're young, just getting to know each other. Give each other a chance. Please. Now, that's better. It's good to see you again, Arielle. Come visit us. I'm going to sit down now. I hope you don't mind." We watched him walk to a table and sit with a group of other older, bearded men.

"I'll take you to see him, but you should know, it's a bit of a shock. He doesn't look good. He's hooked up to machines, barely conscious most of the time."

"That's so sad."

"I know."

"So what's the connection? How does Eliyahu know David and Miri?"

"Oh my G'd, you mean I didn't tell you that either? David is Yehoshua's nephew."

My knees grew weak. I was so surprised. "No wonder he looked familiar. He was there, wasn't he?"

"Yes."

"He was on his left side, helping to hold him up."

"Exactly."

"I can't believe it. Now *I* need to sit down," I said.

"It was a shock for me too. Maybe that's what drew me to David, why we've gotten so close, though I think it would have happened anyway."

"Well, you definitely have a lot in common, with his similar upbringing and all."

"True. He's become a good friend, a bit like a big brother."

"That's great. I can't wait to meet him."

"I'll introduce you." Aryeh said. "That looks like fun. Wanna dance?"

The band was playing Hebrew music with a rock beat, and people had started to get up to dance together. "I'd love to." It was unexpected for such a religious Jewish wedding—men and women dancing together. Some danced in groups, or in pairs, and some people danced by themselves. Everyone danced free-form, with no touching.

"Another thing you're a natural at," I said, leaning toward Aryeh so he could hear me over the din of the music as we danced together for the first time.

"Thanks. It's not so hard; I'm just following you. You're a great dancer. It makes it easy."

"Thanks. You are full of surprises," I said, smiling up at him.

"All good, I hope."

"All good, so far," I assured him.

"They'll probably be *bentching* and doing *sheva brachot* soon. Then we should head back if we're going to go tonight," Aryeh said. "Do you still want to go home?"

I felt torn. "I don't know. I hate to leave, but I don't want to put anyone out. What do you want to do?"

"Whatever you're most comfortable doing. I'm wide awake. The wedding will probably go on for hours. It would be fun to stay. And we're invited for Shabbat and *sheva brachot* Saturday night."

"But we didn't bring anything with us, no changes of clothing, no gifts."

"So at least for tonight, let's stay. We can go back in the morning," Aryeh said. "Do you really want to leave in a few minutes? It's a wedding! How often do you get to dance at a wedding?"

"You're right. We'll stay," I said. "I need to let Nava know."

Nava was thrilled to hear we were staying and even offered to lend me clothes to stay through the weekend. "Nava, you're too much. I don't know how to thank you."

"You don't have to do anything to thank me. We love having you. Go and enjoy yourself. If you don't see us when you're ready to go, it means we've probably gone home. I'll leave the key for you, like I did on Shabbat. Have fun!" She gave me a hug.

I found Aryeh again and let him know what Nava had said. "It's amazing how people just open their homes here."

"They really understand the concept of loving your neighbor and treating everyone the way you want to be treated."

"Totally."

The bandleader raised his hand for everyone to be quiet and spoke into the mike. "Everyone, if you could take your seats, it's time for *Birkat Hamazon,* so please gather round."

While Aryeh and I had been figuring out our plans, a table had been brought into the middle of the room, and people were busy carrying in chairs from outside. Aryeh got two chairs for us, and we sat waiting for the grace after meals to begin. Two silver cups of wine were poured, and when the *Birkat Hamazon* was through, one was passed to a man with a beard sitting beside the groom. He made the first blessing and handed the wine cup back to the man who'd given it to him. Everyone sang a slow and stately nigun between each blessing while the cup was being passed to the person who would make the next blessing. The chanting continued until the last blessing was said, the blessing over the wine, and then the wine was mixed between two cups and the bride and groom were each given one to drink from.

The bride's cup was then passed among the women and the groom's among the men. "Here, it's a *segula.* It will bring you luck. Take a sip," Miri's friend Terry said, handing me the cup after taking a sip herself. I took a little sip and passed the cup on to someone else. Aryeh had a sip from the men's cup. No one seemed concerned about germs.

Many of the guests left at that point, but the band started another set. Chairs were cleared away to the sides, lining the walls of the room, and we danced for hours. The bride and groom danced with each other, enjoying the festivities.

"Where are they staying?" I asked.

"The bride and groom? Here, at Kol Rina. There's a bungalow, a little house they're staying in. The owners are away and offered it to them for tonight and after the *sheva brachot* on *motzei Shabbat.*"

"Miri told me they're going to be living in Jerusalem. In Baka, where she already lives," I said. "But she also told me that eventually they're probably going to move back to the States. After David finishes his studies."

"It's hard to find a job here as a rabbi or a professor," Aryeh said.

"Do you think you'll leave when you finish your studies?" I asked.

"No."

"But what if you have to leave to get a position, what will you do?" I asked, knowing how important living in Israel was to him. My heart pounded at the thought that he might not be planning to live in Israel permanently. Could I continue a relationship with him if it would mean leaving Israel permanently if we married? I hated the thought of it and had ended things with my last boyfriend in the United States for that exact reason—though he loved Israel, he didn't want to live here.

"I'll find a job here," he said definitively.

"How can you be sure?" I asked.

"Because I won't allow for any other possibility. This is my home. I'll take whatever job I get as long as it's here. The salary might not be as good, or the benefits, but I'll stay, even if the only job I can find is flipping pizzas or sweeping floors, but I don't think I'll have to. I'd be fine with any teaching position, and that shouldn't be so hard for me to get with my education."

"I hope you're right," I said. "I know how much you want to live here." I didn't mention how important it was to me as well, not wanting to put any undue stress on him or our budding relationship.

"Forever," he said.

"Forever," I seconded.

"Amen."

*   *   *

It was after midnight when the bride and groom took their leave. The band continued to play, and Aryeh asked me to go outside with him for a break. "I just want to be alone with you for a while before we say good night," he said, pulling me to a secluded area. We sat under a large banyan tree and listened to the revelers.

"Me too," I concurred. He put his arm around me, and we leaned against the big tree's trunk. "I'm so glad we came," I said. The downward streaming aerial roots afforded us a good deal of privacy. "I love these trees. I remember the first time I saw one when I was living on kibbutz. The kids would swing from them, like Tarzan."

"They are pretty cool," he agreed, lifting my face by the chin and kissing my lips. He combed his fingers through my hair, making my scalp tingle. He brought a handful to his face and inhaled its scent.

"Your hair smells like flowers. I love the smell. I don't think I ever noticed the smell of a woman's hair before."

"It's honeysuckle—from my shampoo," I explained.

"Whatever it is, it smells great."

"I'm glad you like it, but I change shampoos all the time."

"That's okay. I don't need your hair to smell like this, but I like it."

"How do you always know the perfect thing to say?"

"Do I?"

"Yes."

"I turned into a prince when you kissed me."

"You were one already."

"Now who's the one who knows the perfect things to say?" He leaned over and brushed his lips against mine. I reached up and held his head, running my fingers through his curls, loving the feel of his silky locks.

"I love your hair. I keep remembering your crew cut, and I'm so glad you let it grow."

"But you'd feel the same about me even if I had a crew cut again?"

"Even if you grew back your *peyot*!" I laughed.

"Don't laugh. I might. Haven't you noticed, a lot of the men here have *peyot*?"

"I noticed. Actually, I never in my life imagined being with a man with *peyot*, but if you decided to grow them back it wouldn't bother me."

"Don't worry. I'm not planning on growing them back anytime soon."

"I'm not worried. It's just the externals . . ."

"It's okay. I love your hair too. Even if it's just the externals, I love your externals." He laughed.

"I've got a thing for yours too." My Mae West imitation was lost on him. I sighed and nestled into his chest. He tightened his arms around me and squeezed me to him.

"I could stay like this all night," he whispered, bringing his head down to my ear.

"That would be nice. Wouldn't it?" We were quiet for a while, soaking in each other's presence, enjoying the moment of intimacy. "This is a great song. Would you like to dance?" I asked, noticing the song the band was playing.

"No. I'd rather stay right here, unless you really want to. I mean, I wouldn't want you to miss dancing to such a great song."

"One of my favorites, but I promise, I'm okay with staying right here." He moved my hair aside and nuzzled my neck, causing goose bumps to surface all over my body. I ran my hands up his arms, around his shoulders, and caressed his chest through his coat, then found the buttons and made an opening large enough to get my hand underneath, pushed the suit jacket aside and stroked his chest, above his white cotton shirt. I inched my hands down the front to his waist and under his shirt, stroking up again to reach his chest. His skin was soft and warm with hard muscles underneath and a smattering of curly coarse hairs at the center.

"Is this okay?" I asked.

"This is wonderful," he replied and kissed me deeply.

*   *   *

We made the most of our time Friday touring the area before heading back to Jerusalem. We took a bus to an area on the other side of the Jerusalem—Tel Aviv Highway and hiked through the hills and caves near Hashmonaim. It started to rain before we got back to the highway, and we took refuge under some trees, praying that there wouldn't be any lightning nearby when we heard rumbles of thunder.

We made it back in time to go back to our respective dorms to pack, take showers, and change for Shabbat. I wore the most *tznius* outfit I could create, then quickly hopped on a bus to Yossi and Shaina's. I had called them from the Tanzers in the morning, and Shaina enthusiastically agreed that it was better for me to stay with them for Shabbat than to walk back to campus from a *sheva brachot* in Sanhedria that David's aunt and uncle were hosting.

"It's great to see you again so soon," Shaina said, welcoming me into their apartment. Yisroel Meir was sitting in his high chair—I had obviously interrupted his meal. Shaina sat down opposite him and went back to feeding him.

"Hi Yisroel Meir. It's good to see you again too," I said in a singsong voice, moving to stand beside him. I leaned down and kissed him on the top of the head, then turned back to Shaina. "Thanks so much for agreeing at such short notice. Sorry for the imposition."

"We love it when you come. It's no imposition. You're family, you have an open invitation. Come anytime."

"Thank you. That means a lot to me, but I also want you to know that you're allowed to say no. You don't have to agree every time I invite myself over."

"You have an open invitation, that's what it means—*you're already invited,* you just have to let us know when you're taking us up on it. If you don't come for too long a stretch, I'll call and remind you. How's that? Not that I want to pry, but *nu,* the last time we talked was before your second date with Aryeh. So, you're still seeing each other?" she prompted.

I smiled. "Yes. We went to Kol Rina together last weekend and had a fantastic time and to the wedding there last night. We stayed over at people's homes again and spent most of the day today hiking around the area. Shaina, it's like a breath of fresh air, he's straightforward and open, and there's no game playing; he tells me what's on his mind and cares about my opinion. He's intelligent, considerate, and fun to be with and seems kind and caring. It's only been two weeks, hard as it is to believe, so it's too soon to really know. The wedding last night was absolutely heavenly. That's the best way I can describe it. Rabbi Yehuda officiated. From the time of the *b'decken* and on I could feel something happening, it was as if the *chatan* and *kallah*'s souls were literally being joined together, and I could feel the Shechina's presence everywhere."

"It's amazing that you could actually feel all that."

"I've never experienced anything like it. It was amazing."

"It sounds amazing. Of course the Shechina is always surrounding us, but to actually feel it, that's really something." Shaina said.

"It was. Have you ever experienced it? Was it like that at your wedding?"

"I didn't feel what you're describing. I was concentrating on not tripping on my dress and counting the number of times I circled Yossi." She laughed. "I shouldn't have worried about counting. My mother was counting too. She wouldn't have let me make a mistake. But, seriously, I was happy to be getting married, amazed that this ceremony would change my life forever from being part of my parents' home to building my own."

"You're right. I've never thought of it that way." I always thought of weddings in terms of romance and excitement. Her view took in the magnitude of the event.

"It was very exciting. Have I shown you the pictures?"

"No. I haven't seen the pictures yet."

"We have a video too, but we can look at pictures and watch the video another time. Tell me more about Aryeh. He sounds like a terrific guy. Yossi only has lovely things to say about him."

"That's good to know. I really admire him. Even if this relationship doesn't develop any further."

Shaina interrupted me mid-sentence.

"Why should it stop developing further?"

"I don't know. It just might not work out. It's just barely two weeks since our first date. I've had a lot of relationships in the past, and I'm still single. I'm just being realistic."

"I don't think it's too soon to know. When you know, you know," she insisted. "Yossi and I only went out on five dates before he proposed.

You've already been on more than that with Aryeh. He definitely likes you, and the feeling is obviously mutual, *plus* he's American and he wants to live in Israel. I wouldn't let him go if I were you."

"I don't want to let him go. I hope that this *does* develop. I never thought I'd be ready at this age to get married, but, and I can't believe I'm saying this, I can see spending the rest of my life with him. We should give it time and get to know each other better. There's no rush. Especially given all the changes he's been through in the past six months."

"True. Take your time then. So tell me again, how did you meet originally? You were working on an assignment for school?"

"Yes. For two classes, actually."

"How did a Chassidic *yeshiva bahur* come to help you with your assignment?"

"It's a long story."

"So, *nu?* I have time to hear it. Tell me the story."

"He should be here any minute, but okay, I'll tell you. Late last May, I was walking down the street and saw a poster on a lamppost that said the Messiah was coming, *Moshiach Ba,* it said. I decided to interview people about it, that's why I told you that I met him while I was working on a project for school."

"Right, so you interviewed him?"

"Not right then. We didn't meet till later." I continued to relate the story of how Aryeh and I had met, ending with the question: "So, Shaina, what would you have done if you'd seen the signs or heard about it? Would you have come to the rally?"

"I don't know," she said, shaking her head. "I honestly don't know."

"Would you have been willing to check into it further to see if it could be true?"

"That's a good question. I like to believe I would have done what you both did, that I would have gotten involved, and I would have gone, but honestly, Yisroel Meir was three months old at that time. I don't know if I would have gotten involved. So you think this rabbi could be the Moshiah?"

"I only saw him for a short time at the rally, and he seemed very pious. Eliyahu also seemed completely sincere."

Just then there was a knock on the door. "Think about it." I put on my coat and said, "Hi," as I opened the door to let Aryeh in.

"Hi. *Gut Shabbes.* Sorry to rush you, but we really should be going. *Gut Shabbes*, Shaina," he said.

"*Gut Shabbes*," said Shaina. "Have a good time."

"You too. Don't wait up," I replied and closed the door behind me.

"That dress was the perfect choice," Aryeh said. "You look beautiful."

"Thank you, but do I look like I belong? I'm a little nervous walking through these neighborhoods. I once had garbage thrown at me when I walked through Meah She'arim with a group of friends, even though we were all dressed appropriately. It was so disgusting. Another time they threw rocks at us. We were lucky none of us got hit."

"How awful. It really stinks that people act that way."

"That garbage really stank too."

Aryeh shook his head. "That's horrible. I'm sorry that happened to you. No one should have to go through it. Ever." Despite it not being his type of community anymore, Aryeh was dressed in his full religious attire, including his black hat. We held hands as we walked through the Shmuel HaNavee neighborhood, then dropped them as soon as we got to Sderot Levi Eshkol and crossed the street into the more religious neighborhoods. As we made our way through a maze of narrow streets, I knew I wouldn't have been able to find my way out of without Aryeh's help, many men hurried past us. Some had children in tow. Some nodded in acknowledgement or wished us a *gut Shabbes*; others gave us curious looks or ignored us completely.

When we found the synagogue we were looking for, Aryeh walked me to a staircase leading to the women's section, then opened a big wooden door and went inside. I climbed the long stone staircase, which led to a narrow room above the main sanctuary. It was difficult to see or hear the service being conducted below through the small windowlike opening covered by an opaque white cloth. Miri, Mrs. Roth, Mrs. Shapiro, and another woman I recognized from the wedding as one of David's aunts, (also a Mrs. Shapiro), sat in a row together. "Mazel tov!" I said, going to stand beside Miri. I hugged her and kissed her cheek then greeted her mother and mother-in-law. Miri wore a white dress and white turbanlike head covering, similar in style to the ones Nava wore. "You look beautiful with your head covered that way, so exotic. Is it difficult to tie that way."

"Nava and Devorah made me a *tichel* party—instead of a wedding shower—and all the women brought scarves and head coverings and taught me the different ways you can tie them. This style is a challenge. Believe me, but I love the way it looks. I'm a little worried they're going to fall off!"

"Well, you look beautiful. I had such a wonderful time at your wedding. Thank you so much for inviting me!"

"I'm so glad you were there. And thank you so much for coming tonight. I don't know many people who will be here, it's just going to be David's family and my parents, and some men from the neighborhood to make the *minyan*."

"I hope it's okay that I came," I said.

"Are you kidding? I'm thrilled. Really. This will give us a chance to get to know each other better," she said. "Come, sit with us." She led me over to where her mother and the Shapiro women were sitting.

"Didn't Devorah come?" I asked.

"No. She wanted to be home so she could prepare for tomorrow night and make sure everything goes smoothly. I don't think they ever go away for Shabbat when Rabbi Yehuda is there."

"Oh," I said. "So how was your first day of marriage?"

"Wonderful. A bit hectic, but wonderful." She laughed, a becoming blush coming to her cheeks.

She told me about her day going everywhere together with David, since for twenty-four hours before and twenty-four hours after the wedding, neither the bride nor groom should be alone as protection against evil forces. "It's such a strong time for the light to come through that the forces of darkness try even harder than usual to stop it from succeeding. So I went with him to shul this morning, then we went back to our apartment in Baka, opened wedding presents, went to the bank and opened a joint account, and then met my parents for lunch at their hotel, and finally, I went with him to the *mikveh*."

"The *mikveh*?"

"Yes, David goes every Friday. It's one of the Chassidic customs he still follows."

"Really. I didn't realize he still kept Chassidic customs."

"Only the ones he finds meaningful and that speak to him spiritually. Did Aryeh tell you, they had very similar upbringings, but David grew up in Borough Park."

"And you? Where are you from?"

"I'm also a New Yorker, from Long Island."

"So am I!" I exclaimed.

The *shaliach tzibur* started *Kabbalat Shabbat*, and we opened our *siddurim* and prayed. Many of the melodies they sang were the traditional ones I knew, while a few were very different, intricate, and hard for me to follow. Looking through the *mechitza*, I saw that the men's section was packed, but we were the only women present. When the service ended, we all walked together to David's uncle's apartment. The women sat at one table and the men at another. Fortunately, I sat next to Miri, and we got the chance to talk between courses, speeches, and *zemiroth*.

We talked about our upbringings and how we grew to love Israel and decided to make aliyah. Miri and I had both been in Young Judaea. She went to Camp Tel Yehuda and on the Young Judea year course, the yearlong program that many members go on for their first year of college.

"I didn't go on year course. I thought it wouldn't be possible to stay observant, so I went to a kibbutz ulpan for six months instead, which wasn't enough for me, so then I went on the one-year program. I think that we were here alternating years."

"You're right. It was hard to be observant on year course, unless you were on a specific section that went to a religious moshav," she said.

"I left in July 1982, and you must have come in August."

"Exactly. I've been here ever since, except for visits to my family."

"That's what I wanted to do, but my parents thought it best that I get my degree before making aliyah."

"I'm sure my parents would have felt the same if my sister didn't live here. They knew I wouldn't be alone. It seems so strange that our paths never crossed before last Shabbat, and we have so much in common. You've been here for how long now?"

"About a year and a half. I made aliyah a year ago August. And you?"

"I've been here five and a half years now. First studying and now working, primarily. I finished my nursing degree and certification as a midwife, but I'm still taking some holistic healing courses on my own. There's so much to learn."

"It all fascinates me," I said. "What are you taking now?"

"I'm studying herbology and the principles of Chinese medicine. I want to incorporate it into the work I do with patients."

"How long are the courses?"

"The ones I'm taking now are yearlong courses."

"Where are you studying?"

"In someone's home. There's a wonderful nurse-midwife from the States who specializes in natural remedies and complementary medicine. She's well-known among religious women in Jerusalem and native English speakers."

"Have you taken other courses with her?"

"With her and others."

"If I want to learn this, what do you recommend I start with?"

"Whatever interests you most."

I laughed. "So there's not some kind of order that you need to take the courses in? Something that's an overview or a prerequisite for other courses?"

"If you go to one of the institutes for complementary medicine, there probably is, but I've just gone by what interests me and what's being offered at a time that fits into my schedule." Our conversation was interrupted when David's uncle started singing *Shalom Aleichem*, followed by *Eishet Chayil,* some mumbled prayers that I couldn't distinguish, and then we all stood for Kiddush. A woman dressed in black, wearing a wig with a scarf over it, came and served us all the traditional Shabbat fare.

Dinner was followed by a lot of singing and dancing by the men. Aryeh was seated to David's left, next to David's father. I wondered how he was getting on. From where I was sitting, I could only see him if I turned, which I did only a couple of times, looking over my shoulder as surreptitiously as possible. Once I caught his eye, and he smiled. David's uncle gave a *d'var Torah,* then his father gave one, and finally, David was asked to give one as well. Each of the speeches was in Yiddish, until David, in deference I assume to Miri and her family, translated what he'd said into English.

During a lull in the speeches, I turned to Miri and asked, "Was it weird for you or hard to adjust to the idea of marrying someone Orthodox? A rabbi no less?"

"At first it was strange for me to be with someone so much more religious, but the lifestyle was familiar. I'd spent a lot of time with my sister since she'd become Orthodox. She and Shimon met at a Purim party her junior year and have been together ever since. They got married right after she graduated and made aliyah, as part of the original seed group that founded Kol Rina. I was six at the time. She was twenty-one and already a follower of Rabbi Yehuda. Whenever they'd visit, they'd tell stories about life in Israel and in the kehilla, and I couldn't wait to see it for myself. I fell in love with Israel even before I ever set foot on it. I was ten the first time we visited and must have driven my parents crazy. I didn't want to leave. All I ever talked about when we got home was Israel and making aliyah like Devorah. We came to visit every year, and I moved here right after I graduated high school. I spent almost every Shabbat with Devorah and Shimon when I first made aliyah," Miri said. "I wasn't *born again* and don't think of myself as a *ba'alat teshuvah.*"

"Really?"

"Really. I love aspects of a number of different denominations and movements but don't define myself by any one of them exclusively. I grew up Conservative and appreciate the egalitarian aspect of it, the right for women to fully participate in all aspects of the service. I loved leading services and reading Torah and *haftarah,* but I don't mind sitting separately from men during services, and I don't care whether or not I'm counted in the minyan. It makes sense to me that men and women are different and that women's spirituality is different; that women's spirituality is more innate and goes inward. I understand why women, especially once they have children, don't have the same requirements to keep time bound commandments, and I don't feel as if the women's role is any less important because of that, in fact, in some ways, it's more important.

"I like some of the changes the Reform and Reconstructionist movements have made to the prayer service, but for me, they've gone too far away from tradition. I love the meaningful rituals and creativity of Jewish Renewal, and the Chassidic spiritual practices and rituals Rabbi Yehuda has reincorporated that most Jews had stopped practicing when they left Eastern Europe or whatever communities they came from. I also love how the liberal movements are all incorporating *tikun olam*, social action, social justice, and a commitment to women's rights, and issues like the environment into our lives, which Rabbi Yehuda and some of his followers are doing as well."

"How did you and David meet?"

"We met at a lecture. David was already a rabbi with *smicha* from YU. I was in nursing school at Hebrew University—Hadassah Medical School, and he was getting his PhD at Hebrew University. We started talking after the program, and he asked me for my number. I didn't have a phone, but I gave him my address and said to stop by or call and leave me a message at the office. He came by to see me the next day, but I wasn't there, so he left me a message with his address. I called and left a message for him, and we just kept missing each other. Finally, he left a message with a time and place to meet and wrote that I should just confirm if I could make it or suggest another time. He wrote that he'd come to see me at that time, regardless of whether he heard from me, just in case I didn't get the note in time to reply. It was a good thing that he did because I didn't see the message until a few minutes before the time he wanted to stop by. Luckily I was there and didn't miss him yet again.

"The attraction was there right from the start, but when he told me that he hadn't made aliyah and that he was just staying for a few years, I told him that I didn't see any point in our dating, but we could be friends." Miri went on. "He said he still wanted to date but would settle for being friends, if that's all it could be. After getting together a few more times and getting to know each other a bit, he convinced me to give it a chance. The attraction was really strong, and I was already crazy about him. It wasn't logical or rational, but it was very romantic. It felt like we belonged together. I couldn't imagine my life without him. I've always been very into psychic phenomenon and following my intuition, so I asked him about his date of birth and had a chart done on him astrologically and one for both of us that would tell about our compatibility. David laughed when I told him what I was going to do with the information, when I asked him his date, time and place of birth, but I think he thought it was cute. A friend of mine did a numerological chart as well before our second official date.

"It turned out, thank G'd, that according to our stars and planets we're very compatible. I know it says that the Jewish people are above the zodiac, and many observant people take that to mean that we shouldn't have anything to do with it, we shouldn't learn about it, think about it, or take it into account, but I don't think that's what the saying means. To me, it means that we have the ability to overcome whatever might be our propensity, or our luck, but sometimes it's a struggle because we have certain characteristics, strengths and weaknesses, and influences affecting us. There are Orthodox astrologers who base their readings on Kabbalah, so they must have found that there's really something to it. Whatever our horoscope, we're not exempt from doing what we can to overcome what's hard for us or from changing our negative personality traits. It's good to know what we have to work on, and what challenges we might have to face.

"David and I have been lucky. I've been surprised at how easily everything has gone. It's completely different than any relationship I'd ever had. They were always fraught with drama and heartache. I don't know what I would have done if our charts had shown that we weren't so compatible. I might have still continued to go out with him because I liked him so much, but I might have decided that it wasn't worth my having to leave the country eventually if the relationship was going to be difficult. Maybe that sounds strange, or not fair, but for me, leaving Israel is a very big deal. I didn't agree to it lightly.

"It's been hard for me to come to terms with giving up on something that's been so important to me and central to my existence for so long. Thank G'd, Dave promised that he'll keep trying to find work in Israel even after we go, if it turns out that way and that we'll come on vacations and sabbaticals, and eventually, G'd willing, we'll retire here if we haven't moved back sooner."

"Sounds like you've got it all planned out. I wish you luck. I know it would be hard for me to consider leaving. I hope David can find a job here so you won't have to go."

"Thank you. That's my hope as well." We were interrupted by more singing, followed by *Birkat Hamazon*, after which came the *sheva brachot*. People started getting up to leave. Aryeh came over and stood beside me. "Are you ready?" he asked.

"Um, sure." I turned to Miri. "It's been so great to share this *simcha* with you. Thank you for all you've shared with me. We'll see you tomorrow night," I said.

"Great! I'm so glad you're coming tomorrow night as well. Do you need a ride? Maybe we can find someone to take you," Miri said, enthusiastically.

"That would be great," I said. "I hope you won't get sick of us."

"Never. I'm so glad you came. Thank you, Aryeh. It means a lot to us that you're here. I know how happy David is to be your advisor," she said.

"The feeling is mutual. I'm thrilled to have him as my advisor and teacher."

"Promise me that you'll come to us soon for Shabbat," Miri said.

"We should give you time to settle in as a newly married couple," I said.

"Nonsense, come next weekend," Miri said.

"Why don't you check with David first?" Aryeh suggested. "We'll see you tomorrow night. Have a great *Shabbes*."

"You too. And a safe walk home," she said, giving me one of her hugs, which I'd already grown to love.

"I have something to show you," Aryeh said after Miri and I had said our farewells. He drew me into the area where the men were seated and motioned with his chin toward some photographs that were hanging along the wall near where he'd been sitting. "That's him," he whispered.

"Who?" I asked.

"Yehoshua."

"Which one?"

"The second one from the left, with the long, rounded gray beard," he said.

"Are you sure?"

"Yes. Doesn't he look familiar?"

"Yes, I remember him."

He continued in a hushed tone, "I'll take you to see him if you'd like."

"Thank you. Why isn't Eliyahu here?"

"I don't know. Maybe he's at the hospital, or maybe it's because David's family doesn't talk to him."

"Really?"

"David was very upset with his father following their rebbe's advice and not even coming in June. Apparently, Yehoshua and Eliyahu were excommunicated."

"Excommunicated?" I asked in surprise. "That's pretty extreme."

"The rebbe in the Chassidic sect David grew up in didn't believe that Yehoshua is Moshiach and tried to stop him from listening to the messages he got, tried to convince him and anyone who'd listen that Yehoshua is crazy."

"That's terrible. He didn't seem crazy to me, and Eliyahu doesn't seem crazy at all. He's so sincere, so sweet . . ."

"As is Yehoshua, I'm sure. David thinks the world of him and refuses to have anything to do with the community, except his parents, since he left."

"So David thinks it's true. Wow. It's amazing that David is his nephew, and that he was there that day."

"His great nephew."

"Have you talked to David much about it? What has he told you?"

"We've talked about it a bit. I feel funny divulging what he's told me in our private conversations, not that it's a secret by any means, but it's for him to tell, though this is obviously not the time," Aryeh said. "You can ask him about it yourself."

"I've still never spoken with him directly."

"I'm sure you'll get a chance to. He's very approachable. Come on, let's go." We left quietly, walked down the stairs of the dark stairwell in silence, and started back through the narrow streets to Arzei HaBirah.

"David's parents came for the wedding, but they didn't believe Yehoshua is who he says he is. Have they seen him?" I asked.

"I don't know. I think it's put a strain on their relationship. How could it not? I don't know if his parents talk to Yehoshua or if they've gone to see him in the hospital. They probably think that either his uncle is mistaken or possibly that he's delusional. They might just not be sure if it was true and feel they have to follow their rebbe's edict."

"But David doesn't follow it."

"No. He's not a member of the sect anymore. He left years ago when he went to college."

"And you? Did you have a rebbe you followed?"

"Yes. I wasn't close with him, but my family has a rebbe."

"That's so interesting. How does it feel to be on your own, without a rebbe?"

"In some ways, very good, in some ways, a little sad."

"Hmm. Do you think you'll get another one?"

"Another rebbe? I don't know. I like Rabbi Yehuda's teachings, but I don't know him well enough, and besides, I'm not sure I want a new rebbe."

"I was just speaking with Shaina about this. I told her I think you want to think for yourself."

"True. It's good to have someone to turn to for advice when you need it, but I don't want to give up my autonomy to anyone but G'd. I'll listen to their opinions, but I don't want to follow anyone's decisions or decrees blindly."

"Amen to that! Shaina thinks I should have a *posek* or someone to consult when I have questions or things come up that I need to work through. She says it's important."

"There are questions that can come up, especially once you're married that it helps to have input on from someone you trust like a rebbe or a *posek* or a *mashpiah*. Do you really want one?"

"Not really, but Shaina seems so happy. She's so calm and sure of herself."

"She's got *bitachon*," he said.

"You're right. Her trust in G'd is very strong. By the way, I don't remember seeing Miri there in June. Was she?"

"In June? No. One of her patients went into labor, so she couldn't make it."

"That's a good reason." We walked together in silence for a while. The Shabbat light was already off when we got to my cousins. As per my instructions, Shaina and Yossi hadn't waited up for me. I didn't invite Aryeh in and, though it was dark and there was no one around, out of respect for where we were, we didn't kiss good night or touch each other in any way.

After shul the next day, Aryeh came for lunch then we went for a long walk. When Shabbat ended, we got a ride to the kehilla with David's aunt and uncle for *sheva brachot*. Voices rising in song greeted our arrival. The evening was in full swing, with table upon table filled with delicious food, as if it were another wedding. Men and women danced in separate circles, until late into the night when Rabbi Yehuda asked us all to be seated.

Rabbi Yehuda spoke about the sanctity of marriage and the bond formed in heaven, how the Baal Shem Tov spoke of two souls that are destined to be together, uniting as one stronger light that shines forth into the world. Beside him, Shimon filled two wine goblets: one stayed on a small table next to Rabbi Yehuda; the other was passed to a different man for each blessing. Planned in advance, they would announce who would get the next blessing, and we would hum a slow, stately melody until the cup reached each new honoree, until Rabbi Yehuda sang the final blessing, motioning for us to join in with him as he sang the final refrain over and over again. Rabbi Yehuda poured a bit of wine from the cup that had been passed around into the other goblet and then poured some wine from that glass back into the first. One cup was then given to David and the other to Miri. David's cup was then passed among the men and Miri's among the women for a special *segulah*—like a good luck charm able to bestow blessings for whatever ails you—whether you are in search of your soul mate, wanting a child, need healing, a new job, or financial assistance. Everyone took a sip of the wine whether they believed in its special powers or doubted but hoped they might be real. People milled around for a while longer; many started to put on their coats and say their farewells.

"We're heading back to Jerusalem. If you want to come with us, we still have room for you," Mr. Roth informed us.

Aryeh looked at me and tilted his head. I smiled back. It was as if we understood each other implicitly without words. "Thank you, but we're going to stay. Have a safe trip home. We really appreciate your bringing us." I nodded.

As if on cue, all the relatives and friends who were not closely associated with the community began to leave, and when only the kehilla were left, Rabbi Yehuda motioned for there to be silence. A strong vibration began to fill me. It started at the base of my spine and moved up until it had reached the top of my head and spread out. It was as if my body was humming. Somehow I understood that Rabbi Yehuda's presence and intention had something to do with what was happening to me. Though I didn't understand it rationally, I knew I had to sit down and that it would be even more powerful if I closed my eyes. Rabbi Yehuda began to play the harmonium and to chant words from prayers, repeating a single phrase again and again as he played. One by one musicians joined him playing various types of drums and strange stringed instruments I'd never seen before—an oud, a tamboura, a sitar, and something called a saz. Rabbi Yehuda would sing a line; then everyone would repeat it. He would sing the same words again, slightly varying the tune, and those present would repeat the variation he had just completed. I opened my eyes to see what people were doing and found that many sat with their eyes closed while others had gotten up and danced to the music. This continued until the chants became faster and faster and the group was almost in a frenzy. I'd never encountered anything quite like it before. I was moved along with everyone else, swaying to the music as I sat, until as if by some force outside myself, I found myself standing and dancing, undulating, rotating my hips and moving around the room along with some other women.

Usually I'd be more inhibited. A part of my brain couldn't quite believe what I was doing—it was as if I was in a trance. Nava and Devorah danced beside me, mirroring each other's movements. I felt as if I'd known them for far longer than one week. I don't know how long we danced, but finally the music began to slow down again until the final chord of the harmonium faded away. We sat in silence for about fifteen minutes; then someone turned up the lights, and people began to open their eyes. The musicians played a few last songs then packed up their instruments. The crowd had already thinned out even further, people having to get up for work Sunday morning, though a long line waited to say a personal goodnight to Rabbi Yehuda or ask for a blessing before he left.

The next morning Nava gave us a tour of her studio, a small barnlike structure with a wheel, a kiln, a workbench, and many long thin tables and shelves displaying her work. There were rings and pendants, *hamsas,* and Jewish stars of all sizes that could be worn or hung on a wall. There were mobiles and chimes, coffee mugs and saucers, and a lot of Judaica. There were Seder plates and Kiddush cups, *Chanukiot,* and *tzedaka* boxes. Some of it was very delicate, like Nava, while other pieces were heavy and bold. "Now I know where to come whenever I need to buy presents. It's all so beautiful. The only problem is I wouldn't know how to choose."

"That's so sweet. Thank you."

"Do you sell them in other places?"

"Some stores around the country. I'm trying to get them into gift shops in synagogues in the States and specialty shops in cities with Judaica stores, but the best prices and selection are right here."

"That's good to know."

"If you ever want to get something, I'll give you a good discount."

"Thanks, but you deserve to make whatever you can on them. This is your livelihood."

"Of course, but friends get special treatment."

"Thank you."

"Come again soon, okay? We love having you."

"Thanks—for everything!"

We took the bus back to Jerusalem, and I made it in time for classes. Aryeh and I made plans to meet Wednesday night and go together to Baka for the last of the *sheva brachot* celebrations.

* * *

"It's so good to see you. It felt like tonight would never come," Aryeh said Wednesday evening when I opened the door. I stepped towards him opening my arms wide, and he drew me toward him for a kiss. "It's been too long."

"It's felt like a long time to me too," I said when we came up for air.

"Now I feel better." He smiled. "Amazing what a kiss can do." He hugged me tightly for a moment before letting go.

"Isn't it?"

"It's great to come here to pick you up, to be able to kiss you and hold you, not like over the weekend. It was hard to keep from kissing you when I picked you up at your cousins'."

"It *was* hard, wasn't it?"

"So you're happy to see me?"

"Of course. Why wouldn't I be?"

"I don't know. You've been in a lot more relationships than I have, and they all ended for some reason. I'm trying to figure out why. It couldn't be that those guys weren't interested in you anymore. I can't imagine how that could happen."

"Believe me, it happened. Sounds like you're feeling a bit worried or insecure," I said. "Have you been thinking a lot about this?"

Aryeh took a moment before answering. "I think it's natural to feel this way. Nothing is as clear-cut as with *shidduch* dating. It's got its pluses, but I can see the downside in terms of knowing where you stand with someone. In the Chassidic community, men and women who are dating have much more in common. Their goals in life and expectations from a relationship are more clearly defined. They're not looking for love right off the bat. They're looking for someone they can build a life with. Of course, attraction is important, but in *shidduch* dating the focus is on compatibility between your personalities and outlooks on life. You know the kind of home you want to create. There's no clouding of what truly matters long-term caused by acting on the physical attraction between the man and woman instead of waiting, so people don't get sidetracked from realizing whether they are really suited to one another and continue to date because of infatuation and feelings of attachment that form when people are physically intimate." He paused for a moment then continued. "This"—his hands moved out from his heart towards mine and back towards his own—"what we have, is very different. Even though we kiss and hug, it's important that we are sure that we're really compatible in all the ways that matter; that we want the same or similar things out of life. We can't let the strong chemistry between us cloud our judgment. It's important to know if we're really right for each other, that we'll be dedicated to being helpmates, inspiring one another to grow and to develop into the best versions of ourselves possible."

I smiled, remembering the words of Miri's blessing, and took his hand in mine. "Why don't we go to my room to talk more about this while I finish what I was doing?" He nodded and followed me to my bedroom. When we got there, I sat down on the bed and picked up my sewing. The hem was coming down on one side of my skirt and I needed to fix it.

He sat on a desk-chair facing me and watched me sew. "They, the ultra-Orthodox, know what they want and what they're looking for in a partner. Right now, I'm still exploring which path to take. You already know that. I don't know exactly where it will lead, but that could be a good thing—life is an adventure. I don't have everything planned in advance. Whatever my goals once were, they've changed, or at least some of them have. I'm still figuring out where I'm headed, but I know I want you to be there with me now and for however long we're together on this journey. I hope it will be for the rest of our lives, but for both our sakes, I think it's best to wait before making any decisions."

"Of course. I understand. It's too soon to make a commitment. But you're happy with this?" I smiled, motioning toward him and back toward myself as he had done.

"This? *This* is great. It's better than anything I ever imagined. Sometimes it's scary, and I do feel a bit unsure, but I don't remember ever feeling this happy. And how is it for you? Are you happy?" he asked.

"Yes. I've been feeling very happy. I love seeing you and being with you, no matter what we do. It's scary for me as well. I have moments when I wonder if this is it, if we're really right for each other, but I don't want us to rush into anything. It's still extremely early to know for sure, at least in the world I come from. It's less than three weeks since our first date." I laughed. "Sure, it's been very intense, and I feel like I've known you much longer. I love your honesty and that there is no game playing between us, like I've often experienced from men. The fact that we're even having this conversation is an indication of that," I said.

"So where does that leave us?"

"Where does it leave us?" I shrugged. "Right where we were but with more clarity about where we stand and how we feel about each other," I said. "What do you think?"

He nodded. "That makes sense," he said. Leaning forward he kissed me softly, tentatively. I responded, deepening the kiss.

I moved my lips up along his neck and nibbled on his earlobe. "Hmm, this is wonderful, but we should really get going." I whispered.

On the bus ride to Baka, Aryeh told me that even though Rob and Terry, who were hosting the *sheva brachot*, often attend a conventional, modern Orthodox synagogue, they prefer kehilla style services, which they attend or create whenever the can.

As we entered the apartment, a makeshift *mechitza* was being hung, separating the living room and dining area. The men congregated in the spacious living room while most of the women were more occupied with last-minute preparations for the dinner, stirring pots on the stove, chopping vegetables for salad, and setting the table.

"What can I do to help?" I asked, handing the bag of pastries we'd brought to Terry, who I had met first at the Shabbat Kallah. I also recognized several of the other women present from that weekend and from the wedding.

"Everything is under control," she said. "Make yourself at home. The guests of honor haven't arrived yet."

"Thanks for having us. Please, put me to work. I'd much prefer it." Just then the *shaliach tsibur* started singing *Ashrei*, the first prayer of the Minchah service.

"Why don't you go in? I hope you'll enjoy the service. It's a little different than Orthodox services and services at the kehilla. It's egalitarian. Have you ever been to an egalitarian service before?"

"I've been to egalitarian services at Conservative synagogues."

"Our services are a little different. They're similar to the services at the kehilla in that we also do our best to imbue them with the spirituality of Chassidut, like they do, but there are some more parts that women lead. Go on in."

"Thanks," I said and joined the women praying in the dining room. Some held their prayer books in their hands, others perched theirs on the dining table. I didn't find any difference between this and prayer services at Kol Rina—men led the prayers, and there was a partition. As soon as the service ended, the men took down the sheet that had been hung up between the rooms.

When I asked Terry about it later, she said that she'd forgotten that there were only men leading this evening. "In an egalitarian Orthodox service, women are allowed to lead certain parts of the davening, in the morning, before *Baruchu*, or the Torah service, on Friday nights women lead Kabbalat Shabbat, and on occasion, if there aren't enough men to make a *minyan*, women may lead other parts of the service."

"Interesting. So it sounds like there's not much of the service women are permitted to lead."

"It's a lot more than in a traditional Orthodox service."

"And less than in Conservative or Reform. Why stay Orthodox if this is important to you?" I asked.

"Well, I don't consider myself Orthodox, but it's important to Rob that men and women are separated and that everything is done according to Halacha. He would have been happy to only go to regular Orthodox synagogues but saw how important participating in the service is to me and was open to finding a solution that works for both of us. I wish it were available more often. We first met when we were studying for a year at the Pardes Institute. Rob is from a typical modern Orthodox background and went to the traditional service or to different Orthodox synagogues around the neighborhood. I went to the progressive service, or to Kol Haneshama, a Reform congregation, which is very spiritual. When we got together, I went back and forth between the two.

"I really love being involved in the service. I grew up with equal rights, and it was hard for me to give that up, even though I love Rob. Rob was okay with the egalitarian services at Pardes, but a Reform synagogue was too much for him. Then we tried a Conservative, or what's called here, *Masorti*, synagogue, but that wasn't comfortable for him either, so we've become involved in creating opportunities and, G'd willing, ultimately a community, like this one. We've thought of moving to the kehilla, but we love Jerusalem and our work is here. We have a big enough group now to rotate between people's homes one Friday night and one Saturday morning each month, plus holidays. It's been hard to keep it up. So many of the people who've gotten involved are only here temporarily. It feels like each year we have to start again almost from scratch finding people who are looking for this type of *minyan*, but I believe in a way that's a good thing. Some of those people take the idea and bring it back to the communities they've come from and start more groups, or find groups and join them there. It's starting to spread, and I believe it will continue to grow and more and more people will choose this type of service."

"I hope you're right. I myself go back and forth between Conservative and Orthodox synagogues. I think an option like this would be a great solution for me. Do you know if it's happening anywhere else in Jerusalem, like at or near the university?" I asked.

"Sorry, not that I know of." She shook her head. "Maybe you could start one."

"Who knows. I would love to attend services like this all the time," I said. "But I'm not ready to take on such a big project like that on my own. I don't even know where to begin to find other people who'll be interested."

"You'll be surprised. Once you make a decision, things start falling into place."

"I don't know."

"You don't have to decide anything now. Think about it, or as we say, meditate on it." Her smile was radiant.

"Looks like people are starting to eat. Don't let me keep you."

"I'm enjoying our conversation," Terry said. "Food can wait, unless you're hungry."

"No, no. I want to know more. What exactly are women allowed to lead?"

A buffet of salads, quiches, pasta dishes, and pies was set up against the dining room wall. Its placement provided the most room for people to move around and mingle. Chairs were set up around the circumference of the room, along with tray tables and small folding tables.

"Well, women are allowed to lead the parts of the service I mentioned before and participate in the Torah service. We can have *aliyot*, read Torah, *haftarah*, and *megillot*. There are rabbis who've researched it thoroughly and came to the understanding that these are the parts of the service that are *halachically* permitted for women to lead."

"So why isn't everyone doing it?" I asked.

"I'm sure it's still not enough for the Conservative or Reform, and most Orthodox aren't ready to accept the opinions of those rabbis who are willing to shake things up and prefer keeping the status quo, even if it means turning off and alienating a lot of women."

"I wonder how many Orthodox women even know it's an option," I mused.

"Good point. I see Aryeh waiting in line. The poor guy doesn't know whether to get off the line or start without you." I looked over and saw Aryeh had just reached the buffet table. He let the person behind him go ahead, then he handed me a plate, looking relieved when I joined him. We served ourselves from a large assortment of vegetarian delicacies then found two seats in a corner, near some friends he'd met over Shabbat meals spent with Miri and David. Several rabbis and friends made speeches. There was some singing, and then the wine cup was filled in preparation for *sheva brachot*. To our surprise, the cup was passed to a woman for the third blessing then to two other women for the sixth and seventh. Aryeh looked startled, but handled it well. The women's voices were lovely, and the singing continued after the seven blessings were completed. Miri and David joined us for a moment then moved on to speak with other guests. Later, on the bus ride home, I asked Aryeh if he had enjoyed the ceremony. "I don't know about this. It's further than I ever intended to go away from Orthodoxy."

"But Terry said it's still Orthodox, egalitarian Orthodox."

"I need to check the sources myself. It surprised me that David was comfortable with it. I want to talk to him about it. I'm not sure how comfortable I would be going back to something like that in the future."

"Well, I thought it was great. I'd love to attend services like that more often."

Aryeh nodded and put his arm around my shoulders. "Then sometimes we might just have to pray in different places. The service was fine, it was just the *sheva brachot* that went beyond my comfort zone, but I'll keep an open mind to it, especially if it's that important to you."

"Thanks. Whatever you decide, it will be okay with me, as long as you're okay with my going when the opportunity arises."

"Sure. That's entirely up to you. I don't have a right to stop you from worshipping in the way that's the most meaningful for you."

"I appreciate that. It's one of the things I love about you."

"Thanks. I feel the same about you. Um, sorry, I forgot to ask you sooner, are you busy tomorrow night?"

"I was kind of hoping we'd get together," I admitted.

"Great. So was I. I want to take you somewhere special."

*　　*　　*

That night, it was after 10:00 p.m. when the doorbell rang. I opened the door to find Jean Marc standing on the other side, as if no time had passed. He swept me into his arms and pressed his lips to mine. "Hold on, Jean Marc. We need to talk," I said, pushing him away.

"We'll talk. Of course we'll talk, but this is all I've thought of since I saw you last."

"It's been two months. A lot has happened in two months," I said. "Everything's changed."

"Just one kiss," he begged, leaning closer again. I evaded his arms.

"No. I'm sorry. It's too late," I said. "What happened? I thought you were going to get off early one night to see me that week, or come see me the following week at the latest. That was October. Where have you been all this time? You think you can just waltz in here and sweep me off my feet? Well you have another think coming. My life's gone on without you."

"Please, you must give me a chance." He reached toward me again and drew me into his arms before I could stop him. He propelled me from the entry hall into my bedroom, and he closed the door with his foot before I could say a word.

"Stop," I said.

"What's wrong?" He shook his head.

"I told you. It's too late. I'm seeing someone. Now let me go." I extracted myself from his hold.

"You're kidding. You're just angry with me, but I can explain. I've been in France. My father was sick. He had a heart attack."

"Oh, I'm so sorry to hear that," I said. Any anger or resentment I'd been harboring melted away in that instant. I wanted to put my arms around him, to hold and comfort him, but I didn't want him to get the wrong impression. I felt torn. I gave him a hug and pulled away. "Is he all right now?"

I opened my bedroom door and ushered him back into the apartment's communal area, which consisted of a kitchen, dining area, and small hallway. "Would you like some coffee?" I asked, motioning for him to take a seat.

"Sure," he said, as he sat down. "He's doing much better. It's been hard for my mother with him being sick. They're very close. She'd be lost without him." I poured two cups of black Turkish coffee, adding cardamom and one teaspoon of sugar. I handed him a cup. He took a sip. "Perfect. You remembered how I like it. I'm surprised you even have Turkish coffee. Most Americans don't."

"We keep it for company, and every once in a while I'll have a cup. I like it for a change." I took a seat across from him.

He sighed. "It's been a hard couple of months. It took us completely by surprise. I guess it shouldn't have, he smokes and has a lot of pressure at work, but there were no symptoms prior to the attack. My mother has been a wreck. It was very hard to leave until he got stronger. Thank G'd he's doing okay now."

"That must be a relief." I realized this was the first time he'd ever spoken to me about his parents' relationship.

"It is. I'm sure no one is ever ready for something like this."

"You're right. I know I wouldn't be."

We drank our coffee in silence for a while. I looked down at my cup, avoiding his eyes. He broke the silence. "*Ani ohev otach*, Arielle," he said in Hebrew. He used the word *ohev*, which means love, but is also used like we use the word *like* in English. "*Tamid ahavti otach*" (I've always loved you), again that word which can mean love or like. He reached across the table and took my hand. I looked up at him.

"Thanks. I like you too," I replied in English, so it would be clear which I meant, though in a way I did love him still.

"I mean—I love you. I still have strong feelings for you. I'm attracted to you; I think you're a beautiful, intelligent, and interesting woman. I've tried to get over you and just be friends, but I still love you. Despite what you might have thought, I'm not a Casanova or a Don

Juan. Sure, I've dated a lot, but I've been looking for the right woman to spend my life with. It's never been my intention to rack up notches on my bedpost."

I laughed. "Your knowledge of English is incredible. Where did you learn that expression?"

He shrugged. "We learn English in school, watch English television and movies."

"But you do have a little black book," I said, "and it's full of phone numbers. I've seen it."

"And you have a phone book too, it doesn't matter what the color," he said, appearing frustrated.

"I was just joking with you."

"Well, you can stop, okay. I'm in no mood for joking."

"Sorry," I said. "I guess I'm just not used to you being serious."

He reached across the table, lifted my chin, and rubbed his thumb across my bottom lip. I know that if things had been different, I would have darted my tongue out and sucked on his finger. Instead, I gently moved his hand away from my face. Looking into my eyes, he spoke again. "I can be very serious. I want to give this another try. I haven't dated anyone in months. You are the only woman I want to be with. We get along so well, we're friends, and you can't deny this attraction."

"No, I don't deny it. But as I already said, I'm seeing someone."

He ignored my comment and continued. "We never fought. It was just a matter of timing back then. We're older now, and I'm ready. We're both committed to living here. That means a lot of me, and I know it's important to you. Please, give me another chance," he implored, his eyes beseeching me as did his words.

"You're serious about this? I can't believe it. It took me so long to get over you the first time. You can hurt me too easily. I was waiting for you to come by again two months ago, but you never did."

"I explained. What could I do? I had to be there for my father, I'm sorry I didn't find a way to get a message to you before I went," he said calmly.

"Or to leave a message for me with the office when you were in Paris."

"You're right. I could have done that, but we've never called each other."

"Maybe that was part of the problem: you never went out of your way to get a hold of me."

"That's not true. I'd come by many times until I found you in, or I'd leave a note. I didn't think of calling. So much was going on, it's not that I stopped caring about you, wanting you, I thought of you all the time while I was gone." How I'd longed to hear everything he was saying, but it didn't matter. I was dating Aryeh, and even if Aryeh and I had never spoken about having an exclusive relationship, I realized it was what I wanted.

"Jean Marc, I'm sorry. This is a complete surprise. I'm happy with Aryeh. I'm not interested in dating anyone else."

"Our timing has always been the problem." He shook his head then got up and walked around the table. He held out his hand, gently drawing me to my feet. "I had hoped that had changed." We stood eye to eye for a moment. He searched my face then tried one last time to kiss me.

I pulled free. "Please, stop. I can't do this."

"You can't be seeing him very long; not long enough for it to be exclusive."

"Jean Marc, it is, and I'm not interested."

"You've had that conversation? Are you sure?"

"I'm sure," I said. "It's not about any conversation. Aryeh and I don't need one."

"All right. I get the message, but if it doesn't work out, let me know. Okay?"

"Thank you. I'm flattered. I hope it will work out, but we can still be friends."

"Of course." He smiled. "He's a very lucky man. I look forward to meeting him."

"I hope you will, at some point."

"But not yet. I understand." He grabbed his cup from the table and took a last swallow of coffee. "I guess I'll be going then. Stay in touch."

"Of course," I said. "You too."

"Of course." He put his hands on my shoulders and looked into my eyes then kissed me on each cheek. "Good luck."

"Thanks," I said and opened the door for him to leave. "You too."

*　　*　　*

I had a hard time sleeping that night. I tossed and turned, my mind flitting from one scene to another of my relationship with Jean Marc. Memories flooded my mind of our time together while I was on the one-year program, from the moment we met during ulpan, how my heart caught in my throat when I first saw him, and how tongue-tied I was the first few times we spoke, how much I wanted him to notice and be interested in me, and how he was always dating someone else. I dated too, but Jean Marc was the one I really wanted to be with. Over the course of the year, little by little, our friendship grew. We'd smile and flirt when our paths crossed, and then one night we had guard duty together. Walking up and down the streets and pathways leading from one dorm to the next, we talked and joked with each other. At some point, he reached for my hand, and I placed it in his. It was a cold night in February, and he placed our joined hands in his coat pocket as we patrolled. I'd known he was funny and quick-witted, but I hadn't realized till that night how intelligent and interesting he was. I was surprised by how easy he was to talk to. Our shift ended at dawn. I remember the beautiful colors of the sky as it grew brighter and brighter. He put his arm around me as he walked me back to my building. I remember how excited I felt as I burrowed into his side, my arm around his waist.

I don't remember what we talked about, but I remember how happy I felt being with him. He didn't kiss me that night or ask to see me again, and for several days I replayed the evening, wondering what I'd done wrong. Then, one day, I came back to my room after classes and found a note on the door asking if I'd like to go out for coffee, signed by Jean Marc with his room number underneath. I went by to leave him a note in return and found him at home. He asked if I'd like to go out for coffee or if I'd rather come in. "Is this a good time, or would later be better, or another day?"

"I'd love a cup," I said, wanting to spend as much time with him as I could, as often as possible. That had been the beginning.

Scenes passed through my mind of our budding relationship and all the time we spent together, of Purim parties, and *tiyulim*, Shabbat meals, and going dancing Thursday and Saturday nights. I remembered going to the beach at Nitzanim and Hertzaleya Pituach. I remembered missing him when I went home for Pesach and how wonderful it was to see him again and how we spent every moment we could together the rest of the year until the war broke out two weeks before I was scheduled to leave the country. Jean Marc got the call and left that day. We didn't know if we'd see each other again. Somehow he got time off and came to the airport to say good-bye. He looked so handsome in his uniform, and I cried when I saw him. It was so hard to leave. I didn't want to get on the plane with Stacey, knowing that this was the end. Amram was there too, also in his uniform. They were sad too but determined to make it work. Stacey and I kept turning around and waving as we went through security. We both must have cried the whole trip to Corfu, the first stop on our travels through Europe.

I knew I'd be back in two years, and a part of me hoped to get back together with Jean Marc, no matter how unrealistic it might be, when I made aliyah, but I had no expectations and wasn't surprised when he told me he'd met someone else. Why had it taken him so long to reveal his feelings? I'd held on to the hope for so long that there was a chance we would get back together. If only we'd talked that day in October. If only his father hadn't gotten sick. But then, I wouldn't have gotten involved with Aryeh, and I can't imagine what my life would be like without Aryeh in it. Whatever feelings I had or might even still have for Jean Marc, I know I'm in love with Aryeh, and I'm not going to do anything to jeopardize what we have together.

*   *   *

The doorbell rang. When I opened it, Aryeh swept me into his arms. "Long time no see," he joked when we finally came up for air. After my meeting with Jean Marc last night, it did feel like a long time. "You look beautiful." He handed me a beautiful bouquet of flowers. I found a vase and put them in water.

"Roses, thank you," I said. "They're beautiful."

"How was your day?" he asked, as I lifted my jacket from the back of a chair.

"It's been good."

"Let me help you with that," he said, taking the coat from my hands and holding it out for me.

"Are we in a hurry?"

"I made reservations at Mama Mia's. I hope you're hungry," he explained.

"Yum. They make the best eggplant Parmesan. I love everything I've ever tasted there, but eggplant Parmesan is my favorite, and I don't know any other place in Jerusalem where you can get it. I didn't know until I came to Israel that there were so many different ways to cook eggplant, and most of them don't include cheese."

"I never even tasted eggplant until I came to Israel, and I've never had it Parmesan style."

"You're kidding? Do you like eggplant? If you do, you're in for a treat."

"I do like it. It's a very diverse vegetable. It tastes so different depending on how it's made," he said as we headed to the bus stop.

"Have you eaten there before? They make great pasta too, so if you prefer that, of course, get what you like, but you must taste mine."

"Thanks. We can share, like when we went to Jan's, if you'd like."

"Well, as much as I generally like sharing, I love their eggplant even more. I don't know if I'd be satisfied with only half a portion of it, if you know what I mean," I admitted. "You didn't answer my question. Have you been there before?"

"No, actually, I haven't."

"Then you're really in for a treat," I said. It was great to see him so lighthearted and happy. He kept his arm around me as we walked to the bus stop and as we waited for the bus. I snuggled into him. As we waited, the weather grew chillier and chillier; when the bus finally came, we were huddled even closer together to protect ourselves and each other from the frigid wind. We continued to hold each other on the bus and all the way to the restaurant.

"It feels strange to me that I want to make movies and you don't even watch them," I said when I finally closed my menu, having settled on what I'd order.

"I've watched a few movies. I thought I told you on our first date. And I have no problem with watching documentaries. It depends on the subject matter. I look forward to the day that I get to watch yours."

"Thanks. It's great to have your support. It means so much to me. I'm just afraid you won't be able to deal with my lifestyle and my career. I don't know if I'll be able to cope with how religious you are, if you decide to go back to being more observant or if you become less observant."

"I don't plan on becoming less observant. I think this is my limit."

We were quiet for a while once the food arrived, other than our exclamations at how delicious it all tasted. As always, everything was fabulous. He had the spinach-and-cheese-filled ravioli in a creamy mushroom sauce and fed me a piece. It was another magical evening. We ordered cappuccinos after dinner, and I introduced Aryeh to the owner, Sergio, when he came over to our table to talk with us. Sergio went from table to table all evening, talking and laughing with the customers, playing guitar and singing, and making everyone feel special and important. He insisted on treating us to dessert when he heard it was Aryeh's first time there. He chose for us, and a waitress brought out servings of tiramisu, chocolate mousse, and *profiterols*, little balls of puff pastry filled with ice cream and covered in hot fudge sauce.

"Sergio, you're crazy and far too generous. We can't eat all this. We're already stuffed from dinner," I exclaimed.

"So eat the *profiterols* before they melt. I'll pack up the rest for you to take with you," he insisted. "Let me play another song for you. Sing with me, *bella*," he requested.

I looked over at Aryeh, making sure he was okay with it. Aryeh smiled and nodded in agreement. We sang a medley of Hebrew folk songs, from *"Chorsat Ha'ekolyptus"* to *"Yerushalayim Shel Zahav,"* then more modern Israeli pop hits by singers like Chava Alberstein, Yehudit Ravitz, Shlomo Artzi, and David Broza. After a last song, a guitar solo this time, featuring his proficient classical finger picking, Sergio bid us good night and moved on to another table.

"He's quite a character." I smiled.

"Quite charming," Aryeh said. "It was very sweet of him to treat us to dessert."

"Yes. He does that often, either coffee or dessert. Tonight we were lucky. He likes to feel like he's entertaining guests, not just customers. He treats repeat customers like family."

"And it seemed like you must fall into that category. He seems quite taken with you. So you've sung with him before?"

I smiled, and my cheeks definitely flushed. "Yes. As you know, I love to sing, so when he brings out the guitar, I can't help but join in if I know the song."

"It all sounded lovely, and together, your harmonies were beautiful," he said.

I blushed even more brightly at his words. "Thank you. I enjoy it."

"I enjoy it too. It's a pleasure listening to you." We fell silent for several moments, drinking our coffee, and eating every bite of the *profiterols*. We tasted each of the other desserts as well and then had the waitress pack the rest up.

"Have you thought about how you're going to stay *shomeret Shabbat* if or, should I say, when, you go off on assignments?" he asked.

"In high school, I was often in an environment that wasn't very conducive to keeping Shabbat, but I found a way. I walked to choir performances, plays, parties, even football games. It's a good thing we lived within walking distance to the school. It's been a while, but I'm sure I can do it. You'll just have to trust me and take my word for it."

"Yes, you've told me about that. You found a way to not break Shabbat, but it doesn't sound like there was much of a Shabbat atmosphere on those occasions. It's hard to keep Shabbat outside of a *shomer Shabbat* community."

"You're right, but it can be done."

"I'm sure it can. Have you thought about what you'll do once you get married? How are you going to have a family with that kind of career? Do you think you can do both?"

"Is this a theoretical conversation, or are you asking?"

"Asking what?" he asked, looking perplexed.

"Never mind," I said, looking down at my plate, suddenly embarrassed.

"Oh! Ohhh! I'm sorry," he said. "I didn't think we were at that stage yet. I didn't think you were ready."

"I'm not saying I'm ready," I backtracked. "Are you?"

"Look, Arielle, I love you. I'm just still new to all this. I don't know if I'm ready, so that must mean I'm not. I guess I need more time, but if I didn't see the possibility of us marrying someday, I wouldn't lead you on. I promise. Are you okay with that?"

"Of course. That's what I figured. I don't even know why I said what I did. I guess it was just the conversation. It's been an intense few weeks."

"You don't need to explain to me, sweetheart. I think about it too. I just didn't think either one of us was ready for that kind of commitment."

"You're right. We're young. There's no rush. We've got time to figure it out," I agreed.

"Plenty of time. Now, listen," he said. He walked around the table and sat down on his haunches beside me. "I meant it when I said that I love you."

I looked up at him, my eyes brimming with tears. "I love you too."

He leaned forward and kissed my lips then wiped the tears from my eyes.

"There's someone I want you to meet," I said when he moved away.

"Okay. I'm happy to meet anyone you'd like to introduce me to."

"Tomorrow, do you have plans after you finish your classes?"

"Um, a little. Shabbat starts so early, there's not much time."

"If not, we can do it Saturday night, or another time. It's my cousin Shirah and her husband. They want to meet you. And I'd like you to meet them."

"Sure. I feel honored that you want to introduce me to more of your family."

"They're like surrogate parents to me, if she'd been a teenage bride, which she was, but she didn't have any kids from that marriage. Andy is her second husband."

"Set it up and I'll be there." He smiled. "If I had any family here I could introduce you to, I would."

"I thought you do have family here."

"Yeah, but none I could really introduce you to. They wouldn't understand, and I don't want to pretend with them or anyone."

"Well, I look forward to meeting your family, when you're ready," I said.

"Hey, cheer up," he coaxed. "It's not about you, okay? I'm crazy about you! Got it?"

"Got it."

"Good."

"By the way, I'm going to be at Shaina and Yossi's for Shabbat, if you want to come for dinner, if you don't have any plans yet, I'm sure they'd be happy to have you," I said.

"Sounds great. I'm sorry we hadn't talked about Shabbat plans earlier. This is the first time since we started dating that we were going to be apart for Shabbat."

"I know. When you didn't say anything, I made plans with Shaina, hoping we'd be able to see each other."

"You should have told me sooner. Why didn't you say something last night? Arielle, never feel that you can't ask me something like that directly. I was going to see my relatives in Bnei Brak. They've invited me several times in the past few months, but I kept avoiding it."

I laughed. "That's funny, I'd been avoiding spending Shabbat with Shaina and Yossi, and look how great that turned out."

"So you think I should go?" he teased.

"Maybe," I teased back. "You never know who you might meet."

"No, I don't think so—at least not this weekend. If you're going to be in my neighborhood, I'll stay. I'll talk to Yossi in class tomorrow about coming to dinner. They said I have an open invitation. I hope they were serious."

"I think Shaina is already assuming you'll come for at least one meal."

"You do?"

"Yes."

"I'll ask Yossi anyway. It's never good to make assumptions. So I guess I'll see you at shul," he said as we arrived at my door.

"Do you want to come in?"

"I don't think I should. It's late, and I've got classes tomorrow."

"Just for a minute?" I pouted.

"You're very hard to resist. Okay. I'll come in for a minute."

About an hour later, we stood back at the door. "So I'll see you at shul tomorrow night?"

"Yes, but if I'm not there, I'll see you at Shaina and Yossi's."

"Right. And Saturday night?"

"What about it?" I asked.

"Um, well, do you want to do something?"

"I'd love to do something. Oh, you mean together?"

"Yes. Of course together."

"Sure. Remember the rules I told you about?"

"I thought we're beyond that?"

"I've been disregarding them, but I don't know that we're beyond them."

"Oh, I think we are."

"Aryeh, it's common courtesy for a guy to ask in advance."

"I am asking in advance."

"More than two days in advance. At least by Wednesday you should ask."

"Arielle, I just assume I'm going to spend every Saturday night with you if we're both in town. I'd like to spend every spare moment with you, if I could."

"Really?"

"Really."

"Well then, I guess we can do that. We can say it's a standing date—every Saturday night, unless one of us is out of town."

"And Thursday nights," he suggested.

"Oh, Thursday nights too? Let me think about it." I giggled.

"How long do you need to think about it?"

"Hmmm, I don't know."

"Just tell me before our date is over Saturday," he said. "I wouldn't mind calling you before each date to ask you out in advance if you had your own phone, but with the way things are, you in your dorm and me in mine, and having to rely on getting the messages in time to call back and being able to get a hold of each other, it can get complicated. I've tried to remember to make plans with you for the next date whenever we've gone out, but it's a pain if I forget and have to rely on the office staff to give you a message and then wait to hear back from you. It's frustrating. I'd like to avoid that as much as possible."

"I understand. You're right. It *is* a pain in the neck."

"Is there anything you'd like to do?"

"If we can, I'd like to take you to meet my cousins, Shirah and Andy."

"That's right. You mentioned that earlier. Sounds great. I'm looking forward to meeting them."

"Really? I hope you like them. You know, she predicted this."

"She predicted what?"

"Us."

"Us?"

"Yes. She sensed some kind of connection or potential, an affinity between us the day of the rally."

"But she wasn't there, was she?" he asked, perplexed.

"No. I went over to visit her and her family afterwards, and when I mentioned you and how we'd been publicizing the event together and trying to get people to come, she kept asking me questions about you and said she had a feeling there was more to it, that we'd be good for each other."

"That's interesting. So she gets feelings, like your mother gets?"

"Yes." I nodded, smiling. "But Shirah's are even stronger."

"Even stronger? That's impressive. Well, what can I say? She was right about us."

"You think so?"

"Of course, silly."

"Good. See you tomorrow. Have a good night."

"You too. Sweet dreams," he said then drew me against him and held me for a moment before he lowered his head and found my lips.

"How could my dreams be anything but sweet after our date tonight? Sweet dreams to you too." I whispered, when he finally let me go. I looked deeply into his eyes then kissed him again. I closed my eyes and breathed in his scent. After several more kisses, he headed out the door. I watched him amble down the stairs, and we grinned at each other and waved when he reached the first landing.

Epilogue

David
Bloomington, Indiana
1994

I woke from my dream with a start. Miri was sitting in a rocking chair nursing the baby. Her eyes half closed. "Honey, are you awake?" I whispered. "I've got to tell you about my dream."

"I must have dozed off. What time is it?" she asked, rubbing her eyes.

"Sorry, I didn't mean to wake you, but as long as you're up, can I tell you about my dream? It was one of *those dreams.*"

"Really? One of *those dreams?* Tell me!"

"There was a big party in a brightly lit room. I saw Yehoshua and Eliyahu dancing. They looked much younger than the last time I saw them, like they looked when I was a child, and they were in good health. Eliyahu turned to Yehoshua and patted him on the back. 'Mazel Tov! We did it,' he said. 'It's their turn now. The next generation is in place. There's no need to despair or worry anymore. It won't be long now. With G'd's help, they will succeed where we failed.'

"I got the chills at his words. Then Yehoshua said, 'May Hashem bless them to build a *bayit ne'eman b'yisrael* and have the privilege to see the ingathering of the exiles. Then Yehoshua said, 'May this new Yehoshua be a *yiras shamayim*, whose deeds will be the final bricks needed to bring *bayit shlishi*.' And Eliyahu said, 'He's been born to the right family, with parents who have already proven themselves in so many ways. *B'ezras Hashem,* they will recognize his gifts and help him develop. They will see the signs and help him to succeed in any way they can. They know what they're up against, but they're strong. They'll persevere and see it through. I just know they will, they have to. This time, he must succeed.' And Yehoshua said, 'And we'll be there to help in any way we can.'"

"I miss them. May your Uncle Yehoshua rest in peace. We should let Eliyahu know."

"He gave us such a beautiful *bracha* when we saw him last summer. It was as if he already knew, as if he had planned it himself."

"Do you know how he's doing? Is he still living with his daughter?"

"I assume so. I should have let him know sooner."

"That I was pregnant or about the baby?"

"Both," I said. "I think wherever he is, he already knows."

"I think so too. So you think it wasn't just a dream?" Miri asked.

"Honey, I believe the message, wherever it came from. After being at Yehoshua's birth and seeing the light around him, I have no doubt. We have a big job ahead of us."

*   *   *

Glossary

Agudah—association, union, society. It is the name of an ultra-Orthodox political party in Israel, Agudaht Yisrael.

Aliyah—to go up, term used meaning to immigrate to Israel, also used to receive the honor of being called to the Torah to recite a blessing during the Torah reading service. Oleh or Olah—someone who goes up, or makes aliyah.

Ba'al Shem Tov—master of the good Name, good name master, Israel ben Eliezer, the founder of Chassidism

Ba'al teshuvah—penetents, newly religious people

Bar mitzvah—boy at age thirteen, old enough to be worthy of and obligated to keep the commandments

Baruch—blessed (first word of most prayers)

Baruch ha-bah—welcome, literally blessed is the one who comes. These are also the opening words to the Jewish wedding ceremony.

Bashert—intended or fated, "meant to be", often used to refer to one's soul mate.

Bayit ne'eman b'yisrael—a faithful house in Israel, a common expression used to describe the type of life encouraged and sanctioned. It is a blessing to the one told this phrase.

Bentching or to bentch—Yiddish for to bless, or saying a blessing, often refers to reciting the Grace After Meals.

B'ezrat Hashem, or b'ezras Hashem—with G'ds help, G'd willing

Bima—stage, podium, the part of the synagogue where the cantor or leader of the service stands and the Torah is read from, often raised, can be at the front or in the middle of the synagogue.

Birkat Hamazon—grace after meals

Bracha—blessing. Also a girl's name.

Brit (Bris—Ashkenazi and Yiddish pronunciation)—covenant, agreement

Brit Milah—ritual circumcision, performed when a baby boy is eight days old

Bupkes—nothing

Chaim—life

Chareidi (pl.—im)—term used to refer to ultra-Orthodox Jews, strictly observant, (literally, shaking or quaking).

Chas v'shalom—phrase meaning "G'd forbid," a similar Hebrew phrase is *chas v'chalila* or *chalila v'chas*

Chassid/im—(literal meaning—pious, righteous, devotee), ultra-Orthodox Jews who are followers of a particular rabbi or rebbe who follow his teachings.

Chatan—a bridegroom

Chayal boded—a lone soldier, a soldier who has no family in the country

Chessed—loving kindness, one of the sefirot

Chumrot—extra stringent interpretation and adherence to the law

Chuppah—wedding canopy

Daven—to pray (Yiddush, Ashkenazi term)

Davenen, davening—the act of praying

Derech—way or path

D'var Torah (plural, divrei Torah)—biblical teaching

Eliyahu ha'navee—Elijah the prophet

Galut—diaspora, dispersion

Geulah—redemption

Gevurah—strength, courage, greatness; one of the sefirot

Goy/im—literally: nation(s), generic term referring to non-Jews.

Har Hatsofim—Mount Scopus

Hashem—literally means The Name, is the permissible term used for G'd by Orthodox Jews but not actually a name for G'd, so it is not considered taking G'ds name in vain.

Hashkafa—outlook, view point, way of looking at the world.

Hechsher—authorization, permit (given by a rabbi)

Kabbalat Shabbat—Friday night prayer service

Kallah—a bride

Kavanah—devotion, intention, focus, direction, aim. Also a term used by kabbalists to refer to specific practices done with intention of a certain spiritual outcome.

Ketubah—Jewish marriage contract given by the groom to the bride specifying his obligations during the marriage and in the event of divorce or his death

Kippah/kippot—a yarmulke, head covering, skull cap generally worn by Jewish men.

Kiddush—the prayer sanctifying wine; ceremonial ritual for drinking wine on Sabbath, holidays and at certain ceremonies, like weddings.

Koninut—periods of high preparedness

Kol isha—literally a woman's voice, refers to the laws prohibiting men from hearing women who are not related to them sing

Kotel—the Western Wall

Litvish—Lithuanians, people who follow Lithuanian Jewish customs, can refer to ultra-Orthodox who are not Chassidic.

Mamash—an expression like "really" also reality or exactly

Mazel—luck, also the word for zodiac

Mazel tov—congratulations, good luck

Mechitza—a partition, divider. A partition in Orthodox synagogues separating the seating areas of men and women.

Meforshim—commentators

Mehadrin—referring to a stricter type of kosher certification. Also literally means adorned or elegant.

Melaveh malka—a ceremony or party after Shabbat to prolong the joy of the Sabbath. Literally, escorting the Queen

Merkavah—chariot

Midrash—genre of rabbinic commentary that expands and explains the biblical text, generally used to refer to nonlegal material (Drash: a deeper level of understanding of the Torah)

Minchah—afternoon prayer service

Minyan (pl. minyanim)—a quorum of ten men needed for a complete Jewish prayer service

Mitnaged, (pl. Mitnagdim)—term used to refer to ultra-Orthodox who are not Chassidic. The term has come out of fashion and been replaced by other terms as it literally means "to go against," as to go against Chassidism, but their way actually preceded Chassidism.

Mitzvah (plural mitzvot/h)—divine commandment, also a good deed

Mo'adon—a club or clubhouse, can be a canteen, a social hall

Moshav—an agricultural settlement

Moshe—Moses

Motzei Shabbat—after Shabbat ends

Narishkeit—nonsense

Neshama—soul

Nigun (pl.—nigunim)—a melody. Often refers to a repetitive wordless melody used to raise spiritual awareness and experience. Many were written by Chassidic rabbis and masters.

Nu—yiddish term meaning "so" (used as a prompting for more information)

Olam—world

Olam Ha'bah—the world to come

Oleh or Olah—usually denotes a new immigrant to Israel, literally to go "up"

Oleh Chadash—a male new immigrant to Israel

Olah Chadasha—a female new immigrant to Israel

Oneg—pleasure, delight, enjoyment, can refer to an Oneg Shabbat (Verb—Ta'anug)

Oneg Shabbat—literally, Sabbath pleasure, refers to a gathering where people enjoy each other's company on Shabbat, often with food, sometimes with singing, Torah teachings, and story telling

Seder—order, a ceremony done in a certain order

Siddur—prayerbook

Pardes—literally an orchard, paradise. Can refer in Kabbalah to the combined levels of understanding of the Torah: p'shat (literal), Remez (hinted at), Drash (allegorical) and Sod (Secret, mystical)

Peyot—side locks, side curls worn by ultra-Orthodox men, most often by Chassidim. Adherence to the law not to shave or cut the five corners of the face/head.

Pesach—Passover

Posek, pl.—poskim—authority to make halachic decisions or rulings when one is needed. This is done by a Rabbi. (Can be conjugated as a verb—to paskin, he paskined . . .)

P'shat—the literal translation, the direct or simplest interpretation, from the word pashut, simple

Rabeinu—our rabbi, our teacher

Rechov—street

Rosh—head, the beginning or first

Rosh Chodesh—the new moon, new month, celebrated every month with additions to the prayer service and grace after meals. It's considered a special holiday for women due to women's connection with the moon and cycles.

Rosh Hashana—the Jewish New Year, celebrated the first and second days of the Jewish month of Tishrei

Rosh yeshiva—the dean or principal of a yeshiva

Ru'ach—spirit, soul in the World of Formation, considered to be the emotional level of soul in the five levels of soul in Kabbalah

Ru'ach hakodesh—the Holy Spirit, the spirit of G'd, refers to divine inspiration, receiving prophecy

Sderot—boulevard(s)

Sefirot—levels of energetic emanations in the process of creation, can refer to various qualities and attributes as well

Seudah—a meal, often refers to a big festive meal

Seudah Shlishit—the customary third meal of the Sabbath, eaten toward the end of Shabbat, before sundown

Shaharith—the morning prayer service

Shabbat (pl.—ot)—the Jewish Sabbath

Shabbat Kallah—the bride's Sabbath, a tradition where friends and family of the bride keep her company and happy before the wedding

Shabbes (pl.—im)—Ashkenizic pronunciation for the Sabbath

Shalom—peace, a greeting that can mean hello or good-bye

Shavuot—weeks, or the festival of weeks. Takes place on the fiftieth day after Pesach (Passover)

Sh'ma (or Shema)—listen or hear, as in "Sh'ma Yisroel" the prayer: "Hear O Israel, the L'rd is our G'd, the Lord is One"

Sherut—shuttle, service

Sheva brachot—the seven blessings recited during the wedding ceremony, and daily for the week following a wedding, to bring blessings and joy to the bride and groom. A minyan/quorum must be present for the sheva brachot to be said.

Shidduch (pl.—shidduchim)—matches; being fixed up on dates with the goal of getting married.

Shirah—song, poetry

Shomer, shomeret (pl.—shomrim, shomrot)—to guard, keep, observe

Shomer or shomeret negiyah—someone who observes the laws regarding no physical contact between men and women before marriage

Shul—Yiddish for synagogue

Simcha—happiness, joy, a celebration or joyous occasion

Smicha—rabbinic ordination, to cover, also the word for a blanket

Succot—Fall harvest festival, also plural for succah

Tallit—a prayer shawl. A "kosher" tallit must have tzitzit on the corners. See below.

Talmid chacham—great Jewish scholar

Talmud—compilation of discussions, discourses and arguments of Jewish law completed in the fifth century

Tefillin—phylacteries, small leather cases containing passages from scripture worn on the arm and head by Jewish men during morning prayer except on Shabbat and festivals

Tehillim—Psalms

Teshuvah—answer, return, repentance

Tikun—perfection, correction, refinement, fixing, or repair

Tisch—a table, or a ceremony where Torah is taught around a table.

Torah—The Five Books of Moses, can also refer to all of Jewish learning

Tzibur—public or congregation

Tzaddik—a righteous person

Tzitzit—the strings on a four cornered garment worn traditionally by men, strings sewn on the corners and tied in special knots as commanded in the Torah, specifically discussed in the *Sh'ma* prayer.

Tznius—modesty, chastity

Ufruf—a ceremony for a groom on the Sabbath before the wedding. He is honored by being called to the Torah for an aliyah, where he often recites the maftir and haftarah, and sometimes a part of the Torah.

Ulpan—intensive Hebrew school, done generally as a complete immersion

Yeshiva—academy of Torah and Talmud learning, a Jewish school

Yeshivish—People who are Ultra-Orthodox, but not Chassidim, are often referred to as mitnagdim.

Yesod—foundation, one of the sefirot

Zemiroth—songs, generally refers to liturgical songs

Edwards Brothers Malloy
Thorofare, NJ USA
September 10, 2013